Melting Stones

The Circle of Magic Books

TAMORA PIERCE

Melting Stones

SCHOLASTIC INC.
New York Toronto London Auckland
Sydney Mexico City New Delhi Hong Kong

This book was originally published in hardcover by Scholastic Press in 2008.

ISBN 978-0-545-05265-8

12 11 10 9 8 7 6 5 4 3 2 1   10 11 12 13 14 15/0

Printed in the U.S.A.   40

First Scholastic paperback printing, August 2010

The text type was set in Adobe Caslon.

Book design by Steve Scott

This book is dedicated to Bruce Coville, Grace Kelly, Brett Hobin, Todd Hobin, David Baker, Dan Bostick, Moe Harrington, Timothy Liebe, Alice Morigi, and the rest of the wonderfully talented cast of the original, Full Cast Audio production of *Melting Stones*. Each of them left their own, unique stamp on this book. Without their voices and their commentary, it would not read as it does. It is their book as much as it is mine. I give them my heartfelt thanks. I hope that you will, too.

Contents

1

Lost at Sea

H ey, kid — stop hanging off that rail!" A sailor, one of the women, was yelling at me. "We've only told you a dozen times! If you fall overboard, we'll not turn back!"

"Can ya swim all the way to the Battle Islands?" another sailor called. "If ya can't, ya'd best keep alla yerself on th' ship!"

"If I fall in, will I sink all the way to the bottom?" I yelled back. I didn't pull myself up off the rail. If I sank, I would be lying among stones again. I would be among my own kind, with no fathoms of nasty water between me and solid earth.

The sailors laughed.

"The salt water holds ya up, wench! You'll float whilst the fishies pick at ya!"

"But my *bones* will sink. *That's* what matters," I replied. And I muttered, so I wouldn't be scolded for rudeness, "I can take care of myself."

I dropped until I hung from my knees, my back against the ship's hull. Then I stretched out my hands. The choppy water was still dozens of feet beyond my reach. I let my magic stream through my fingers into the sea. It plunged through water and salt. I strained and strained, but the sea has its own magic, a power that hates mine. I couldn't feel the earth anywhere below me.

I hate traveling by ship. Hate it. As soon as I can't feel the stone of the ocean floor with my power, I'm lost. It's like the day my mother sold me. She left me with no family and no way even to speak to my new, foreign owner. Aboard a ship, when I wasn't trying to feel the approach of land, I huddled in a corner. There I placed my own stones around me and held my friend Luvo in my lap.

Luvo helps me some. He's about eighteen inches tall. He has the shape of a bear made of clear, deep green, and purple crystal that's been rounded and smoothed by water. His face is a gentle point, not a muzzle. He's not *truly* a rock, though he has the magic of a thousand stones. He is the heart of a mountain, a living creature with power for blood. So even though Luvo is a good friend, and company as I travel, he can't make up for the feel of rock under me.

I shouldn't have been on that ship. Dedicate Rosethorn — my guardian — was the one who had been called to Starns, one of the Battle Islands. They needed her to see why their trees were dying. She was packing to go when I had a problem with some rich boys who were students at Winding Circle temple. They were bothering some of my friends. I said I would hit them with my staff if they didn't stop, and they drew swords and daggers on me. It wasn't as if I actually broke any of their bones. They *were* disobeying temple rules. Rosethorn told the temple council that the boys got what they deserved, and their parents could put their complaints someplace tender. But I also heard her tell Dedicate Lark, my other guardian, that she would take me to Starns, so the wealthy parents would have time to calm down.

"I won't have anything to do!" I cried, when Lark and Rosethorn gave me the news officially. "These island people want Rosethorn because their plants are dying. That's no bread and salt of mine. And I hate ship travel."

"Then you may partake of confinement to Discipline cottage," Rosethorn told me. "That's the punishment the council wants for you, since you pounded those boys *after* you disarmed them. Travel to Starns and help me find what is killing their trees, or stay inside this lovely, tiny home of ours. Your choice."

So now I hung from the rail, stretching my magic as far as it would go and feeling lost.

"Do you know, Evumeimei, that ocean rocks do not swim to the surface?"

Luvo always said that when he found me hunting for the sea's floor. The hearts of mountains apparently never get tired of telling the same jokes.

They also never get tired of hearing the same answers, so I told him what I often did, "There's always a first time."

I think the reason Luvo came out of his mountain to meet me, and the reason he's stayed with me ever since, is because I make him laugh. Though I don't actually hear him laugh, I know he does.

"The sailors have told Dedicate Rosethorn that we should see the island of dying trees tomorrow, if not today," Luvo said. "You will be able to sense the ocean floor soon, I promise you."

"I know," I replied. "*You* never lost touch with it. I'm sorry I'm not centuries and centuries old. I'm sorry I'm not even a great mage. I bet you Rosethorn knows each and every plant below us, however many fathoms deep they are right now. But I've only been at this mage business four years. I have some catching up to do —"

The hairs on my arms stirred, then stood up. My belly rolled, like that first cramp that warns you the sausage was bad. My magic flexed. Far under the sea I felt power move. The Pebbled Sea had earth tremors and earthquakes, plenty of them, but this one was different. It was thick and heavy, like molten stone. My body filled with a deep, bone-tugging hum. It swamped my teeth and made them itch.

I began to slide off the rail. I swung, twisted, and grabbed. I clung tight to the rail with both hands and one leg. My hold was strong — I was used to climbing mountains. I waited for the world to settle, especially my magic. Right then it was still bouncing up and down, making my bones rumble.

"Did you feel that?" I called to Luvo. I thought I might pop out of my skin, I was so excited. "What was it? Is it going to happen again?"

"It is a waking tremor." I heard Luvo's voice as clearly as if he hung beside me. "It may well happen again. You should climb back on board, Evumeimei."

"Evvy! There, you see? I warn and warn you, and now it's happened. You *never* listen."

That was Dedicate Fusspot calling out from the deck. His real name was Myrrhtide. I called him Fusspot, for good reasons.

"You went over the rail. You nearly dropped straight into the ocean just now. How many times have I said dangling like a monkey is a good way to drown. You never know when a swell like that one will overtake us!" Myrrhtide was coming closer to me from the sound of his voice. I dragged myself back on deck and faced him. Myrrhtide annoyed me. He wasn't *old*. He wasn't in his forties, like Rosethorn — more like his early thirties. Yet he always moaned about his gray hairs. I couldn't even *see* any among his red ones. He just carried

5

on about being old, when he hadn't earned the right to do so.

He also couldn't learn that I don't like to be touched. The first time he bothered me about hanging over the rail, he had grabbed me by my sash. I forgot that I was supposed to behave. I drew a knife on him. Rosethorn got angry. Since Lark and my first teacher, Briar, had ordered me never to upset Rosethorn, I was careful not to let Myrrhtide grab me after that.

I got on deck just in time. He was reaching out to take hold of me. "Swell?" I asked him, keeping my hands behind me, away from my dagger. "What swell? Luvo says it was a waking tremor."

"Myrrhtide sensed the same thing in water that you felt in stone, Evvy." Rosethorn came forward to join us. She had to talk extra-carefully because she was dead once. Briar and his sisters made her alive again, but everyone knows that Mohun, who guards the dead, has to be paid something for his trouble. For Rosethorn, he didn't take the sharpness from her tongue, but he did take some quickness in her talking. "Evvy, I thought you couldn't feel the stone at the bottom of the ocean."

"This was too big for me not to feel. It was like the whole bottom rose up, only it was underneath."

Myrrhtide sniffed. "It was power transferred *through* the water, not under it."

"And *I* know when stone's moving." I hate it when he corrects me.

"Don't start, either one of you." Rosethorn glared at us so hard I felt crisp around the edges. "The world's strength was on the move. Leave it at that."

"I don't know why you support her." Myrrhtide could never let anything be. "She is only a *child*. I am a dedicate mage of Winding Circle. I am far better able to judge the movement and manner of power below us."

Rosethorn's eyes sparked. She was going to say something dreadful, I knew it. Then the breeze puffed and blew her wide-brimmed hat overboard, into the sea. "Blight and beetles. Myrrhtide, Evvy has had *specialized* education. Now would you mind? My hat?" She pointed as it floated on down the length of the ship.

Myrrhtide stared at her. Then he walked off, his Water-blue habit fluttering behind him. I heard him mutter, "Specialized education, indeed!"

Rosethorn ran her fingers through her hair. She kept it cropped short like a man's, which I didn't understand. It was a beautiful dark carnelian red. I'd have let it grow even longer than my own black hair, which came down to my waist when I let it out of its braid. Not Rosethorn. Except for keeping her skin white and soft with creams, and wearing hats, Rosethorn didn't care about her looks, and she had looks. She didn't have a long, flat-ended nose, like mine. Hers was nice and small. Her lips were even a natural reddish color. Mine were just wide. My skin is Yanjing gold brown, so I don't have to worry about the sun as much as she does, but if I ever get interested in romance, I'll have to pay attention to my looks.

"You could try harder to get along with him," Rosethorn told me. "You're a stone mage. You could borrow patience from your rocks."

"I'm no butter of his," I grumbled. "He doesn't have to try and churn me all the time. Don't worry about Myrrhtide and me, Rosethorn."

"I'm not *worried*. I just don't want him carrying bad reports of you to Winding Circle."

I didn't like that thought, so I changed the subject. I looked at Luvo, who sat on the deck between Rosethorn and me. "Does the earth do waking tremors often?" I asked him. "It's not like ordinary earthquakes, where two slabs of rock are slipping together. This is more like —"

"Molten rock. Magma," said Luvo. "It is moving. I have sensed such tremors for several days, but not of this strength. Prepare yourselves. Another comes."

I put my feet on the deck and gripped the rail. Luvo hardly ever gives orders. Far below the ship, stone power rose to meet the outermost feelers of my magic. It felt so strange, pressing like hot, solid water on me. I gasped. The wave passed on, but the sense of stone didn't die, not completely. I felt touches of mica at the fringes of my power, and quartz, and granite. I was brushing ocean floor.

A ridge! There was a ridge underneath the ship, three hundred yards below! I could feel basalt — good, calm, steady old basalt, long slabs of it!

Myrrhtide came back. Alongside the ship came a long arm of seawater with Rosethorn's hat on top of it. It passed the hat to Myrrhtide, who patted the tentacle as he'd pet a good dog. The water dropped back into the sea. Myrrhtide offered the hat to Rosethorn.

"Thank you." She ran her fingers over the hat. The seawater dropped out of it. I guess she made the straw chase it out: She could get plants, or things that had been plants, to do almost anything.

"Waking tremors." Her voice was quiet. "What is the earth waking up to, Luvo?"

"It may only be waking enough to turn in its sleep, as you humans do, Rosethorn. Or tremors may come from movement that began in a distant place. It is hard to say."

I could feel the ridge start to drop away from me. It was just a sharp peak, not a rise in the land under the ship, and we were sailing away from it. "Nooo!" I leaned over the rail. "Come back!" I didn't want to lose the tingle of all those beautiful rocks this soon! I had been so lonely, even with all my old stones and Luvo to keep me company. "Stay close! Stop this stupid ship!"

"Evumeimei," Luvo called.

"Let me alone!" Far below, the floor had dropped out of the range of my magic. "I'm sick of the sea! I'm sick of being away from rocks!"

"Evumeimei, if you will stop making that dreadful noise, I will show you a thing," Luvo said patiently. To be honest, I think Luvo has few moods other than patient. It's part of being a mountain's heart, I suppose. It's really annoying.

"What she's doing is called 'whining,'" I heard Rosethorn say. "I don't think you should reward her for it."

"Young mountains are restless and impatient, Rosethorn. As such, they can be dangerous. They must be kept amused. Although Evumeimei is not a young mountain, my spirit urges me to guide her as one. And that noise she makes is quite grating. Evumeimei, sit on the deck and place your hands on me."

When Luvo speaks to me firmly like that, I do as he says.

I felt ghost hands reach through his clear skin and wrap around my wrists. He pulled me into his crystal insides. We fell through the ship, ghost Luvo mingled with ghost Evvy. It is a powerful thing, being a ghost before you are dead. In Yanjing, they would say I was cursed forever for being a ghost while I was alive. So many things are different when you're a mage.

We dropped into the water. It ran through me, cool and tingly with salt, warm from the sun. I would have gasped, but I had no lungs. We zipped through a huge school of fishes, their skins slick and slippery. The water got colder as we went down. Bright flashes sparked along my insides. I looked at myself. I glittered.

They are flecks of stone borne by the sea. Luvo's voice sounded in my mind. *Once the sea has ground rock down into tiny grains, it is light enough to float. The sea carries the grains. They are so little you could not sense them with your magic. I feel them all.*

More fishes dashed by, blurs in the water. I was starting to wonder what they ate, to make them rush so, when I understood. It was not the fishes, but Luvo.

Is this how you see Rosethorn and Briar and Myrrhtide and me? I asked. *Dashing around like someone had turned us into crazy flies? Because we're meat creatures and you're stone?*

I made an adjustment to see you as you see yourselves. It was necessary. I shall make one now, Luvo replied.

The crystal ladders and spirals that made up our ghost body seemed to go loose, then twist. The dashing fish twinkled. Suddenly they slowed. Jellyfish appeared — I hadn't even seen those until now. Luvo and I continued on down, onto the ocean floor. The ridge I had felt lay before us. Beside it was a deep canyon. Luvo took us into that. I reached my ghost hands out to feel its stony sides.

It's volcano rock. Why is there a volcano canyon in the ocean? I asked.

Volcanoes exist everywhere. Once — long before my time — the world was born of volcanoes.

Long before his time? Luvo was *thousands* of years old. I couldn't imagine anything older than he was.

I have spoken with the mountains from those times, he continued. *They were only pebbles by then, but they were very wise. I learned much by waiting patiently to hear their wisdom.*

Is that "patiently" thing a hint to me? I wanted to know.

I would never hint to you about patience, Evumeimei.

The lower we fell in the deep canyon, the warmer the water got. *Shouldn't it be freezing by now?* I inquired. *What makes it warm?*

Luvo said, *Look, and you will see.*

2

We Meet Our Guides

Below us lay a deep, deep crack in the canyon floor. Strange, death-colored plants grew there, food for the pale fishes that nibbled on them. Around one hump in the crack, bubbles streamed from an opening, boiling up through the water. It looked like a miniature volcano. I touched it with my magic, naming the minerals heaped around it: sulfur, magnesium, and other volcano leavings. The crack itself was limestone.

The vent belched. It threw out a boiling cloud of bubbles that passed through Luvo and me. *Where does it come from?* I wanted to know. *Where does whatever air that is in the bubbles come from? What made this crack, and why did it burp just now?*

It "burps," as you comically put it, because the heart of the earth is forever in motion, Evumeimei, said Luvo. *This seam reaches down to the molten heart, which is gas and liquid stone. These things come to the earth's surface through such vents, be they under water or under the land. That is where the ocean rolls to the earth's pulse.*

So where does this seam go? Under the Battle Islands?

Many do, he replied. *I have heard it said that earthquakes often take place in this part of the world. It is because many seams are here. I had thought that if I showed you these things you might have fewer questions. Instead, you have more. Are you never unquestioning?*

I could tell Luvo was teasing me. *I'm quiet when I sleep. Besides, you said you wanted to stop me whining. You didn't say you wanted me not to ask questions. I'm not whining, am I?*

We began to rise along the canyon wall. The creatures that had been blown out of the way when the vent belched were returning to it. *Do they worship their ocean volcano, Luvo?*

I believe it is only you human meat creatures who worship things, Evumeimei. These animals eat the small creatures that live on its sides, the little gray ones that crawl there. They draw strength from the warmth of the volcano, as well. Volcanoes are good to those who live on them. The soil on the ones above water is richer for plants. Humans farm there, and animals come to graze, just as these sea creatures do.

Above us I saw the ripple of sunlight on the water's surface. *Have you ever been to a volcano, Luvo?*

I was born in one. That was sufficient. Exposure to a second volcano would be the death of me, Evumeimei, just as it would be the death of you.

He let me go. I felt myself turning and twisting on his crystal paths again. Then heaviness clamped around me: a suit of hot, thick meat. That was my body. For a moment I didn't enjoy it very much. Luvo calls humans "meat creatures." For the first time I felt like one.

Someone breathed fish and garlic in my face. Hands shook me. A voice made ugly noises that banged in my ears. In the sea every noise was softened by the swish of water. These noises grated. I flinched. The hands grabbed me harder. I opened my eyes.

Terror flooded me. I forgot where I was. I thought I was a captive. A man's face was too close to mine. I couldn't breathe. Was I back in Gyongxe? That was it — I was the prisoner of the emperor's soldiers. They beat me last time! They'd beat me again to make me tell on my friends!

I screamed and slammed my head forward, hard, into the soldier's nose. Then I lashed sideways and bit deep into his arm. Except his arm wasn't the silk-covered leather of an imperial warrior. I was biting into flesh covered by blue linen.

"Make her let *go* of me!" Dedicate Fusspot tried to shake me off. His voice was muffled.

"Evumeimei, you are far from Gyongxe," Luvo said.

"Myrrhtide, I warned you not to lay hands on her."
Rosethorn sounded like she was close by.

I stopped biting Myrrhtide. My feet were throbbing.
They were remembering the emperor's soldiers, too.

"I thought she was having a fit." Myrrhtide's nose was
bleeding. "I thought she was dying. I was trying to save
her life. The ungrateful brat broke my nose!"

"When I told you don't touch me to wake me, ever,
because I've been in a war and I react violently, you
respected me." For a plant person, Rosethorn could sound
like iron when she made a point with someone stupid.
"Evvy was in that *same war*. She fought as hard as any
adult — harder, sometimes. Yet you refuse to acknowledge
that she may suffer the same effects. I told you not to grab
her. I said she might panic if she saw a man's face so close
to hers when she came out of a trance —"

"She is too young to do a mage trance!" Myrrhtide
groped his pockets for a handkerchief. He was bleeding all
over his habit.

"Looked like a mage trance to me," one of the sailors
muttered.

Fusspot Myrrhtide glared at her. The sailor shrugged
and gave me her water flask so I could rinse the taste of
Myrrhtide from my mouth.

As I spat the water over the rail, Rosethorn dragged
Myrrhtide's hand away from his nose. "It's bleeding, not

broken. I have something that will fix it in a trice. Don't touch Evvy again unless it's a matter of life or death, understand?"

She looked at me sidelong. I knew what she wanted.

I sighed. The trouble with learning manners was that sometimes you had to do and say things that stank. "I'm sorry I almost broke your nose, Dedicate Myrrhtide." I tried hard to sound truthful. "I thought you were one of the imperial soldiers who whipped my feet."

He was about to say something mean, I could see it in his eyes. Suddenly he let all that air out in a whoosh. "They whipped your feet?" he whispered.

I nodded. "I knew where people were hiding. The soldiers tried to make me tell by hitting the bottoms of my feet with a cane. See?" I leaned on the rail to show him the scars on the sole of one foot. "I put crystal around my heart, so I wouldn't tell. They gave up finally."

He was going to ask something else, when the sailor up in the crow's nest yelled, "Land ho!"

I turned and squinted northwest. In the distance rose a tall mountain, floating on the horizon. We were in sight of the Battle Islands at last.

"Enough reminiscing." Rosethorn wrapped her arm around my shoulders. "Evvy, time to pack. Myrrhtide, come below and I'll fix your nose."

I had little to pack: clothes, books, my mage kit, and the stone alphabet that Briar gave me. Soon Luvo and I were back on deck, watching as the Battle Islands grew larger ahead. They were a clump of islands in the middle of the Pebbled Sea. Their reputation was shady. Briar said people came there when they got tired of their home countries interfering in their business. Lark just said that island people liked to keep to themselves. They must be really nervous if they were sending for Rosethorn.

"The place used to swarm with pirates." Myrrhtide's nose was as good as new. Rosethorn's medicines really are the best. And he'd surprised me. I had thought he'd be packing until after we had docked, but here he was, all ready to go. "It was a pesthole. Any vice you can think of was available here. I served in a temple on one of the northern islands, and I got quite the education. Then Duke Vedris of Emelan led *three* attacks on the Islands, to break up the pirate nations. He was joined by navies and soldiers from the other Pebbled Sea lands who were sick of pirate raids. The place is almost respectable, these days."

"You don't have to be nice to me just because I have scars on my feet. It was a long time ago."

Myrrhtide stiffened. "I am trying to be civil because we will be the only three from Emelan in an environment which may be uncomfortable. Just because they invited us does not mean we will be welcomed with open arms. It would be nice if we could get along." He sniffed at me, winced, and left.

"He's stiff-rumped, that 'un," said the woman sailor who was coiling rope nearby. "Ignore him. Look there. The isle with the tall mountain? That be Starns, where you're bound. The peak is Mount Grace. Starns is grand. Olive groves and orange groves. Grapes burstin' with juice. The plumpest goats and sheep and cattle I've ever seen. And hot springs, where a girl can relax with a friend or two."

"And the island folk are real friendly," joked another sailor. "Now, they're not too good for common sailing folk. They've no pirates to dangle trinkets and coin in front of them!"

"At least you won't be bored, waiting to take us home." I said it mostly to be polite. I could feel the ocean floor again. I didn't even have to stretch my magic to do it. I wasn't interested in grapes and friends, but Lark told me that I should practice making conversation.

"Bored is the last thing we'll be!" The man laughed. I suppose they were talking about fooling around. People always think they have to discuss it like I don't know what it is. That's grown-ups for you. I let them do their sideways joking about sex, while I let my power trail along the ocean floor.

Sustree wasn't much of a town, but it had plenty of docks. Our crew brought us up to one nice and smooth. I hardly noticed. I was saying hello to every stone on the harbor bottom, and in the walls along the docks.

Rosethorn poked me. "You'll feel better ashore. Let's go."

We said good-bye to the crew after they carried our bundles to the dock. I had a cloth sling that I used to carry Luvo around, those times when it's easier than letting him walk. I arranged it around my shoulders, and tucked him in. Then I gathered up my mage kit and alphabet, two saddlebags' worth, and followed Rosethorn and Myrrhtide off the ship. The moment I set foot on the ground, I felt like a different person. There were so many rocks under my feet that I couldn't count them. They filled me with strength.

"It's like I was breathing with only one lung."

"You said that when we sailed home from Gyongxe." Rosethorn looked around. "Do you suppose there's an inn here?"

"Excuse me — are you the dedicates from Winding Circle?" A white man came over to us. "I'm Oswin Forest, from Moharrin village. I'm honored to be your escort. My headwoman, Azaze Yopali, sent me to meet you." He was about six inches taller than me, which made him almost six feet tall. He had blue eyes as bright as turquoises, set in heavy lids. He must have been blond when he was younger, but most of the hair on top of his head was gone. What was left at the back and sides was cut really short. He had a long nose that tipped up at the end, and a nice-looking mouth. He dressed like most of the men around there seemed to, in a tunic shirt — his was bright blue, like his eyes — and tan breeches, and soft brown boots. In one hand he held a book, marking his place in it with a finger.

"We were just wondering about the arrangements. I'm Rosethorn, and this is Dedicate Myrrhtide. Your head-woman wrote that you've had water go bad as well as plants and trees dying?"

Oswin nodded. "It seems to be random, all around the mountain. I've never seen anything like it, and I can't find anything in the village records or here in Sustree. Our mage says there were some incidents, when she was younger, but they started and stopped abruptly. People thought the usual things — the gods were angry, mostly —"

"If you could take us to our rooms now?" For someone who was always after me about *my* behavior, Myrrhtide could be *rude*. "We would like a proper meal, as well. Dedicate Initiate Rosethorn's and my skills and senses will be at their sharpest for a night's rest and an hour or two spent in a bathhouse, perhaps a good massage . . ."

Oswin's nose twitched. "I don't think there's a bath-house *on* Starns. We have hot springs everywhere, so no one bothered to build one. Headwoman Azaze could have one set up for you, if you need it for your rituals and privacy. We have your rooms prepared in Moharrin, along with a decent meal."

Myrrhtide drew himself up. "Are we to *walk* to your village? It is not at all what we expect, nor what is due to us. I have delicate instruments for water scrying and communication with Winding Circle's Water mages. I certainly cannot carry all of my own packs. Dedicate Initiate Rosethorn, moreover, is not in the best of health. She cannot bear heavy loads like a peasant."

I winced. Rosethorn talked a little slow, and maybe she wasn't as bouncy as me, but she was tough as an old root. I stood back, in case plants started shooting out of the ground to strangle Myrrhtide.

"Sorry, Oswin, sorry!" A boy maybe three years older than I am, seventeen or so, trotted down the street, towing a string of horses and mules. He was about an inch taller than me, with light brown skin and short, kinky black hair. He had a funny nose, like a long brown fat drip of wax that got frozen before it dropped, and merry black eyes. He was chubby inside his loose orange shirt and breeches. His voice was rich, like butter tea. "The old woman took forever to wrap up the herbs I bought. Then she seemed to think I would look at her dog's sore tooth for nothing because I buy from her, and the poor thing was in pain —" He stared at Rosethorn and Myrrhtide. "Oh. Dedicate Initiates, you're here already. I'm sorry." He bowed low. "I've brought your horses, and they're already saddled. I'll load your things on the pack mules. Are these all of your belongings?"

22

"Here." I put Luvo on my saddlebags. "I'll show you. I'm Evvy."

"Jayat. The message said there would be an assistant. We'll get you packed up in no time."

Oswin came over to collect Rosethorn's and Myrrhtide's horses. Once he'd settled the dedicates' saddlebags on their horses' backs, he helped Jayat and me finish loading the packs. From the way he and Jayat worked, they had almost as much experience as I did. It was nice to deal with people who knew what they were doing.

They weren't chatterers, either. In fact, they were so quiet, we could hear Rosethorn talking to Myrrhtide, even though she kept her voice down.

"I should have left you at Winding Circle. We can't demand the royal treatment here! If they could afford all the luxuries, they would have gotten a mage for pay. They wouldn't have sent all the way to Winding Circle in the hope that we could spare someone!"

"It's important to demand respect," Myrrhtide snapped. "Otherwise, people think they can get the world of you. I have no intention of sleeping in a hovel. This place they have prepared for us — I'm sure it has fleas."

"I brought fleabane," Rosethorn told him.

"And rats."

"I brought ratbane, you idiot."

"Have you brought foolsbane?" demanded Myrrhtide. "I don't doubt this matter of poisoned water is simply one of sewage draining into their water table. I have experience of these Battle Island peasants. I know whereof I speak!"

"Should we let them know we peasants can hear?" Oswin spoke softly as he finished tying the last packs into place.

"No," I replied. "I'd say put rats and fleas in his bed, but Rosethorn's ratbane and fleabane are really strong."

"They can *hear* you, Puffbrain!" Rosethorn gave Myrrhtide a shove. "Mount up, and be quiet. I am six months fresh from a war. You have me a sesame seed away from declaring a new one on *you*." She looked at Oswin. "Forgive Dedicate Myrrhtide. He was dropped on his head as a child. Often."

Myrrhtide turned garnet red.

"May I?" Jayat offered Rosethorn his hands so she could use them to mount her horse.

I held my breath. She actually let him help her into the saddle. I guess she was trying to be nice. "Tell me — Jayat, right? What is your place in Moharrin?"

As I scrambled onto the little mare Oswin held for me, I heard Jayat say, "I'm apprenticed to Tahar Catwalker. She's our mage and healer. Me and Oswin will be the ones to show you all the sick places. He knows where they are, and I know where the lines of the island's magic are. I — I guess Dedicate Initiate Myrrhtide will let me know what you need, apart from what you brought?"

"No," growled Myrrhtide as he checked the third saddled horse. "She's the great mage, after all. She's in charge."

"A great mage?" Oswin, who was starting to mount his own horse, missed the stirrup and stumbled. He stared at Rosethorn. "They sent a *great mage* to us?" Jayat gaped at Rosethorn, too.

"I am a *green* mage. That's the important thing, and all you have to worry about, Oswin. You too, Jayat." Rosethorn doesn't like it when people fuss over her being a great mage. She cures diseases and destroys castles with plants, but if you ask her what she does, she'll tell you she gardens and makes medicines and jellies. The green habit with the black stripe on the cuffs and hem that says she's an initiate? She hardly wears it. She keeps her mage's medallion, the one marked so people know she has power at the great mage schools, under her habit most of the time. Myrrhtide *always* wears the blue initiate robe for Water temple. If he could make his mage medallion glow on his chest, he would. To Myrrhtide, Rosethorn is a cat who insists on acting like a dog.

Rosethorn gathered her reins in her hand. "I *would* like to reach our destination and have that night's rest before we look into your problem. May we get moving?"

3

The Mountain Is a Restless Sleeper

The road to Moharrin followed a nice river called the Makray. As roads went, it was all right. There were farms on the side that wasn't a river. The farms had lots of cows, sheep, olive trees, orange trees, and grape vines, just as the sailors had said. It was very pretty, if you like that sort of thing. I was more interested in the stones all around us.

There was plenty of basalt, but that wasn't special. There was lots of basalt on the ocean floor. As soon as I touched it, I sent my magic on for something new. The stone walls that hemmed the farms and orchards sparkled in my magic. The rocks were granite, specked with quartz and feldspar. I was so glad to see crystal that I let it soak a bit of my power in. The granite shimmered like heaps of jewels in the sun when I finished.

"Evumeimei." I think Luvo had been trying to get my attention for a while, because he was making his voice boom in my bones. He knows I don't like that. "This young man wishes to speak to you."

Jayat was riding on my left. His eyeballs were bulging in his head. "Your rock made a mouth and it *talked*." He said it as if he'd never heard of such a thing.

Well, maybe he hadn't. *I* hadn't heard of any others like Luvo.

"He's not my rock. His name is Luvo. He's the heart of a mountain. Only I suppose the mountain can go on living, because it's still standing, back there in Yanjing." I looked down at Luvo in his sling on my chest. "Isn't it?"

"My mountain is quite well, thank you, Evumeimei." Luvo turned his head-lump to Jayat. "You may call me Luvo."

Jayat swallowed hard. Being addressed by a rock does take getting used to.

"I'm Jayatin Holly. Mostly people call me Jayat." He bowed to Luvo. I knew it was to Luvo because I'm not the sort of person people bow to. If they think I am, I discourage it quickly.

"I will call you Jayatin, then. That is more fitting," Luvo said.

"Luvo doesn't usually like short names." I explain things so Luvo won't try to. Sometimes his explanations are on the long side. "He always calls me Evumeimei, which is the full form of my first name."

"So, Evvy, which dedicate are you apprenticed to?" Jayat asked. "Rosethorn, or Myrrhtide?"

I shook my head. "I'm a student *stone* mage. Rosethorn brought me because they don't feel kindly about me at Winding Circle just now. She and I are used to long trips together. What kind of magic do *you* have?"

"Just the kind that's done with charms and spells. It's good enough for Starns, but that's all. You won't see the likes of me at Winding Circle. I could no more hear the voices in nature than I can fly. I don't know how you natural mages do it." Jayat grinned. "Hearing stones or plants or water talking to me would make me half-crazy."

"Well, for one thing, it's not natural magic, it's ambient magic." I had to show off my Winding Circle learning. "Not everyone's magic goes through things in nature, you know. My foster-mother Lark has hers with thread and weaving. And there are ambient mages who work with carpentry and cooking and metalwork. That's all things that are made."

Jayat chuckled. "Excuse my error, O wise woman from across the water."

I stuck my tongue out at him, feeling better about this trip. It looked like I had a new friend who wasn't all serious and temperamental, like the grown-ups I traveled with. Rosethorn is fun in her crackly way, but dealing with strangers makes her cross. And I knew Myrrhtide was a fusspot before we weighed anchor. Meeting Jayat was a big relief. Oswin seemed all right, too. He actually had Myrrhtide smiling as they rode together.

"What were you doing in Yanjing?" Jayat asked.

Luvo was explaining about Rosethorn's and Briar's trips to see new plants when I felt a wave coming. It was just like the one at sea. The problem was that we were on solid ground. It wouldn't adjust to moving power so well.

"Tremor!" I yelled.

For something with a tiny mouth, Luvo can sound like a landslide in a small canyon. "Off your horses."

My body was on the ground. I clung to my reins. My mind and magic darted into the earth to ride the wave in the stone as it raced toward us. The wave roared under our feet, making everything shake. The horses whinnied and reared. A gap opened beside the road, swallowing a few trees before it closed. Our people staggered, clutching their mounts' reins, as the frightened animals tried to escape. Then the tremor was over.

"Evvy?" Rosethorn meant, did I feel any more coming?

Luvo? I put my hand on his smooth, cool surface.

"There will be no more waves for now," he said. "It is safe to ride on."

"Amazing." Oswin shook his head as Rosethorn and her horse trotted back to us. "Can — who is that? What is that? Can you tell tremors are coming all of the time?"

I let Rosethorn explain Luvo to Oswin. I took Luvo out of his sling so Oswin and Jayat could have a better look at him. Luvo looked at them, too, turning his head knob this way and that. Oswin asked a dozen questions: Where Luvo was from, how he'd left his mountain, when he could first remember walking, things like that.

He might have asked a dozen more, except Myrrhtide interrupted. "We *would* like to reach our destination before next week."

"Probably we should get moving, then." If Oswin knew Myrrhtide was scolding him, he didn't act like it. "It's wonderful to meet you, Luvo. Dedicate Rosethorn, it must be quite useful, in these parts, to have your own earthquake-warning creature."

Rosethorn rolled her eyes, but didn't speak. Luvo never minded things that *I* would take as insults. Unless Rosethorn or I explained that Luvo was more than an earthquake-warning thing, Luvo wouldn't set Oswin straight.

As we rode on, Oswin said, "The tremors are the cost of life here. See our mountain? That's Mount Grace. The wisewomen say that the goddess Grace was deserted by her lover on their wedding day. She sleeps restlessly, waiting for him to come back. Her tossing and turning causes the tremors. Our rich fields and forests are the home she made to lure him back to her."

Rosethorn pursed her lips. I looked down so nobody saw me grin. I would have bet any coin I had that Rosethorn was thinking unkindly of a goddess who waited around for a man who treated her so badly.

Suddenly I felt a shimmer in my magic, like sunlight glancing off water. This time I didn't care if Rosethorn rode on without me. "Mica!" I yelled and jumped off my horse. "There's sheet mica here!"

Mica lay scattered over a heap of rocks that had tumbled from a cliff face. It lay to the right of the road in sheets of a single thickness, delicate amber-colored glass that would chip away at a breath, and in clumps of different sizes, some of a hundred sheets or more. I picked up a few thick clumps to keep.

"You like this stuff?" Jayat had followed me. "What's it good for?"

"Scrying, if you need to have a *use* for everything." I showed him glittering flakes that fell from my hand like snow. "But mostly it's just wonderful — so delicate, and yet it's stone."

I flicked a tiny burst of magic up the slope. Flakes, sheets, and clumps of mica flashed, thousands of flat crystals in the sun. Everyone who rode by would now see the stone as I did, glittering in the light.

"Beautiful." Jayat liked what I had done. "I never thought of it like that. It was always just glassy stuff, laying around."

Luvo looked at Jayat. "That is what magic is for, Jayatin. To help us to think of the world in new ways."

I went back to my horse, though I didn't mount up. I hung Luvo in his sling from my mare's saddle horn. That way I wouldn't bounce him around as I searched for rocks. Then I carefully wrapped the mica I had gathered, before I stowed it in one of my packs. After that I walked beside the road's edge. Jayat stayed with Luvo and the horse. I meant to find some excellent new stones for my collection. Briar would be sorry he went to boring old Namorn with his sisters, instead of coming to Starns with Rosethorn and me.

It was a mistake to think of Briar just then. I started missing him, and brooding as I walked along. Briar was my first true friend. He saw the stone magic in me. He taught me how to use it. I learned other things from him, too, like reading and writing and table manners. We saved each other's lives constantly, from our meeting in Chammur through our time in Yanjing and Gyongxe. The problems came at Winding Circle. Briar could barely stay there for more than an hour or two. Being inside a temple city just reminded him too much of Gyongxe. I didn't understand. I had been in Gyongxe, and I was just fine at Winding Circle. Rosethorn told me that everyone recovers differently from war, and not to blame Briar.

I did visit Briar practically every day after he moved in with his sisters. Then they took him to Namorn. Just four months home, and he's off on the road again! *I* didn't want to go on some journey that might last all summer. I had a stone mage at Winding Circle who could teach me new and tricky things. So off Briar went, while I smiled and waved. I thought, I'll bet he's glad to leave me. Of course. I'm finished business to Briar now.

"Evumeimei," Luvo said, "will you mope, or will you regard the obsidian to your left?"

Obsidian?

I stopped feeling sorry for myself. Standing beside the road, I cast my magic out until I could feel it slide over *pure* obsidian. Before Rosethorn could say anything, I scrambled down the riverbank. It lay just offshore, not too far under the tumbling water. Here the river was somewhat wilder than it was closer to Sustree. On the far bank the ground rose into the air as if it had been shoved straight up. Its bare rock face was colored in pale sidelong stripes. They were made up of quartz layers and cemented with glasslike sand. Through the centuries the sand had been pressed into a mortar that could fight the river's long rubbing. That rock face was a marvel all by itself. Then there was the river bottom. It was covered in fine white sand, the kind glassmakers praised to the skies. The obsidian shoved up through it in shelves.

I slid into the shallows to reach it. Feeling underwater, I gathered a handful of small pieces that had broken from the larger ones. I didn't care if I made a mess of my clothes. Obsidian chipped in curved surfaces. It sent my magic swooping back to me like gliding seabirds. My power chimed off colored bands and sang from clear ones. It hummed on obsidian flecked with gold, then slid sharply from clean edges. I bathed in fiery magic and music.

"Another day you may admire the pretty rocks, my dear." Someone wrapped a hand in my collar, then dragged me from the water to land on my bum.

If it had been Myrrhtide, I would have dumped an avalanche on him. Seeing that it was Rosethorn, I behaved. "I'm sorry. I'll walk now," I said. "I was just admiring the obsidian. There's rainbow obsidian. And gold streaked, and translucent . . ."

I wasn't arguing with Rosethorn, mind. Just before he left, Briar had told me, "Evvy, you have to watch out for her. She won't care for herself, you know it as well as I do. Don't let people work her too hard, all right?"

And because I was being brave, pretending that it was fine by me if he went off for months and months with his sisters, I had said yes. Rosethorn was mine, too, after Yanjing and Gyongxe. If the emperor and all his armies hadn't made trouble between Rosethorn and me, then this sleepy island in its sleepy ocean would never do it.

I got to my feet, but Rosethorn still held on. "You can walk only if you stop slowing us down, Evvy." She towed me along. "Otherwise I'll tie you to your horse. Why are you acting like a child who got into the honey jar? I know you missed stone while you were at sea, but usually you calm down once you're on land. It's not like you to make visible displays like those farm walls or that rock slide."

34

I didn't think she had noticed that I made the granite walls sparkle. "But it's all right if I play." I said it, rather than asking. I was afraid that if I asked, she might say no. I never ask a question if I don't think I'll like the answer. "It's not as if the woods are full of enemies waiting to pounce."

"No, but usually you aren't so, so prodigal."

"Prod — hunh?" Educated mages like Rosethorn and Fusspot always talk as if you know every long word they use.

"Prodigal. In this case, it means profligate — no. Giddy. Reckless. Tossing your magic around, as if you shouldn't save it for an emergency. Spending it without regard for the future." She let me go.

"*I* would have just said that I don't go around wasting magic." I stowed my obsidian pieces in the front of my shirt. One of them had cut me. I hid the cut before she noticed it. As I followed Rosethorn onto the road, I explained, "It's *these* rocks. So many of them are fire-born."

She looked around at me. "Fire-born?"

I shrugged. "From volcanoes. I keep finding the kind of rock that my stone teachers say is made in fire. I've never seen so much in one place, not so close to the surface. There's some at Winding Circle, but all underground, mostly. There's granite here, and feldspars, and obsidian — obsidian is *really* hard to find. And they're all volcano rocks. Starns is one big basket of treats for the likes of me."

We reached the road. Dedicate Fusspot looked as if he was about to complain. He changed his mind when Rosethorn and I both glared at him.

"Play with your obsidian treats in the saddle, please," said Rosethorn. "No more delays."

She leaned against my horse's shoulder as I climbed onto its back. I felt guilty as I looked at her. Coming home from Gyongxe, Briar and I had made her rest. She had relaxed after we got to Winding Circle, but she still got tired easily. Rosethorn had ordered Briar and me not to talk about all she had done to fight the emperor's armies. She had put so much strain on her body and heart. Seeing her lean on my horse, hidden from the people who rode with us, I wished Briar and I had disobeyed her. I wish we'd told the Winding Circle council that she was in no shape to go saving villages, not so soon.

"Did you drink your medicine tea?" I asked her. "The kind that smells like boiled mule urine?"

My horse was nervous, pawing the ground. Rosethorn pushed away from it. "I will have it in the village, if we can get there with no more —"

The other horses snorted and stamped. Birds flew out of the trees, shrieking.

"Evumeimei . . ." Luvo said in warning.

I felt it coming, too, from under my feet — liquid stone on the move, rich and heavy. Now was the time to use tricks I had learned from the riders of Gyongxe. I wrapped the reins tight around my right arm, locked my legs around my horse, grabbed Rosethorn's arm, and hung on. I muttered prayers to Heibei, god of luck. This time the weight of the earth's power drove straight up through the ground underneath us. It boomed under the horses' hooves and rattled down the road, away from the island's heart. On the far side of the river, stones dropped from the cliff to hit the water with huge splashes. Behind me I heard the sound of tearing wood and the crash of a big tree as it fell. I clutched Rosethorn with both arms and the horse with my legs, to keep Rosethorn from tumbling down the riverbank. She clung to me, her lips tight and her eyes all business.

Then we had silence. We listened for a time, waiting for a second shock. The horses quieted down. Finally, the birds began their usual chatter.

"You may let go now, Evvy." Rosethorn gave me a little push.

I let go. People tell me sometimes I have a grip like stone. I think I must have used it. Rosethorn's wrist was marked where I grabbed her. The cloth of her habit was as wrinkled as if I'd ironed it that way.

Rosethorn rubbed her white fingers to get the blood flowing into them, then looked at Oswin. "If I had wanted to bounce like this, I would have stayed aboard ship. Is your island normally so lively?"

"We've had a lot of tremors in the last couple of months. Times like this come and go, Dedicate Initiate. You — *we* become accustomed, anyway."

"Charming." Rosethorn went to grab her horse's reins. "I can't wait to become accustomed."

We stopped for a cold lunch Oswin had brought, then rode on — and up. Moharrin was high on the side of Mount Grace. As it got later, and the river and the road entered forested mountainsides, things turned cooler. I dug out Rosethorn's coat and rode over to her.

"Evumeimei, she dislikes it when you try to put warmer clothing on her." Luvo had seen me do this dance with Rosethorn before.

"You just have to wait until she isn't paying attention," I whispered to him. "Hush."

"Stop." Rosethorn climbed off her horse and walked away from the road. With her eyebrows together and her forehead crinkled, it was clear she was in a thinking mood. Myrrhtide reined up his horse and grumbled. He didn't like to ride, I could tell, but he wouldn't say so. Oswin and Jayat dismounted. Jayat went to refill their water bottles.

"Perfect, Luvo. If I move fast, I'll get Rosethorn's coat on her before she even notices." I slid to the ground and caught up to her. She was busy inspecting two dead trees.

I danced around her back and sides, working her arms into the sleeves, while she ignored me. Of course, I made sure not to get between her and the dead trees.

"I can get my own coat, Evvy." She looked at a big patch of dead plants behind the trees. In the dim woods light, that spot looked as if it was filled with plant ghosts, the dead leaves pale against the living shadows of the forest beyond. At the heart of the ghost space, dead birds lay beside a slab of basalt that jutted from the earth.

Do birds and trees have ghosts? I wondered. In Yanjing and Gyongxe, everything human has ghosts. That's what I was raised to believe. Were there bird ghosts here? And wouldn't Rosethorn believe that plants have ghosts? Plants are her people, just as stones are Luvo's people, and mine.

"Briar told me to look after you. I could see you were shivering." I answered her in a whisper. I didn't want the attention of bird *or* plant ghosts. "What killed them, Rosethorn?"

She gathered some dead limbs and leaves, gently cutting them from bushes and saplings with her belt knife. *I* wasn't going to say that if they were dead, they couldn't feel the cutting. "If I knew that, we might be able to go home." Raising her voice, she said, "Stop rolling your eyes and sighing, Myrrhtide. If there's anything I hate, it's a person who rolls his eyes and sighs when he's impatient. It just makes me move that much slower." Under her breath she added, "Twitterwitted Water temple bleat-brain."

I grinned. She learned "bleat-brain" from Briar.

I put the dead stuff in her workbasket while she mounted up again. Then I got on my own horse. "I'm sorry about all this getting on and off," I told the horse. "It seems to be that kind of day."

"You are always hopping about, Evumeimei." Luvo was still in his sling, hung from my horse's saddle horn. "I was telling Jayatin and Oswin about our travels in the East."

I wrinkled my nose as we rode on. "Not the nasty parts, I hope. Nobody needs to remember those."

"Only that there was fighting, and that we were caught in it."

"He was describing the temple of the Great Green Man," Jayat explained. "I can't even imagine a solid jade statue over a hundred feet tall."

"It was *wonderful*," I said. "The jade was the color of that grass over there. It sang to my magic. Alabaster the color of the moon. Some rubies, though they weren't very good. It was hung with ropes of pearls, too. They're well enough in their way. Briar really liked the blue and pink pearls, the ones as big as his thumb. He said you could get very good prices for those in the markets in Sotat and Emelan."

"But you weren't impressed." Jayat sounded like he was laughing at me.

"Well, they're pearls. They're just fake stones, you know. Cheats. They're dirt an oyster puts around grit to keep it from itching. You'd think there'd be a law against trying to cheat people with fake stones like that. Now, jade — the Green Man statue had it carved all kinds of ways, so it sang back to you in different tones."

We talked about my travels as we rode onto the shores of Lake Hobin. We'd finally reached Moharrin, just as dark was setting in. Torches were lit on the road along the lake, to guide us past farms and orchards to the village.

"Jayat, go let Azaze know we're here." As Jayat rode ahead, Oswin told Rosethorn and Myrrhtide, "I know you're too tired for a big reception, but Azaze — our headwoman — also owns the inn. People tend to gather there as a matter of course. There will be some of them to greet you."

"As long as there is a decent meal, they may greet me as they choose." Myrrhtide snapped his horse's reins and moved ahead of us.

"I don't think you have to worry." Oswin sounded very innocent in the dark. "Azaze gives a decent meal to almost everyone."

I saw Rosethorn slap Oswin lightly. "Naughty."

I don't *think* Myrrhtide could hear. Or if he did, he pretended he didn't.

4

The Inn at Moharrin

I hung back as the grown-ups rode on. People rushed out of the houses as we reached the outskirts of the village. They surrounded Rosethorn and Myrrhtide, giving me the shivers.

"Evumeimei, you are unhappy," Luvo remarked. "Are you so weary from your journey?"

Luvo sees in the dark. I *think* he sees, anyway.

"People," I grumbled. "Look at them. They swarm around Rosethorn and Myrrhtide like ants at a feast. They do everything but wag their tails —"

"Ants do not have tails, Evumeimei."

He couldn't distract me so easily, not when I was cranky at seeing the old game begin again. "Don't play logic games, please. Just listen to them for me, will you?" I asked. Luvo could hear at great distances. It was very useful.

"They say it is an honor for their village and their island, that two dedicate initiates of Winding Circle temple are here. They say they could not have hoped for such blessings. They are happy, Evumeimei."

"They're happy *now*, Luvo. People always *start* out being grateful," I reminded him. "But under the gratitude? They're already telling themselves that Rosethorn owes —"

"Not Myrrhtide?"

Luvo was learning too many human tricks, including trying to distract me. It wasn't at all becoming for a rock to be so sly. I ignored him. "Fusspot, too, if you *insist*. That our people *owe* them work and magic. That they should half-kill themselves in the service of this, this beetle-spit village next to its chicken-piddle lake on its donkey-dung island. You watch. Fast enough their requests will turn into demands and orders. That's what people are like. If you do things for them? You turn from friend, or even helpful stranger, into a slave."

I hadn't noticed that Jayat had returned on foot. He'd come through the trees on my right. That was why I hadn't noticed him getting close to me. He'd heard some of what I told Luvo. "Evvy, how can you say that? Surely you don't believe people are so cruel."

I slumped in my saddle. I *hated* having this argument with others, even more so when they seemed like they might be sensible. I squinted so I could see Jayat's face better in the shadows. "I *know* they are that cruel. See here. My mother sold me as a slave when I was six. It was because I was one mouth too many, and only a girl. I understood that. The part I minded was *where* they sold me. They brought me all the way from Yanjing to Chammur. Why didn't they just sell me in Yanjing? At least I was born there, and I knew the language."

"You would have *liked* it if they sold you before they left?" Jayat sounded shocked.

"It would have made more sense," I answered. "In Chammur I was a stupid slave who could barely talk. I had to run away, my master beat me so much. Then I lived on the street. You *really* see the good side of people that way. They chase you from their garbage heaps with brooms and rakes. They dump chamber pots on your head. They scream 'thief!' when you walk by, they steal what little you have, they kick you when they pass. . . . For every person who did me a kindness, I knew twenty who left bruises on me."

Jayat took my horse's reins. "I'm sorry, Evvy. I must have sounded like an idiot." He looked up at me. "But people are different here. We won't take advantage of either of your dedicates. You have to trust me on that. She'll see, won't she, Master Luvo?"

Luvo was as silent as clay.

Jayat glared at him. "Master Luvo?"

Luvo clicked and said, "My knowledge of humanity is most incomplete, Jayatin. The samples of it that I have encountered until today have been of a mixed kind."

Luvo always could say something bad so politely that it almost sounded good.

"We were in a war," I told Jayat. "It sours you, kind of."

We had reached the circle of light in front of the inn. Rosethorn, Oswin, and Myrrhtide had already given their horses to stable hands for care. I slid off mine and hit the ground with a wince. My knees and thighs moaned. I hadn't done so much riding in months. My bum felt like crumbling sandstone. I hung Luvo's sling over one shoulder, and my stone mage kit over the other. A stable boy took my reins.

Jayat got my saddlebags, lifting them down with a grunt. "What have you got in here, rocks?"

I grinned at him.

"So what happened?" He showed me inside and up a set of stairs. "How did you come to be traveling with Dedicate Rosethorn, if you were a street kid . . . where?"

He opened a door and ushered me into a room with two beds. I saw that Rosethorn's gear was already there. I also saw a basin of warm water, soap, and cloths to dry with.

"Luvo, would you tell him while I clean up? I feel like I have a mask of dust on my face."

"I do know the story. Evumeimei was nine human years of age when she heard the song of stones out of harmony with themselves. She was in the city of Chammur." I had put Luvo and his sling on my bed. I peeked over. Jayat sat beside him, watching Luvo as if Luvo was the village storyteller. I giggled and began to scrub off the dust.

"She followed the disharmony to a merchant who sold stones," Luvo went on. "She offered to clean them for coins, and in cleaning them, she restored their harmony. A year later, young Briar, Rosethorn's student, saw Evumeimei's magic in the stones. Briar pursued Evumeimei for days, to inform her that she had magic."

"He sounds very determined," Jayat said as I dried off.

"He would have to be." Oswin stood in the open doorway. "From what I hear, the mages of Lightsbridge and the Living Circle have strict rules. Regarding new mages, if a graduate of those schools finds one, he has to make sure that new mage gets an education. If he doesn't, the penalties are harsh. The graduate mage will lose his credentials. Or hers."

I nodded at Oswin. "That's right. The only stone mage in Chammur was a fungus on legs. I refused to study with him. Briar had to teach me the easy stuff until he found somebody who wasn't. He and Rosethorn were just visiting Chammur on their way to Yanjing, so I went with them. That's where we met Luvo. Oswin, you know a lot about mages, for somebody who isn't one. You *aren't* a mage, right?"

"You can't tell?" Oswin crouched by the bed so he could have a better look at Luvo.

"No, that's Briar. And his sisters. They can all tell if someone has magic in them." I squinted at Oswin. I always do that, squint at people, though I can't really *see* magic. At the same time I reached out with my power to try to feel Oswin's. I felt only air, like I do with most people. I'd only felt air with Jayat. "Are you a mage, then, Oswin?"

He gave me a twisted, sideways smile. "No, but I've studied what they do, every chance I get. How they use herbs, how they clean wounds — whatever helps the magic along. You'd be surprised how many of those things a normal human can put to use."

"Oswin's the reason why Starns hasn't *needed* to call on outside mages in *years.*" Jayat said it with as much pride as if *he* was the reason.

"That's not true." When Oswin blushed, he did it from the collar of his tunic all the way to the back of his skull. There wasn't any hair to cover it. "Tahar is good for most problems, and you're coming along, Jayat."

Jayat chuckled. It was a deep, rich sound, like warm honey. "Tahar would tell you herself, she can't even predict the weather with a spyglass and a tall rock to stand on. Maybe once, but she's too old now. She's good enough for the likes of me, with my cupful of talent, but what does that say? None of us is up to Winding Circle standards. If we were, we'd be somewhere else, earning a *real* living."

47

"It is a wise mortal who knows his limits, young Jayatin." Luvo cocked his head knob to look at Oswin. "And what kind of man is it who is more valuable than mages?"

"I'm *not*." Oswin turned even redder.

"Oswin fixes things." Jayat leaned back on the bed. "Let's say you have a problem. Maybe your well's gone dry, or your barn roof is falling apart. You have no money for a new roof, or the mage can't find water to fill your well. So you go to Oswin's with a loaf of bread or a crock of pickled eggplant, and you tell him your problem. Oswin comes to your place with a slate and chalk and looks things over. He starts drawing things and telling you what you have to do. Sometimes it involves helping another fellow who comes to help you. Sometimes Oswin builds a device to fix your well so you have water again. Then you send him home with a roast leg of lamb or a sack of couscous. They always need food at his house."

"Oswin fixes things." I said it again just to be sure I had it straight.

Jayat nodded. "Now, he might see what your Rosethorn does for plants. Next time he'll remember what medicines she used besides her magic. If we use the medicines first, before the plants are dying, maybe we won't need the magic."

"Now, then! Is this how you show folk Moharrin hospitality?" a woman asked from the doorway. Oswin and

Jayat leaped to their feet, as if they were boys who'd been caught raiding the pantry. The woman looked them over with snapping black eyes. She was queenly tall. She looked even taller with her henna-red hair pinned in a knot on top of her head. Her dress was plain brown cotton with yellow and orange embroideries, under a sleeveless yellow robe. Still, the emperor didn't look so regal in all his silk. When she frowned, her thin black eyebrows snapped together over an eagle-beak nose. "This child has been riding all day. Now I find you've kept her here, gabbling like a goose, when doubtless she's starving. In my house!" She looked at me. "Your Dedicate Rosethorn tells me that you are Evvy. I am Azaze Yopali, headwoman of Moharrin. My apologies for these two scapegraces."

"We didn't mean —" Jayat hurried to say.

"We were just explaining a few things." Oswin was sweating a little. I stuffed my sleeve in my mouth so, if I giggled, no one would hear.

"Forgive us, Azaze Yopali." Luvo reared back on his bottom end. He stretched up as high as he could, though that wasn't very far. "I am unable to reply to questions speedily. I fear the delay was mine, and the blame is mine."

For a moment the lady could only blink. Then she said, "I wasn't told of a talking rock."

"I prefer to be known as Luvo, though it is not my complete name. 'Talking rock' is unflattering at best."

49

Again Azaze was briefly silent. "Are there more of you about?"

"They prefer to keep to their mountains. I am an unusual sample of my kind."

"I don't know what to feed you," Azaze said.

"You need not concern yourself, but accept my thanks," Luvo told her politely. "I dine on the power within the earth, and take it as I need it. As to my housing, I remain with Evumeimei. We have traveled together for some time and are accustomed to one another."

Azaze smoothed her hair. "Well." She looked at me sharply. "There's more to you than meets the eye, *that's* plain. Come down and be fed. And — Master Luvo is welcome for his company, if he likes." She turned and walked downstairs, muttering to herself.

"We should have taken you to supper." Oswin still looked sheepish. "I'm sorry, I just wanted to get to know Luvo better. Come on, Evvy. Azaze's as prickly as a thornberry bush, but her girls know how to serve a meal."

"Do they ever!" Jayat said eagerly. "Master Luvo, may I take you down to the common room?"

"Do you want to walk, Luvo?" I asked. "I know you don't like steps."

"Thank you, Evumeimei. I would prefer to be carried on the stairs."

Before I could warn Jayat to let me do it, Jayat put his hands around Luvo. Luvo's size being what it was, I knew

Jayat had expected Luvo to weigh four or five pounds at most. Jayat lifted, and almost fell over.

"You'd better let me carry him," I warned. "Me being a stone mage, it's a lot easier."

"No, I can do it. Excuse me," Jayat told Luvo.

I looked at Oswin. He stood just outside, a finger on his lips, watching Jayat try to pick Luvo up. His eyes were interested, but distant, like Briar's when he was thinking. I wondered if that was the look Oswin had when he was deciding how to fix something.

It was a good thing for Jayat that Luvo is the patient sort. When he likes someone, he only weighs about forty pounds. Once, he adjusted himself when someone he *didn't* like was lifting him. It didn't go well for that man's back. I hadn't liked the fellow, either.

"Can your Briar carry him?" Jayat staggered as he carried Luvo to the stairs.

"Briar knows to leave stone things to me," I said. Oswin and I followed them. "Actually, that's what I liked about him, once I got to know him. He was the first person I knew who ever treated me like I had a mind of my own. See, he was a street rat, once. He knew how bad people could be. So he knew what would help me understand things."

"He . . . sounds . . . like a . . . paragon." Jayat was puffing when we walked into the main room of the inn.

Paragon — I knew *that* word!

Jayat set Luvo down on the table closest to the door and collapsed onto the bench.

"I'll get the food." Oswin patted Jayat on the shoulder. "I think you've done enough for today."

I giggled at both of them as Oswin walked off. "Briar's no paragon, Jayat. He likes pretty girls and picking locks and making jokes and playing with knives. And he's a realist. We both are." I looked across the room. "And we both look out for Rosethorn."

She and Fusspot sat with Azaze and a few people who seemed to think they were important. They had a table near a big stone hearth. There was a fire burning there, even though it was the middle of the summer. The room needed the heat. The air up here was even colder than it had been when I'd gotten Rosethorn's coat on her. There were more grown-ups at other tables around the room, eating, drinking, and eyeing the main table.

"You watch Azaze." Jayat had caught his breath. "She won't let people impose on your Rosethorn."

It was true: Two men approached the table, only to leave when Azaze glared at them. I was impressed, but how long could it last? There had to be people about who weren't afraid of Azaze, headwoman or no. And I'd seen plenty of headwomen and headmen who would do what they were told, if enough rich people told them to do it.

At least they were feeding Rosethorn. Girls in aprons were putting bowls and plates before Rosethorn and

Myrrhtide. They already had bread, hummus, and olives in front of them. Fusspot smiled and nodded to everyone, as if he was king of the Battle Islands. Rosethorn listened to Azaze and ate with a serious appetite. That was good. She wasn't too tired to pick at her food.

Oswin gave us bowls of chicken stew and pulled spoons wrapped in napkins from his sash. The stew smelled of ginger and cinnamon. My belly growled. Behind Oswin, a maid brought us a tray of plates: hot bread, olives, chickpea and yogurt dips, lentils cooked with noodles, and pastries stuffed with eggplant. I swallowed my saliva and dug into my stew. It was delicious.

"Is the death of your plants and trees so unusual, Oswin?" Luvo had settled on the table where he could watch the room. He never got tired of looking at things, human or natural.

"I haven't seen anything like this, Master Luvo." Oswin scooped up hummus and olives with his bread. "Trees, strong, healthy ones, gone dead overnight — actually overnight. And I've never seen something that killed plants *and* animals in the same spot. It's happened all around Mount Grace. The same thing with water sources. A pond that was good one day is acid the next, the fish, the plants all dead. It's like the place has been cursed, but it's a random curse. It doesn't strike any one family or village. I'll tell you, it's the saddest thing in the world, to go to a place that was living a month ago, and find it . . . dead." His mouth made a hard line. "If it's a person who's doing this, I'd like to dump him in one of the acid ponds. There's an old pine in the grove by my place — it was there in my grandfather's day. I'm going to have to cut it down, before it drops on one of the children."

Jayat looked up and swallowed hard. "Speaking of your household."

I turned around. A beautiful girl about Jayat's age had come in. She walked over to lean on Oswin's shoulder and steal a piece of bread. She moved like a dancer, swaying and graceful, as she whispered to Oswin. Her hair was the color of dark honey. She had a tiny, delicate nose. I tugged at the end of mine, trying to give it a little point. It stayed flat.

Oswin swore. "I told Treak if he started one more fight he was out on his ear."

"I think that was the ear he *wasn't* listening with," the girl replied. Even her voice was pretty.

"All right, I'm coming. Nory, this is Evvy. Evvy, this is Nory." Oswin got up. "It was very nice meeting you, Evvy." He looked at Luvo. "And *amazing* to meet you. I actually wanted to ask —"

Nory dragged on his arm. "Treak is breaking furniture and you're talking to a *rock*?"

"Furniture?" Oswin was red again. This time, from the way his eyes were bulging, I think he was red from anger. He hurried out, the girl trotting beside him.

54

"Remember I said he always needs food at his house?" Jayat asked. "A lot of kids were orphaned or left behind when the pirates were cleaned out. Oswin found homes for plenty of them all around this island, but not all of them. The rest live with him. They can be a handful."

I wasn't listening very closely. I was looking at my tea instead. I hadn't touched the cup or jostled the table, yet the tea rippled, as if a stone had fallen into its center. On and on the ripples went. I looked at what was left of my stew. There, too, the liquid shivered. I closed my eyes. Grimly I concentrated on what I could feel. Under my feet and my behind I felt the ghost of a vibration in the floor and in the bench.

I rested my hand on Luvo. *More earth-pulses?* I asked him.

The earth can be as restless in its sleep as you, Evumeimei. I didn't like his tone. It was troubled. Luvo had faced armies in Gyongxe without even grinding his crystal jaws. I hoped that whatever troubled him would go away soon, before it started to trouble me as well.

5

Dead Water

ven after two years in this aboveground world, I still love to watch the sun rise." Luvo was speaking quietly to Rosethorn as I woke up. "This is a gift you and Evumeimei and Briar have given to me. When I was safe in my mountain body, I did not understand the glory of the dawn."

Rosethorn explained, "Having to do midnight temple services for worship of the Earth gods puts a dent in my admiration for sunrise." When I cracked my eyelids I could see Rosethorn pour her morning wash water into the basin. She went on, "I'm too tired to appreciate it, most of the time. On the road it's different."

I looked out of the window. Ever since Luvo had first told me about his love of daybreak, I remembered all the sunrises *I* had missed, living in my burrow deep inside the stone cliffs of Chammur. Usually I watched for dawn with him. I could see it from my cot now. The sky was the pink of rose quartz.

As I tossed aside my blanket, I noticed that Rosethorn was staring at the water in the basin.

"Rosethorn?" I asked. "The water's shivering, isn't it? Making ripple circles?"

"Yes. Last night, my tea did the same. Myrrhtide didn't mention it, but I saw him try to make his stop moving. He failed." She looked at me. "A water mage of his degree couldn't get a cup of water to stop quivering, Evvy. That's . . . interesting."

"What do you think it means?" I wanted to know. "Earthquake?"

She shook her head. "No earthquake I've ever been through was so regular in its warnings. Nor did it send greetings by water like this." She took a breath and started to wash.

When I joined Luvo at the window, I saw that he wasn't looking east, where the hills were gold around the sun's rim. His head knob was turned north. There, at the western edge of Lake Hobin, stood Mount Grace. It was tall enough to have snow at the peak, even in summer. Trees covered the lower slopes.

"Luvo, do *you* think there's an earthquake coming?" I asked him. "Rosethorn says not, and she's been through plenty. Have you ever been in one?"

"Small ones, many. Large ones? Only when my mountain — when I — was born, the earthquakes, and the volcano that created me. I know of that because the older mountains told me of it. Though some of what I feel now reminds me of my earliest memories. Terror, fire, bursting into freezing air as the warm earth spat me out. Growing higher, rising into the air, above everything around me. But I do not know if these are true memories, or what I was taught."

"Then what is a true memory?" I wanted to know.

Luvo began to pace along the windowsill. I had to sit on my bed, I was so startled. Luvo *never* paces. He's not the pacing sort. He's the standing sort, or sitting. He did the new pacing slowly, but still . . . I glanced back at Rosethorn. She had stopped in the middle of tying the belt to her habit. Like me, she stared at him.

"I remember slow stiffness that began on my skin, and grew into my flesh, turning it from lava to stone," he said. "I got hard and cold. I felt crystals and minerals form. The stiffness went on, bringing with it stillness. Silence. Indifference. It came closer to my heart. To this piece of me, that you think of as Luvo." His stone feet thumped on the wood. "I had to make my first choice. I could let my heart, as well as my body, go solid and silent. I could dream my days away. So many of our kind choose that, unless they are awakened by great events. I could also choose to fight. I knew the battle would be hard and constant. It is easier to be still and to dream, harder to move around as I do. But I wanted to know more about the green things that were growing on my sides. I wished to see the water as it shaped my flanks into something different. I needed to feel the air as it remade me. I desired to meet the creatures that came, like the birds, and you. Those were my first needs. Evumeimei, Rosethorn, I have not thought of my birth, for many spans of your time." He stopped, and looked at Mount Grace. "I do not know why this place makes me think of it. Why it makes me think of pain."

Rosethorn came over to his window, drying her face. "Do you wish to return to the ship, or to Winding Circle? I'll make the arrangements, if you aren't comfortable here. I can find someone who will take you. . . ."

But Luvo was shaking his head. He sat on his haunches. "I want to know why I feel these things here. And I do not wish to leave Evumeimei. You are a teacher, Rosethorn. You know the most dangerous students are half-taught ones."

"Well, I like that!" I put my hands on my hips. Rosethorn was laughing softly.

"With the earth in motion, you might find yourself in a predicament," my friend the upstart piece of gravel told me. "I must look after you and keep you out of trouble."

"That's not funny," I cried.

Rosethorn was still laughing at me.

"Of course it's not." She gave me a wicked, wicked grin. "Come down to breakfast dressed for riding. We have another long day."

Azaze was up, too. "I have everything ready for you," she told us as we finished breakfast. "You've horses saddled and waiting, and a lunch packed. Jayat waits outside. Oswin will come to you later. He's work of his own to see to, first. Your Dedicate Myrrhtide says he'll be down as soon as he's finished his breakfast."

Rosethorn pursed her lips. "He had breakfast in his room?"

When she sounds like that, I'm really grateful if she isn't talking about me.

"I was just as pleased." Azaze filled Rosethorn's teacup a second time. "He kept fussing at my maids. Men like that are best left locked away, where they can't meddle with folk doing honest work."

Rosethorn choked as Azaze walked off to see to something in the kitchen. When she caught her breath, she said, "I'd say our headwoman can handle Myrrhtide."

Hearing that Fusspot was coming had taken the edge off my excitement. "Do I have to come if Myrrhtide goes? You don't need me to look at plants or water."

"But we need you as we go higher on the mountain, in case of rockfalls. Yes, you're coming. Just think, Evvy. You could be snug in your bed at Winding Circle right now, if you'd kept your temper with those boys."

I *knew* she would make me go. "Would *you* have done it differently? Would you have let those boys bully my friends?"

"That's different," Rosethorn told me. "I'm a dedicate initiate. When I pick on bullies, it's called an object lesson. And *I* know when to stop. *You* didn't."

I hate it when she says things I can't argue with. I finished my breakfast and went to get her mage kit. I left mine in my room, even my stone alphabet. I wouldn't be able to study any magic on horseback, for certain. Myrrhtide chatters at me when I take out my alphabet stones around him. He's afraid the magic I have stored in them will get out.

Like Azaze said, Jayat was waiting in the courtyard with the horses. I put Rosethorn's kit on her horse myself. Then I slung a little pack I carried, in case I found new rocks, in front of me on my saddle and perched Luvo on it. Luvo wanted to see everything. By the time I was ready, Rosethorn and Myrrhtide were set to ride. The sun was all the way up as we followed Jayat east, on the road through Moharrin.

By day we could see more of the village. It was set on the inner edge of a gigantic, gently sloping bowl ringed by mountains, or at least very tall hills. Mount Grace was the queen of them, towering over the others. Lake Hobin was where the water ran at the lowest point of the bowl. There were patches of farmland and orchards around the rim. The country seemed prosperous enough, earthquakes and all.

"Have you been in the lake yet?" Rosethorn reached over with a foot and nudged Myrrhtide.

61

He glared at her. "I have not. It looks very, very cold."

"It's snowmelt, a lot of it." Jayat was much too cheerful for that hour of the morning. "You'll be wide awake if you have a swim."

"I thought you Water temple types didn't care about the temperature," Rosethorn said. I don't know why she kept telling *me* to behave with Myrrhtide. She was always after him like a needle with the mending.

"Will you *please* be quiet?" Myrrhtide rubbed his forehead. "I can't hear the adorable little birdies greet the thundering sun."

The road followed the shore. We had a wonderful view of Lake Hobin and all the birds that fished and swam there. The sun turned the water into a bright silvery mirror. Now and then a fish would splash, rising to grab a bug. I half-expected the lake to show us those same weird ripples Rosethorn and I had seen in our wash water and tea. Only the animals ruffled its surface. Not even the wind stirred it. The air was still.

At last we turned down a new road, away from the lake. It took us past a few of those small farms. "This is Oswin's place." Jayat led us through a rickety gate. "He was the first of us to find a dead patch on his land."

A little girl stood on the doorstep of the main building, sucking her thumb. She was six, maybe, a mix of races, with light brown skin, brown hair, and long brown eyes. Her nose and chin were sharp. She was a pretty thing. She needed better clothes, though. Her dress was the color of butter amber, but it was patched. The sleeves had been ripped out of the armholes. She stared at us, walking out into the dooryard for a better look.

The beautiful girl — Nory — who had come for Oswin the night before ran out of the house. "Meryem, I told you to change out of that old rag!" She grabbed the girl by the back of her dress, then glared at us. "Don't even think of waking Oswin. He didn't get to sleep until long after midnight, with one horse having croup and us needing a rebuilt table for breakfast."

I felt watched and looked up. Faces in the upstairs windows of the house, boy and girl, watched us. They were all colors: black, white, brown, and mixes like Meryem. These would be the pirate kids Oswin had taken in, the ones left over after the adults had been killed. They looked like street kids I had known in the old days, before Briar had found me. They had that wary expression, the same as feral cats.

"Dedicates Rosethorn and Myrrhtide need to see the pond, Nory," Jayat said. "We don't have to wake Oswin to do it."

Nory scowled at all of us. "There are plenty of dead spots all around here. Why don't you go poke your noses into them?"

"Because we're here. We won't be any trouble." Jayat was almost pleading with Nory. I wondered how long he'd been sweet on her. Quietly he said, "Come on. You'll wake Oswin before we do, with your growling."

The older girl took Meryem inside the house. Jayat looked at us and shrugged. "Oswin says she's getting softer, looking after the kids. You just have to know her, I guess. This way." He led us around the house, down a rock-lined path into the trees.

I drew up even with Jayat. "I don't get it. Why are *you* showing us around, if you and your master are the only mages for this whole area? Won't you be needed someplace, sooner or later? Couldn't someone else play guide for us, if Oswin isn't available?"

Jayat shook his head, making his curls bounce. "It isn't just that the plants and water are getting poisoned." He looked older this morning. Maybe he just didn't like what he was saying, or thinking. "Too many of the dead patches are on places where this island's lines of power lie." He pointed to a rough granite post beside the path. It was as tall as my hip. Carved in the top of it was the Earth symbol, the circle that enclosed a cross.

I had seen them the day before, but had been too busy looking for new rocks to care. I studied the post. "It's tilted. And there's a crack in the middle of the granite. A bad shock and it will split right down the middle. You haven't been taking care of it."

Jayat scowled at me. "Then we'll replace it. We have one of those every ten yards to mark where the lines of the earth's power are hereabouts —"

"Are they all stone?" At least this was something I could take an interest in. "Are they all granite?"

"How would *I* know?" Jayat seemed grumpy. "They're just rocks that tell us where we may draw on the force of the earth, to give us strength for our spells. That's how lesser mages like Tahar and me can be of use to our kindred. . . ."

I felt for the line of power that was supposed to be under the cracked granite post. I didn't sense anything. I let my magic sink through the stones beneath it. There was some power in them that fizzed, but nothing big. There had *been* strength beyond the normal in those dull bits of stone. The quartz there clinked with an echo of it, but it was just an echo.

I let my magic run deeper and deeper. I sensed a hum, way down. It reminded me of how my own magic had once felt. It called to me. It was like a kid, wanting me to come and play. I kept reaching out, trying to grab that fizzing sense of being alive . . .

Then I fell off my horse.

It's not as if it never happened before. I start to chase some fire or crackle in my magical senses, and my body forgets to hold the reins, or to keep my feet in the stirrups.

My horse doesn't know what's going on because I'm not telling it anything, so it does what the other horses do. This time, the other horses had stopped in a clearing of dead trees around a dead pond. My horse did, too, only suddenly, because it almost walked into Fusspot's horse. Fusspot's horse objected to mine coming so close. It turned its head and snapped. My horse backed up and stamped — that's what Jayat said, when he stopped laughing. The stamp jarred me enough that I slid down my horse's side.

At least my body knew what to do, even if my attention *was* somewhere else. I tucked and rolled like a Yanjing acrobat.

Rosethorn grabbed me before I landed in the pond. This time my collar ripped. I was about to argue when she pointed at the water.

Dead fish floated there. Dead animals lay at the water's edge. The skin of the fishes was eaten away.

"Acid." Fusspot looked absolutely miserable. "This water has turned to acid."

"These plants and trees have been poisoned by it." Rosethorn dragged me to my feet, away from the water. I didn't complain, not after a look at those fish. I didn't want my shoes burned off my feet. "There, now, Myrrhtide. It's not sewage, as *you* thought."

"Not here, anyway. It might be sewage in the water table elsewhere."

Myrrhtide never knows when to give up.

"Evumeimei?" Somehow Luvo had stayed on the horse even while I fell off. "You are all right?"

"I'm fine. Just my dignity hurt. Jayat, listen, nobody could have drawn earth power here." I got up. Rosethorn let me go, once she knew I wouldn't stumble into that nasty-looking brown pond, with its scum of dead things. "The stones were touched by something great, but not lately. They fizz, but it's all leftovers. Maybe you and your Tahar Catwalker were chewing funny leaves. The shamans of Qidao do that, to imagine they can talk to the sky and horse gods."

"We didn't teach you how to be *rude*." Rosethorn was using her this-is-your-only-warning voice.

I'd been rude? I was impatient. How was I rude if I was just honest and wanted a straight answer?

"That's what I've been trying to tell you." Either Jayat didn't agree I'd been rude, or he was really easygoing. "We *used* to be able to call up the deep power with the right spells. Mages here have done it for centuries. The veins along these trails are so accustomed to this use, they almost offer the power at a touch. But at least close to Moharrin and the lake, it's all gone out of reach. And if I can't reach it, my master can't — I'm stronger than she is, even if I don't know a quarter as much. Further up the trail, there are more bad places. In one of them, there's a spot where the power is too close to the surface, and there's too *much* of it."

Myrrhtide frowned. "What do you mean, too much? You're a mage, you need to learn to be more precise in your reports. 'Too much' is hardly definitive."

Maybe I was wrong about Jayat's patience. He *did* scowl at Fusspot. "Master Tahar was called to help a woman who was having a difficult childbirth. She lives out by that place I mentioned. It's a power spot Tahar has used since she was my age. She was going to save this woman and her baby, with spells she's worked all her life. That time, when she set the spells to channel the power, it swamped her magic and her control. It was, was . . ." He shook his head. "It was a river, an ocean. Tahar would have killed them both if she'd used it. Instead she turned it back through herself. They died anyway. Master Tahar couldn't leave her bed for two weeks. She couldn't work magic for a month."

"What would make it do that?" I asked Rosethorn.

She shook her head. "There are all kinds of reasons. The earth lines are part of nature. They aren't an easy source of power for academic mages who need a bit extra. Too many things can go wrong." She frowned at Jayat.

He shrugged. "You're a dedicate initiate of Winding Circle temple. You can say that. I bet you've never had to call on sources outside yourself for help in your life."

"You're wrong about that," Rosethorn said. "I draw from the green world all the time."

"Because the green world is you, and you are it," replied Jayat. "Master Tahar and I aren't so lucky. Our people depend on us to help them live, Dedicate Rosethorn. You and Dedicate Initiate Myrrhtide here will leave when you've solved our problem."

"Of course." Myrrhtide sniffed, as if Jayat smelled bad, not the water with the dead things in it. "You could hardly expect us to remain *here*. We have other demands on our time and skills."

"Well, *Moharrin* is the demand on Tahar's time and skills. She's in her eighties. She needs all the help she can get." Jayat didn't even look grumpy as he spoke. It makes me cross just to *see* Myrrhtide when he sniffs that way. "So we do what we must to satisfy the village's demands, since we are the only mages here. If doing our work right means tapping a vein of power, as the mages before us did, you can't blame us for using the tools we have."

"Except there's nothing here but cold earth and stones that remember something," I reminded Jayat. "I can stretch down half a mile, and it's all ghost fizzing."

"I can reach even further," Luvo announced.

From the way Jayat flinched, he had forgotten that Luvo rode on my saddle. I wondered why Luvo always had to be so slow. Didn't he understand that life was just whooshing by?

Luvo went on talking. Slowly and pokily. "There is no crack below the ground, though it may be there was at one time. Some of the rock faces a mile to the west are cloven, as if they were sheared off. As if they were once small fault lines in the earth. But that shearing is no longer evident. You could no more reach the power in the faults under the heavy cloak of the earth than I could fly."

Myrrhtide sniffed. "Nonexistent fault lines are all very well, but I understand our little tour of inspection will take us up on the mountain today. You may talk rocks at another time. Let's go."

"No." Rosethorn pointed to a big, brown-needled pine tree on the far side of the pond. It was leaning, half-uprooted from the soft earth. "That's a hazard. It needs attention."

"You certainly don't expect me to get an ax and hack at it," Fusspot told her huffily.

"Oswin said he would cut it down," Jayat called to Rosethorn.

She was already walking around the pond. "He took in the children the pirates abandoned. Azaze was telling me about that. He's got enough to do with his days. I can handle this."

Jayat turned his horse. "I know where Oswin keeps his saw."

I put a hand on his arm. "She'll hate it if you cut. She wants to give the tree a proper funeral."

He frowned at me. He didn't understand, but he had the sense to halt and wait to see what happened. I picked

Luvo up and cradled him against my chest. *But we can do something to help, right?* I asked him through our joined magics.

Luvo and I mixed our power and let it sink into the ground. Under the pond we flowed from stone to stone. I winced at the burn of that water on each rock we passed through. Even with a foot of mud between us and the pond itself, we could feel the acid in it.

Did some evil mage poison it or something? I asked.

No mage has been here, Evumeimei, Luvo told me.

That was that. When Luvo was definite, he knew what he talked about. I don't know how he understood things, but he did. He tells me I'll know, too, in a few thousand years. I can't get him to see that I won't be around all that time. It makes me wonder if he knows something I don't.

Ahead shone the white blaze of Rosethorn's magic. She jammed vines of her power into some shadowy thing. The threads spread away from her to fill the shape of a leaning tree. Slowly and clumsily they tugged, trying to move its dead roots.

Luvo and I entered the stones around and under the tree. There Luvo went very, very still. I felt us flex, as if Luvo had swallowed with our magics. A wave of coolness from outside Luvo and me bore down on us. It was an invisible power that filled the earth, calling to the children of iron in the surrounding stone. The iron in fool's gold,

71

hematite, and olivine, even specks of iron no bigger than pinheads in the granite around us, all stirred like waking bees.

Rocks don't like to move. Still, given a choice between their iron's pull to that immense force, and battling the loose soil to stay put, the rocks chose to move away from the tree's roots. Luvo and I drew them back from Rosethorn, too, so she wouldn't be knocked off her feet.

With no rocks to help keep it standing, the tree slowly lay down on the ground. Luvo and I thanked the earth power that called the iron *very* politely. Luvo talked to it then for a while. My head was a bit woozy, so I drew back to my body alone, and leaned on my horse.

When I could, I drank some water and ate a peach, then looked around. Rosethorn was speaking the Green Man's prayers over the dead pine and the other dead trees. Myrrhtide, who grumbled that he should do *something*, collected pond water as he waited. He worked spells on it, to see what was wrong.

Jayat's face was covered with sweat. "What was that?" he whispered when he saw me smile at him. "Something went through me. It came from you and Luvo. I — I didn't know what was up or down, where the village is, where the mountain or the lake is . . ."

"There are more important things in the world than this village and lake." Myrrhtide was definitely cranky. Maybe he was as touchy about sick water as Rosethorn was about sick plants. "Even a half-trained bumpkin like you should understand that."

I was taking a breath, getting ready to teach Fusspot some manners, but Luvo had come back from talking with that great force. He stood in front of me. I steadied him as he spoke in his thundering mountain voice. "Respect a mage in his lands, human. You know nothing of those things that Jayatin has put into this place. You do not know the dedication and sacrifice that he and his masters have given this lake, this village, this mountain. You preen yourself on your learning. Take shame instead for the fear that bars you from true work and true devotion. You have not the heart for it. You have not the soul to understand those whose measure will always be greater than yours."

Myrrhtide went dead white. He kicked his horse into a trot on up the trail, away from us.

Rosethorn came over. "Luvo, remind me to stay on your good side. It was very well done, though." She mounted her horse and looked at Jayat. "I hope Myrrhtide went in the right direction."

Jayat wiped sweat from his face and nodded. His dark cheeks were scarlet. He took a drink of water. "I don't think I was worthy of that, Master Luvo."

"I am thousands of years older than you, Jayatin. I know what you deserve."

6

I Fuss with Fusspot

We caught up to Myrrhtide. Nobody said anything for a long time. I believe none of us could think of anything that wouldn't sound like fake jewels after Luvo's thunder.

The trail followed those earth lines marked for the island's mages. It often came close to places where plants and water had gone bad. Not all the water places — ponds or streams — had turned acid, but there were plenty of dead patches of land. Rosethorn got quieter and quieter. Her eyebrows came together more often in her puzzled look, until they just stayed that way. Myrrhtide fussed over each bit of dead water as if it was his child.

We crawled up the mountain's shoulder except for halts at dead spots. I kept searching the ground for the fizzing rocks, for something to do. They were hard to find. The strength in those ones I touched was fading, without their source of power to renew them. I was getting bored to *death*.

"The whole world is hurrying by while we poke along," I muttered when we stopped for the thousandth time.

Jayat shrugged. "We can only ride so fast. Here's where the earth's power swamped Tahar." He pointed to the farmhouse that sat back from the road. "The farmer's mother looks after him now." He and Rosethorn went to the house to talk to the family.

Myrrhtide glared at me. "Magical investigation takes time. A proper student would be taking notes."

I smiled at him. "I'm not Rosethorn's student."

"You think you don't have to obey temple rules because you have her and Briar Moss and that rock for friends?" he asked me softly. He kept an eye on Rosethorn. "In two years you'll be sixteen. It won't matter then *who* your friends are. You'll be out on your ear, *Evumeimei*. Out on the street where you belong." He smiled cruelly. "Unless you take your vows to the temple. But you'd have to care about us — and that's not a thing you can lie about."

Something around my heart pinched me. "I'll be on my way to magecraft, Dedicate Fusspot." I said it with as much sass as I could, pretending I didn't care. "I won't need your precious temple then."

"Spoken like a true guttersnipe." He sounded pleased. "Take, take, take. Never give anything back. Why the temple keeps allowing the likes of you in —"

"Shut up." I turned to face my horse. "Rosethorn's coming, you stupid man." I climbed back into the saddle, thinking, He's just a nasty old fusspot. I don't care what bile he spits.

"What were you talking about?" Rosethorn looked suspiciously at us. "You both looked very passionate about something."

I dug a smile up from somewhere. "Midday. I'm always passionate about food, you know that. He wants to wait awhile, and I didn't eat enough breakfast."

She looked at Fusspot, who was getting back on his horse, then at me. She didn't seem convinced. "Luvo, were they discussing the midday meal?"

"I was inattentive, Dedicate Rosethorn." Luvo's head knob was pointed toward the cliffs to the west. "My thoughts were on the fine-grained volcanic gabbro and quartz crystals higher on the mountain. Some of the crystals have a pleasing violet-pink color which I have never seen."

Jayat looked awed. Rosethorn could tell something was not right, but she could never bring herself to call Luvo a liar. Not that he was lying. Luvo's thinking is funny. It works like the rope of clear crystals that runs through his body. Each crystal is a little mind. Luvo has thoughts in all of them going on at once. He probably *was* thinking of gabbro and quartz, in part of him.

"Let's move on." Rosethorn mounted her horse. "Myrrhtide, you will ride beside me, if you please."

Off we went. Luvo sat in front of me and didn't move for a long time. Jayat rode ahead of Rosethorn and

Myrrhtide, thinking about something. I tried to sit quietly, but it got harder as the morning wore on. I swear, even the sunlight made my blood itch to move faster. My flesh throbbed inside my skin.

Is this how Luvo feels when he watches us? I wondered. Birds and small creatures dashed past and around the trail, living their real lives at a *real* pace, not crawling along. Does Luvo feel as if life is passing him by? Or does he like being *slllllooooowwww*?

I ground my teeth.

At yet another halt, Luvo looked at me. I don't know how, because he didn't have to turn his head to do it, but I felt his eyes on me. "You tremble. You give off heat. Are you ill?"

"Just restless. I feel fine," I retorted. "I feel better than fine. I just want to *ride*, not trudge along like a snail. I'm not hot. I don't feel the ground trembling one bit. *I'm* not trembling."

But I looked at my hands on the reins. They shook, as if I had a fever. I didn't *feel* sick.

I felt it then, far below the stone and earth under us. The little hairs on my arms stirred as I called the warning: "Shake coming!"

We all dismounted. I held Luvo with one arm as I clutched my horse's reins with the other. Now everyone else had the sense of it. The birds and little creatures were silent. Our horses stamped and yanked at the bits. We hung on as the earth rattled the loose leaves from the trees and the stones from their places. When the shock struck us, I felt like a thousand fingers were tickling me. I giggled. Then the power was gone. Life got slow and boring again.

As we rode on, those neglected stone markers started to vex me. What if they didn't show the local mages where strength could be drawn from the earth anymore? That was no reason to leave them untended. They had done generations of service. Some of them had fallen over. Some were just tilted, which made them look undignified.

When I found moss covering most of one granite marker, flaking its carvings away, I couldn't bear it anymore. "Rosethorn!"

"Evvy, I'm thinking," she said.

"It's moss on a rock, and the rock doesn't want to be changed. It likes being all neat and carved." I was jittery and aggravated. "If you won't clear it away, I will, Rosethorn, you know I will. I have followed like a good dog all morning. Now I would like to tend this marker."

She sighed and dismounted.

"I can't believe you're doing this." Fusspot turned his horse around in the road. "We're going about important work, looking at serious problems. Why do you cater to that spoiled brat you *insisted* on burdening us with?"

Jayat rode a little way up the trail, to get away from us.

Rosethorn glared at Fusspot. "Evvy and I have an understanding. There are plenty of reasons for doing things as we do them. She is no burden to *me*. Since I am senior *and* in charge, I will thank you to hold your tongue!" She came over to me and muttered, "Don't make me have to defend your behavior to him again."

I didn't tell her I could defend myself. I was eager and nervous and vexed, but I was not ready to die. It was one thing to snap at Fusspot. I had learned early on, a person who snapped at Rosethorn had best be armed for war and prepared to take casualties.

"What is the matter with you, anyway?" Rosethorn demanded. "You don't normally care if there's moss on stone or not. Didn't you tell me in Yanjing that you don't even think vines are rock killers now? That since rocks have no bodies like ours to grow and change, they are dependent on forces from the outside to change them, and that includes plants?"

I scuffed my foot in the dirt of the road. "This marker wants to stay the way it is for now." Normally I would have told the rock not to be silly, but my veins were filled with hot, fizzing blood. It was like what I'd sensed in those old power places, only stronger. If Jayat and Tahar had drawn this kind of strength from there, I was surprised Jayat could bear to ride along so pokily.

"And stop *jittering*," snapped Rosethorn. "Mila save us, Evvy, it's like you've been sniffing dragonsalt. Enough!"

Carefully Rosethorn put her hands on the moss. She talked it into letting go of the stone. Piece by piece, she lifted it free and moved it to a shady patch. I called a fistful of lesser stones in the soil to come together, bracing the marker. They helped me to push it until it was straight again. When that was done, Rosethorn and I mounted up and followed the others along the trail.

Fusspot couldn't keep still for long. We hadn't gone more than five more markers up the slope of Mount Grace when he drew his horse even with Rosethorn's. "I want her left at the village next time! She is a distraction and a nuisance! She is —"

"What in the Green Man's mercy?" Rosethorn turned her horse down a path among a tumble of rocks. Myrrhtide might think she was riding off in a temper, but I knew better. She hadn't even heard him. Something else had gotten her attention. I looked at Jayat.

"There's a better place to see it from," Jayat called to her, and turned to me. "How did she know?"

"How did she know what?" I asked. Fusspot shoved in front of us to ride after Rosethorn. Jayat didn't answer; he just followed Fusspot, and I followed him.

Rosethorn led us down among rocks that got taller and taller. These were big, *gorgeous* slabs of flat stone. They looked like some giant had cut them from the mountainside with an ax. We came out on a ledge. Stone rose behind us, and the ground sloped far below. The slope ended in a small canyon filled with dead trees.

Jayat sighed. "This is the worst place. My uncle and I found it two weeks ago as we were hunting."

I dismounted and put Luvo on the ground. The fizzing in my blood was starting to annoy me. It made me fidget, when I am not by nature a fidgeting person. I rested my hand on one of the slabs behind us, hoping the nice, steady granite would calm me down. Instead its roots warned me of what was rising under our feet.

"Shock!" I yelled. How did it come up on us so fast? It must have welled up under the mountain. "Earth shock!"

The others threw themselves off the horses, which were panicking. The animals had felt the coming shakes almost as soon as I had. *That* was embarrassing. I should have known faster. "Luvo, why didn't you warn me?" I cried.

"It is too quick. Too close," he said.

I dragged my horse's head down. It fought, until I yanked my jacket off and covered its eyes.

The earth shuddered and crackled. Trees fell into the dead canyon from its sides. Boulders tumbled along with them. Everything smashed to bits at the bottom. The wave of power struggled to reach the surface, fell short, and sank back.

We waited and did nothing, only listened. Luvo and I sent our magics into the ground, feeling for more waves.

We found nothing. On the mountain and in the canyon, more stones fell. Big ones, little ones . . . They welcomed the chance to change themselves. I wished them well on their journeys to new shapes.

"That was very, very close." Jayat, like me, had covered his horse's eyes to keep it calm. He began to unwrap his shirt from his horse's head.

I stared at the long scars on Jayat's back. He shrugged and said, "Not everybody was sad when the foreign lords killed as many pirates as they could find."

I nodded. I could see that he wouldn't be too upset at that. "Luvo? Are you all right?" I asked.

Luvo wandered over to the ledge to look down into the dead canyon. "The crack in the earth beside the road closed, but a new one opened down below. I do not recommend that you try to use the new line of power, Jayatin. There are seams of quartz crystal around and below it. They will make any magical strength drawn by a human somewhat irregular."

"Are you sure we would do so badly, Master Luvo?" Jayat smiled patiently, as if he spoke to a child. "We've gotten pretty good at finding ways to draw on this stuff, you know. We have to, you see. We're just a little bit desperate at the moment. Perhaps our skills don't look like much to you, being stone . . ."

"The strength you used is affected by certain laws, including those of crystals, Jayatin." Luvo was in his teaching mood. I was glad it wasn't me who brought it on. "Magic passes into quartz as light does. It is reflected from the inner walls of the crystal. You would gather it up quickly, if your magic passed only through one crystal. However, along the seams below and around the crack in that canyon are large clusters. Within each cluster the crystals are turned in their own arrangements. They will reflect each bit of power back upon itself, then to other crystals. You would be trapped here, chained by your magic, until it wore out."

I heard a grinding noise above our heads.

So did Rosethorn. "Luvo, be quiet." Her brown eyes searched for the source of the sound. "Everyone, back up —"

Higher up the mountainside, a huge slab of granite gave way. The shock had broken it from its roots. It slid toward us, collecting a train of smaller boulders and gravel as it came. As it fell, it gathered the strength of its falling, picking up speed.

And then it flipped, like a coin in a street magician's hand. In my head I had been set to send it on a neat detour around us — until that flip. When it leaped high in the air and came down like a six-ton ax, there was no time to be pretty. I even forgot Luvo was there. I just threw up my hands and my power, sucking the strength of the mountain granite in through my feet. I hurled it around that slab and the worst of the boulders.

They locked into place over our heads. They were as solid in the air as they had been on the mountainside. I held them still, wondering what I was going to do now.

Luvo's power slid into place over mine, cool opal slabs over my thin mica sheet. "I have it, Evumeimei. We are fortunate that you are so quick."

He gently lifted all that stone away from me. I've seen parents set infants in bed with a careful gentleness, as if one slip might break the baby. That was how Luvo settled the slab and its boulder friends in the canyon below, as if they were his children, and he didn't want to disturb their sleep.

"Still wishing she had stayed at Winding Circle?" Rosethorn raised an eyebrow at Fusspot. One of the smaller rocks that escaped me had bruised her cheek. I winced in shame — I should have caught those stones, too. She took a little pot of something from her saddlebag and dabbed some of its contents on her skin. The bruise faded to a yellow spot. Then she did the same for Jayat, Fusspot, and the horses, who had all been dinged by smaller rocks. Jayat gaped at me even when Rosethorn was mending his cut.

"What?" I was feeling cross. "Are the flies lonesome? Are you offering them a warm, wet home?"

"Hunh?" Jayat blinked at me.

Rosethorn pushed Jayat's chin up until he realized his mouth hung open. He closed it.

84

"It's just raw power. There wasn't any art to it." Fusspot was red-faced as he fiddled with his horse's reins. "Thank you." He said it to the horse's side.

Despite the banging in my head — it hurts to work so fast and so hard — I had to grin. I bet the horse didn't get thanked every day. That night it would probably tell all the other horses about the strange human who snapped one moment and said thanks the next.

Jayat was still staring. "Stop goggling," I snapped. "You don't do that to Rosethorn or —" I almost said Fusspot, which Rosethorn wouldn't like. "Myrrhtide."

"They're dedicate initiates. You're *my* age." Jayat tugged at his collar like it was suddenly too tight.

"Luvo did the really hard work. I just stopped it. Ogle Luvo," I ordered.

"Ogle no one." Rosethorn gathered her mare's reins in her hand. "Let's go someplace safer and eat our midday. I don't know why it is, but sudden peril and rescue always improves my appetite."

7

Fizzing

We returned to the trail. Jayat led us up a few hundred yards, to a broad open space covered with grass and flowers. "This is as high as we will go," he said as we stared at the huge peak of Mount Grace towering over us. "The road circles the mountain but doesn't climb. We can't clear it in the winter. But there are advantages to keeping it open this far." He gestured for us to look toward the north side of the clearing.

From there the mountainside fell away. We had a glorious view of the neighboring Battle Islands. Two of them were smaller than Starns. They looked sunbaked and dusty in the blue-green sea. Behind them rose another island, a big one, with real forests on the ridges that faced us. Cliffs rose out of those forests like castle walls. They seemed to frown down at the tiny fishing boats on the water between the islands.

"If the weather's good, we can see if the neighbors are sending trouble our way." Jayat took a spyglass from his pack. He gave it to Rosethorn and Fusspot, who viewed the islands with it. When they were done, he offered it to me. "Moharrin and the other villages take turns manning a watchtower just a mile from here, to give the alarm if that happens."

Once we had all looked, Jayat put the spyglass away. Rosethorn and I unpacked the lunch. Azaze didn't mean for us to starve: She'd sent bread rolls filled with spinach and lentils, pickled beets, and grape leaves stuffed with rice, pine nuts, and currants. While we ate, Jayat, Rosethorn, and Myrrhtide talked about the Battle Islands.

"Jayat, why don't you go study with the mages on the other islands and learn more stuff?" I picked up some chunks of rock to juggle. "I don't know about you, but the more teachers I meet, the more tricks I learn."

He made a face. "I wish I could, but I can't be spared. We're both so busy. Tahar's health isn't good. She —"

"But you said yourself you're stronger than her." I know interrupting is bad manners, but I think I had my bad manners skin on that day. "She has to know you need more education than you'll get here. Doesn't she realize it does more harm than good to keep you ignorant? Just because she's spent her whole life here doesn't mean that helps —"

"*Evumeimei Dingzai.*" This time it wasn't Luvo who used my whole name, but Rosethorn. And unlike Luvo, when she used my whole name, it wasn't a good thing or even a normal one.

I looked at her.

"Since when do you have the right to comment on the way others choose to conduct their lives?" She had her eyebrows raised — a bad sign.

I felt very, very warm, and strange. I looked at Jayat. He stared at the ground. What had I been saying? I thought about it for a moment, and choked. Kanzan the Merciful forgive me, I thought, she's right. "I just — I didn't mean . . ." I whined, and clapped my hands over my mouth. For a moment I sounded like a street beggar again! What was *wrong* with me today?

We all heard the voices at the same time. "— ridiculous for both of us to come all this way —"

"It won't kill Treak to see how hard it is to manage without us. You might never get a second chance for him to prove he's learned. Oswin, you said you'd leave the management of the house to me. You either meant it or not."

"That's Nory's voice." Jayat stood as Oswin and the girl Nory rode into the clearing.

I sighed in relief. Now everyone would pay attention to them, not me.

"I told her she was to wake me the *moment* you came, so I could help take you around." Oswin glared at Nory, who tossed her hair. "What have I missed?"

"Evvy stopped an avalanche." Jayat was trying hard not to look at Nory. "Dedicate Rosethorn and Dedicate Myrrhtide have gathered a lot of dead plants and bad water."

I sighed. "Luvo did the hard part with the avalanche."

Rosethorn actually *smiled* at Oswin. "Once young people get the idea that they're taking care of you, they become perfect tyrants. Besides Evvy, I have four others, so believe me, I know. Sit down and eat something, Oswin. All we did was collect samples from the destroyed areas."

He got off his horse, which didn't look as if it had liked its trip up the mountain road. "*Five,* Rosethorn? You have *five* of them doing this to you?" He passed his reins to Jayat, who took over unsaddling his horse. Nory dismounted and cared for her own animal.

Rosethorn patted the ground beside her. "My student Briar and his three foster sisters hover over me whenever they're given the chance. Evvy here makes five young tyrants. Have a spinach roll, Oswin. Tell us when you first saw these dead places. Jayat, I'll need the same information from you." After she passed the food to Oswin and Nory, Rosethorn felt around with her hands.

I stuck my juggling rocks in my pockets, then got her map, notebook, and writing kit from her saddlebag. She opened her map on the grass and anchored it with cups. While she did that, I broke a piece off of her ink stick and ground it to powder, then mixed it with water until her ink was the thickness she liked. Jayat had brought his own notebook and writing kit. He set that up.

I could see that they were settling in for a long, dull meeting. I wandered across the clearing and through the stones that marked its limit. A short walk brought me to the dead canyon, among the sharp-edged granite slabs that made its rim. I squatted on my hunker bones and plucked a stem of grass to chew, looking at the streak of brown that marked the canyon floor.

Under the carpet of dead trees and brush, I felt stone that had been soured, touched with some nasty air. It had tainted the surface of the granite down there. I let my magical body pop free of my real one and slide down those poisoned surfaces, into the distant earth. The touch of bad air covered all the stones beneath that ground, as if the poison had swelled around it before bursting into the free air above.

These stones *fizzed*. The power that Jayat and the mages before him had drawn on had been there recently, filling them. I plunged deeper, hunting the source of that wonderful feeling. Here was the quartz Luvo had mentioned. It glinted in the crack, throwing the reflection of my power back at me from hundreds of its facets. There was enough white, clear, and smoky quartz to keep

Winding Circle and Lightsbridge supplied for centuries. Bits of the fizzing power that had passed through here clung to them like echoes of a lightning storm.

Now I was having fun. Quartz has as many aspects as Rosethorn has medicines, from agates to tiger's-eye, in shades from darkly smoky to colorless. There were agates at the canyon's bottom, as well as amethysts and pure white quartz. I shimmered through the white vein, then bounced along hexagonal rods of amethyst. The faces and chunks told me their stories, about the times this bed had moved up as the earth shifted, then down again. I slid through the long sides, seeing my magical shadow ripple along their surfaces.

Evumeimei. Luvo's voice was thunder in the ground, echoing off of every stone there. I shrieked and shot upward. I opened my body's eyes and looked for him frantically.

He sat next to me, seemingly just a green and purple and crystal bear worn down by water.

"Why did you do that!" I shouted. "That *hurt!*"

"We have company," Luvo said quietly. You would never believe he had made every rock underground within miles bang with the sound of his voice. "You should greet her."

"I was fine! I was minding my own business! I was just —"

Nory stepped into my view. "What are you screaming about? And where did you find the talking rock?" She stood next to us, her arms folded over her chest.

I glared at her. "Why are you here anyway?" My head hurt badly enough from Luvo's voice that I didn't care if I was rude or not. "*You're* not a mage or a fixing person or a person who looks after her mage."

"Treak's all full of remorse for being bad last night. I am taking advantage and getting free of the house for the day. Not that it's your business, Person Who Looks After Her Mage. As titles go, that's not very impressive. Will you answer my question or not?"

I stared at her. How did someone so pretty get so hot-tongued? "Do your parents worship at the Fire temple every day of their lives?"

"My mother worshipped money. Then her ship got hit by lightning and sank while it attacked Winding Circle eight years ago. My father and older brother worshipped Urda and Lakik like sensible people, praying to Lakik's good-luck side. Pirate chasers mistook them for fierce outlaws and killed them. I'm skeptical on the whole question of gods at the moment." If saying these things bothered Nory, it didn't show on her face. "You still haven't told me where you got the talking rock."

I took out the juggling stones I had stuck in my pockets. Luvo could handle this snapdragon himself.

He walked toward her, his short legs thumping on the dry grass. "I sensed the coming of Evumeimei and her friends when they approached my home in the Heaven Wind Mountains of southern Yanjing. I had never felt the spirit of any human like Evumeimei before, and so I left the inside of my mountain to meet her."

"Stone mages are a copper a pair," Nory told him scornfully. "At least, they are in the real world, not this pile of droppings in the Pebbled Sea."

"But none like Evumeimei. She is alive. The world is hers, or she will make it hers. She sparkles."

I spat on the ground. Luvo is a dear, but being a mountain for thousands of years made him a dreamer.

The fizzing in my veins was bothering me even more. I tossed my juggling stones in the air, but my hands shook too much. I dropped one and smacked a finger with the other. That hot, itchlike tingle made me want to scratch my own skin off. Did I bring it back with me from the stones in the dead canyon? Now that I was up here, I knew that I felt the power that Jayat and his master had used. Luvo was right. It was down below the canyon floor.

I picked up my juggling stones. "The earth strength found new paths. If I reach down far enough, I could maybe touch it." I spoke out loud, forgetting I wasn't by myself. "I could maybe find out what happened to the old lines, what made them shift." The rocks I held were puzzling me. One was pumice, littered with long holes. Another was obsidian. One was feldspar. What were volcano rocks doing up here? I brushed the area around me with my power. More volcano rocks. Mount Grace was covered with them.

Never mind those, I told myself. What of all that power far beneath the canyon? That line went someplace, but where? I sent my magic down to touch it. The line passed out of my reach under the mountain. I wondered if I could pick it up on the far side of the peak.

At our present rate of travel, we'd be another couple of hours riding around the top of Mount Grace, even if the grown-ups were done talking. My body's itch was getting worse, the fizz spreading into my bones. By the time we got down the other side of the mountain, I would be chewing my arms.

I can't explain what I did then. I just did it. I ran back to the clearing and threw the bridle on my horse's head. I got the bit on faster than I had ever managed before. I think I had taken the animal by surprise. Once I had done that, I was in too much of a hurry to bother with a saddle. I simply jumped on the horse's back, grabbed the reins, and kicked it in the sides.

I don't even remember hearing anyone, though I am very sure Rosethorn and Fusspot had things to say. I rode, galloping madly along the rocky, twisty mountain road. At least I knew enough of what I was doing to stop and rest the horse now and then. I would wipe it down with hand-fuls of grass. I even remembered to give it water from my bottle, since there might be acid in the streams.

I'm surprised I thought of it. Otherwise, my mind was on the cracks and seams of Mount Grace. I let my magic seep into them, searching for the feeling of power. I wanted that sure sense that greatness had touched these stones. I searched far ahead of me and to either side, let-ting my magic sink deep into the ground. The fizzing grew into the thunder of waterfalls through my veins and bones. I had to stop guiding the horse and trust it knew the road, because I couldn't see anymore. My eyes were filled with magic. I saw only stones.

She says she will drown you in the lake tonight, so say your prayers. Luvo's voice in my mind was a cool bath that soft-ened the roar of the power in the mountain stone. I sighed in relief, it felt so good. *She is very, very angry. She cannot defend your actions to the others, and that makes her angrier.*

I couldn't answer him. Crystals — moonstone, quartz, garnet, the indigo-in-green gem called black moon-stone — sang through the roar. Their power was raised to heart-piercing levels by what had passed through them. I had found the place where the magic was loudest.

Hands helped me off of my horse. My legs crumpled. I wasn't used to riding a grown horse bareback for so long.

"Evvy, here are some rocks." I think that was Jayat. My memory wasn't good for anything but the voice of my magic. "Luvo, she can't walk. Does she have fits like this often?"

"Never. However, I know the nature of what possesses her. If you wish to ride on, Jayatin, I will remain with her. We may be here for some time."

"You said yourself you couldn't run for help and get to it in time for anything. And you can't ride. Oswin can show them the old power trail as well as I could have. I don't like the way *you've* been acting, either. I mean, our acquaintance hasn't been long, but you've been quiet and tucked into yourself this last bit of the road like you're ailing. Do you even get sick?"

"I do not. Moreover, I cannot tell you what it is that makes me so uneasy. I only know that Evumeimei pursues it."

Jayat helped me onto a tumble of basalt — cool, black, rational basalt. In this shape it was six-sided columns, broken in spots, lying in a pile. He shooed away some lizards and arranged my body so I could sit, then dribbled water between my lips.

"My master goes on spirit quests sometimes, and her body gets like this." After a moment he closed my eyes — I dimly remember they were starting to hurt, they were so dry. He yanked off my headcloth. Soon after that I felt cool wetness on my forehead, cheeks, and eyelids. He had dampened the cloth and laid it over my face.

I pulled my magic in from all around me. Two hundred yards or so under the ground, about fifty yards downslope from the basalt, there was a new crack in the earth that bled strength. It would take me closer to all that wonderful magic. I gathered my power and fell into it.

Evumeimei, you do not know what you are doing. Luvo followed me. He didn't sound like the Luvo who had taken me down into the Pebbled Sea, or the Luvo who had fled with me through Gyongxe mountain canyons. He sounded . . . old. And frail. *The earth's molten heart is too close to the surface here. It may overwhelm us.*

Don't be silly! It's melted stone! How can melted stone be anything but wonderful *for the likes of us? Honestly, Luvo, if you're going to natter and scold, don't come with me!*

You are young. You do not understand the great forges below the blanket of rock. None of us do. We are all born in fire, with no memory of that birth but pain.

That's what I mean about nattering and scolding, Luvo! In my magical shape I swooped through a vein of rockwater, the indigo crystal cooling me as I passed. I had reached the depth that was usually as far as I could go. This time, though, I could keep traveling through the earth. I could do the same as Jayat and his master, using the power I had followed here. I wrapped it around me like a shell of fire. It threw off colored flashes to rival the ones from the crystals I passed through: scarlet, violet, flaming orange, amethyst, sea green, midnight blue.

Luvo slowed behind me, then stopped. *Do not go further. I will not stay with you. There is no good to be found down there.*

My soul was on fire. *Luvo, where's your spirit of adventure? The heart of the earth is here!*

Finally the crack was starting to open up. Power and heat filled it, welcoming me. I dropped into it, grabbing all the magical protection I could wrap around myself. I screamed with victory over the treasure of power I had found. No *wonder* I had been restless and half-mad, with an abundance like this close by! It was a miracle I didn't split in two. Those first minutes of bathing in that wealth exploded in me. If I hadn't protected myself on the way down, it might have eaten me like a chip of wood.

Floating there, the part of me that still had sense knew I was in danger. It found a mess of spells I had made once to soften, then harden, rock to trap an enemy. I used the spells now, with some changes. I grabbed power, not stone, and turned it into a tough shell of protection around what I already had.

Then I drifted, my magical eyes taking in my surroundings. I had come to the ceiling of an immense chamber under Starns Island. Below me was a huge pool filled with melted stone. Minerals, metals ... they all swirled together in different colors of hot. The chamber squeezed them together in a stone vessel that melted even while it kept them underground. The moving colors enchanted me, calling to me. I thought I saw faces in them and hands. They beckoned me to join the fiery spirits that swam in that pool. I could feel myself melting around the edges. What would it be like down there? Maybe it would be like joining one huge lake of melted stone and magic, with no beginning, and no ending.

I thought I would like that.

8

Flare and Carnelian

I was starting to sink down through the air toward the pool when two shapes rushed out of the stone-melt. They grabbed my protection-sphere, hauling me back up to the crack I had just left.

Hello, hello, look at you! one of them cried, twirling around me.

You're new, you're not old, you're not cold and dead, who are you? the other demanded, twirling the other way.

You're sparkly and you came from the cold place above, said the first. *How did you get in? Show us! Take us out of here!*

They danced me around like two kids who had found a new playmate. Then they wrapped their hot, snakey bodies around my shell. Now I was *really* glad for my protections. Even with three layers of magic around me, these two kids felt *hot*. Quickly I dragged more strength from the melted rock below. I put it into my layers to keep from being eaten. My magical body was all ideas and power, controlled by my mind, but I was certain that if my magical self burned to ashes, my real body would die, too.

Who are you? I asked. *Where did you come from? Are you mages? What are your names?*

What are mages? The one who felt more like a boy slowed down. He trailed a shock of sparks and flame from his top end, like a flare. To keep them straight, I decided to call him that. *We came from below to here,* Flare said. *Now we want to go* up. *We* must *go up.*

Can't you feel it? The other one had a prettier voice, more like a girl's. Her core fire was a darker, cooler orange, like carnelian. I thought it would make a good name for her. *How important it is to go up, and* out?

Slowly, though they kept spinning me around, they were changing. When they'd first grabbed me they were like a pair of comets, gripping me with long, molten stone tails. Now they were shifting, their bodies getting shorter. The tails became two legs; arms split off from the trunk. The ends at their heads settled into their bodies until they had formed necks. Were they copying the shape of my magical body? I had always liked to appear human, maybe so I wouldn't forget.

Once they had simple bodies, they changed even more. Flare was sapphire blue, still with his trailing flame of hair. He had black-rimmed eyeholes around flame eyes. Carnelian had turned her fiery hair black like mine. She made herself a nose and mouth, as well as eyes.

What are you? I felt like an idiot for having to ask again. A real mage would know, it seemed to me. *What are you doing here?*

We're the children of the pool. Flare spun until he was a blur, then stopped and took his humanlike shape again. *We were born there. We swim there, too, sometimes, but that isn't all we are anymore.*

We want other things than just melting together now. We want to go out. Carnelian obviously thought I was quite slow. *Don't you? Don't you have the pool where you come from? Aren't you bored with the pool? Don't you want to go somewhere new?*

Don't you want to be *someone new? Someone who isn't always from the same places?!* Flare spun against the roof of the chamber, melting a hollow spot there. Liquid stone dripped through my magical body, its power making me shiver.

No. We don't have anything like it. I looked down at the pool and felt the tug of it again. What would it be like to give up my edges completely? To melt and join all those other spirits? I could be stone forever. Why did these two want to leave that?

I came to myself and looked at Flare and Carnelian. *I have never met anyone like you in all my travels through the earth.*

You mean the cold stuff? You travel in that? Who do *you meet, then?* Flare asked.

Stones. Crystals. Metals, I said. Both of them cocked their heads at me in just the same way. How could they not know what those things were? Then I realized that if they were spirits from magma, they might only have seen the walls around them. If they approached anything that was hard, it probably melted. *When all of that* — I took my hand from Carnelian so I could wave to the hot world below us — *goes cold, it turns into those things. It stays in one place and never moves. Like the walls that keep us here.*

But those are just rock. They aren't like us. They aren't even like the others, the ones who are old and never want to do anything. Carnelian pointed to the lava pool.

The others. Flare sounded impatient. *Like us, only boring and sludgy. They're everywhere.* He pointed like Carnelian had.

Now I could see that the pool was made up of thousands of spirits. They had the shapes that Flare and Carnelian had when they first came to me. Apart from that, the spirits were every size, fat and thin, tall and short. All of them watched me with faces that looked greedy and worried at the same time.

They made me very, very uncomfortable. I asked, *But aren't you the same as the others? What makes you different? Why do you want to go out when they don't?*

Flare laughed. *Oh, they do. They just want someone to lead the way. We're tired of waiting for someone to come along and lead us. We're going out by ourselves.*

Come on! Carnelian dragged on my arm. *Come with us. We have a wonderful game, it's called Let's Find a Way Out!*

They pulled me along the roof of the big hollow chamber, above the pool. Melted stone dripped through my magical body where Flare and Carnelian touched the roof. I felt the weight of the mountain overhead, pressing down. How many tons of stone, earth, and water lay on top of me right now?

Look, up there, Flare cried, *a crack in the walls!*

Flare towed me through it, thinning himself as he did. Carnelian swam in my wake: I could feel her heat through my magic. Flare and Carnelian were groaning. It was even harder for them to move in that stone split than it was for me. They were solid with their melted rock bodies, even if magic shaped the way they looked to my eyes. At least my magical body took up no more space than the width of my arm. That was only because I'd covered myself with hard protection spells.

All around us the rock growled as they pushed it apart. At last it refused to budge any more. We didn't get very far.

Failure. Carnelian sounded heartbroken, like a little girl who had lost her favorite doll. *Again.*

I sent a tendril of my power up through the crack. There was poisoned air on the stones above us. In two hundred feet or so I broke through into the open, above the ground. Suddenly I wondered: What happened to the trees there? Heat from my two new friends and air from the chamber would have come from that crack in the soil. I felt no stones washed by water, so there was no stream to poison, or a pond, but . . . what about the grass, and the bushes?

Let's go here! Flare dragged me back into the big chamber. Carnelian caught up with us and leaped on Flare. They swirled around like kittens play-fighting for a moment. Then they grabbed me.

I thanked every god I knew, from Yanjing to Emelan, for the protections I had put on myself. Without them, Flare and Carnelian's white-hot touch might have made even my power burn. *I can move on my own!* I told them. They ignored me, towing me to another crack in the stone ceiling that might lead to a way out.

Three cracks later, I was so very tired. If magic could bruise, I was bruised. I wanted to go to my body and face Rosethorn and Luvo. I wanted a chance to think about these two lava creatures. Floating high above a pool of lava, I tried to imagine asking Oswin if he could take in two new kids. Oh, I'd say, they're a little hot-tempered, or a little hot at hand, or a little hot under the collar. . . .

Let's try the top way, Carnelian announced. *The way the Oldest said some break free. We go a little farther every time.*

But it's hard. Flare whined like any human kid. *It's hard and we push and push and only get a little farther along and it hurts!*

105

But now we have Funny Spirit with us, and she can help, Carnelian said.

My name isn't Funny Spirit. It's Evvy. I've been calling him Flare, and you Carnelian. If you have real names, you could tell them to me now. I suppose I wasn't very polite, but I *did* feel bruised and weary.

Names? We never had them in the pool. Everyone knows everyone else. . . . Flare for you, and Carnelian for me. Names . . . Carnelian sounded awed.

What's Carnelian? Flare I understand, he said. *I flare all the time. But Carnelian sounds funny.*

It's the name of that darker color she likes, I explained. Since they didn't seem to have a high opinion of stones, I wouldn't say what a carnelian was. *Where I come from, everyone doesn't know everyone else, so we have names.*

My color. I like it because it's nice and it has a gentle feel to it, said Carnelian. *Not hard, like the brighter colors. And you are Evvy. What kind of name is that?*

It would take too long to explain, I told them.

Who cares about explanations? She's Evvy. You're Carnelian. I'm Flare. Creatures from the cold world have names, so we will, too. We are going to leave the pool and become famous, even if we die.

Then let's try the hardest way . . . Flare. If there are three *of us pushing, maybe we can break out this time,* Carnelian suggested.

I'm not sure I want us to break out... I spoke too late. The problem with these creatures seemed to be that they never ran out of strength. I suppose that made sense. They did live in a constant source of it. They grabbed my hands and raced straight up with me. The chamber rose to a high peak just off the center. The walls closed in slowly as we flew, higher and higher. We were in a cone-shaped area, with Flare and Carnelian bound straight for the cone's narrow tip.

The three of us rammed into it. I screamed, crushed. I knew they felt the same way, but they were pushing, grinding all three of us into that tip. I saw the tiniest of cracks ahead of me. They jammed us into it. Grain by grain the crack spread. With each grain that broke free, I was forced tighter into that opening. My protections against them creaked and shuddered. My concentration was breaking up. If I lost that, I would lose my hold on the spells. My magical body would evaporate.

I panicked. I fought Carnelian and Flare, wrestling until I popped between them. I sped back to the huge chamber. There I flailed about until I saw the path back to my body. I flew up through earth, water, and stones. I scrambled to reach my meat body, my meat lungs, and cooler air. When I shot onto the basalt where my shell sat, my mind went black.

*   *   *

Everything hurt. *Everything.* There were pins in my muscles. Big, rusty needles stabbed my joints. I tried to draw the coolness of the basalt into myself, to make the hurting stop. I drew nothing. My magic was as dead as ash. Playing with Flare and Carnelian had used it up.

I tried to lift my head off the columns and was sorry I'd ever thought of it. My neck was one big ache. I opened my eyes. Those worked, thanks to the damp cloth on my face. I tried to lift my arm, to move the cloth. A new cramp the size of Mount Grace made it seize up.

Jayat took the cloth away and put a lantern on the rock beside me. I was surprised — it was dark. Briskly he kneaded the cramping arm. "I've never seen a living dead person before." He acted like that was a perfectly normal thing to say. "She said to come back with a coffin, because that's how she's going to ship you to Winding Circle. She was very convincing. Should I believe her?"

I tried to nod, and cringed as my neck locked.

Jayat massaged my shoulders, loosening knotted muscles. "You ought to be ashamed, scaring Master Luvo like this. He's been curled up in a ball for hours right next to you. He'd tell me you were all right, just 'traveling.' Then he wouldn't say another word for the longest time. The others came past here about mid-afternoon. She came over and checked your heartbeat and your breathing. Master Luvo talked to her and said you were well.

Dedicate Initiate Myrrhtide was in fine fettle, now that you're in disgrace. Oswin wanted to leave you some food, but Dedicate Initiate Rosethorn said to let you starve. When she went away, though, it turned out she left you these." He held up a cloth with some cold dumplings in it.

Lucky for me he knew the signs. Jayat rolled me on my side with my head hanging over the ground, not the boulders. I started to puke.

That went on for a time, long after I had anything to bring up. Luvo came out of his ball. He walked up and down my cramping thigh, kneading out the bunched knots. When I finished vomiting, Jayat and Luvo worked on me until I could sit without screaming, then till I could stand. I rinsed my mouth with water, and kept from looking at the dumplings as Jayat ate them.

"What happened to you?" he asked, saddling the horses. "Your whole body was as hard as a rock. You didn't even move when I slapped you or jostled you. I waved stinkweed under your nose. Nory fainted a year ago. I used stinkweed on her and when she came around she punched me. She has a good punch, but then, her mother was a pirate queen. I guess she comes by it naturally. Master Luvo, do you eat *anything*? Can I give you some water, at least?"

I turned facedown on the basalt to let Luvo walk up and down my back. His weight pressed my spine back into its proper shape, making the bones crackle. His feet worked my bunched-up muscles. They tired of clenching, and lay like they were supposed to again.

"I would like to have a little water poured over me, thank you, Jayatin." Luvo stepped down from my back.

As Jayat fumbled with the stopper on his water skin, I whispered to Luvo, "You were afraid. I could feel you, very far back in my magic. You were *afraid*."

"Do you know where you were, Evumeimei? You were *below*. Not in the place where all rocks are melted down, but in a higher chamber to that place. I do not understand how so many spirits of molten stone have come so close to our world, but they should not be here. Their touch on our kind — yours and mine alike — is death."

"But Evvy's still here. She's alive." Jayat carefully poured a trickle of water over Luvo. "Tell me when you've had enough."

"Thank you, Jayatin," said Luvo. "I am not a creature of fancies, yet I cannot rid myself of the idea that my skin is hot and stretched. The water is very good, and also sufficient. Evumeimei went as a creature of magic. Because she is not from that world, she can shield herself. I cannot."

"It cost me." I sat up again. My hair fell all around my face. I had to do something about it. The stuff was down to my waist and flopping everywhere since Jayat removed my headcloth. I tried to lift my arms to see if I could wrap the cloth, but my shoulders knotted with pain. *That* wasn't going to work.

"Had you been stone, it would not have cost you, Evumeimei. It would have killed you."

"Instead it milked every drop of magic I have." I couldn't even braid my hair.

Jayat saw. "My master has arthritis. And I have little sisters. Now, shall you have a turban like Azaze Yopali, or a band and braids, or a wrap like your old one?"

"Anything, as long as it's out of my way." I rested my face on my hands. Jayat wrapped my hair in my cloth, and coiled and tied it as I would do it. I said, "You didn't have to stay here. You must have been frightfully bored."

"Tahar gave me spells to practice. I did that for a while. Then I gathered some mushrooms and herbs she's been wanting. And there are garnets around here I can sell down in Sustree, for extra cash. Once you were back in your body, Master Luvo told me about where he's from, and the things you have done since you met. Your friend Briar sounds like quite the fellow."

"He's usually the first to tell you so, too." I sat up and managed to plant my feet on the ground, which was a start. "Are we ever going to meet Master Tahar?"

"Not if she has anything to say about it. Her attitude is that it's bad enough the people who live here know who she is and bother her." Jayat frowned, then said, "You know, Master Luvo *could* mean the source of the heat that feeds the hot springs."

"What?" Maybe the time underground had slowed my brain. I couldn't understand what he was talking about.

"There are hot springs on the far shore of the lake from Moharrin. People go there for curative baths, or to get warm when the winter's really cold. My master says they draw their heat from deep within the earth. That's probably what you found." Jayat hung the lantern on a tree branch and looked at me. "Can you ride? I'm starting to get really cold, and you have to face her sometime. I can maybe smuggle you into Oswin's house, or the barn behind the inn, if you'd rather face her tomorrow."

I lurched to my feet, hanging on to the rocks for balance. "No. If she has to wait to tell you what she thinks of you, she just gets worse. And she's right to be angry. I don't know what possessed me. It wasn't ghosts."

"It was the heat fever." Luvo shifted on his feet. "The excitement of magma and the earth's strength, so close to the air. I felt it in the closed-off sources of the power you had once used, Jayatin, but I did not recognize it, at first, because it was so faint. I knew it a little better in the dead trees canyon, because it was so fresh there. By then it had moved into Evumeimei's blood. When I saw it in her, my fear overtook me."

"But the ghost of power like that can't hurt you, Master Luvo. Can it?" Jayat levered me into my horse's saddle with a grunt. I nearly slid off the other side. Then I tangled one arm in the reins and grabbed the saddle horn with the other. The horse looked back at me. I saw white around its eye in the dim lamplight.

"I'm sorry." I patted the animal's neck clumsily. "I don't blame *you* for being angry, either."

Jayat didn't trust my control over my body. He walked around the horse to make sure my feet were in the stirrups. Under the circumstances, I was kind of grateful. My feet seemed far away and not exactly connected to me. Once I was settled, he set Luvo's pack on his own saddle, then put Luvo on it.

"Oh." I felt like an idiot. "*That's* how you got here."

"Actually, I found him halfway down the road." Jayat secured the pack to his saddle. "He ran after you. I was held up because I had to ready my horse and bring your gear." He took down the lantern.

"Thank you," I said. "And how did you know we'd need a light?"

"I didn't. Your Rosethorn sent it with one of the boys from the inn. Is she going to beat you?"

We rode out onto the road as I goggled at his back. "Does your master beat *you?*"

113

"She did when I was younger and wouldn't mind her," Jayat explained, "or snuck off to go fishing. That's what masters do."

I sat back. I cringed as my hips told me I might *think* they had forgiven me for that afternoon, but they hadn't. Jayat was right. My owner had beaten me when I was a slave, after all. Jooba-Hooba, who was going to be my first master in stone magic, would have beaten me. I bet he would have smiled as he did it. The lady, who tried to buy me for her house and her pet gang, would have beaten me. No, she would have *had* me beaten. She wouldn't have soiled her hands with me. But Briar, who never hit me, kept me away from the lady and Jooba-Hooba.

And Rosethorn?

"She'll set me to weeding acres of gardens for weeks." I tried to sit more comfortably and failed. "Or put me in a small, hot room to cook up nasty messes that have to be stirred all the time. Or cook nasty messes part of the time, and dip candles part of the time. But she would never ever beat anybody."

"But she seems so *fierce*," Jayat said with awe.

"Have you ever made soap?" I asked. "Let me tell you, a temple needs a *lot* of soap. She's quite happy to tell them you'll make it *all*. You watch. I'll be on my way to Winding Circle tomorrow, with orders to make soap and dip candles *forever*."

9

How to Get Out of Trouble

The ground floor of the inn was lit up. I didn't wait for Jayat to help me dismount. There was no point in trying to put it off. I slid out of the saddle, hung on for a moment until my body stopped cramping, then lurched inside. I ignored Jayat's shout for me to wait while he saw to the horses. I didn't want him to witness Rosethorn's laying down the law to me. He was bound to hear some of it, but it would be nice if he wasn't there for it *all*.

Inside, the important folk were seated near the hearth fire, as they had been the night before: Rosethorn, Fusspot, Oswin, Azaze. Other grown-ups from the town were there, too. Splendid. More witnesses for my disgrace.

"Well. Her Highness graces us with her presence." Myrrhtide looked as if he'd just swallowed the Midsummer goose whole. "I suppose you're just bubbling over with excuses, aren't you? They won't do you any good this time."

Rosethorn looked at me and folded her hands on the table. There was no way to tell what she was thinking.

"I'll go pack." I headed for the stair, trying not to stumble. If she wasn't even going to speak, I was in worse trouble than I thought. There was no point trying to explain when she was that angry. I may be silly and I may be reckless, but I know better than to make excuses. Sometimes I have to keep my mouth shut and take what's coming.

And maybe, just maybe, she didn't want to humiliate me in front of Myrrhtide. Perhaps she would task me in private, when she came up to bed.

"It appeared to me as if she were under some kind of compulsion," Oswin said thoughtfully.

I froze with my foot on the stair, holding on to the rail. Why did Oswin stick his neb in, as Briar would say? If Rosethorn despised people who were supposed to obey and didn't, she hated mages who couldn't control their magic even more. I turned my aching head to glare at Oswin.

"Look at her." Oswin talked as if I wasn't trying to burn holes in his face with my eyes. "She's pale and sweating. She was that way at midday. She was fidgeting then, too — unable to sit still. She gnawed her nails to the quick by noon today. They weren't chewed at all on the way here from Sustree. Her lips are dry and cracked. She looks as if she had been taking poppy or was under a spell of compulsion —"

"Nonsense," Rosethorn told him coldly.

Jayat came in. He put a hand under my elbow to help me stay on my feet. I tried not to lean on him too much. I have my pride.

"You told Dedicate Initiate Myrrhtide Evvy's behavior is highly unlike her. Surely you'll let her explain before you send her packing." Oswin was mad-brained stubborn, to keep hammering with Rosethorn, Fusspot, *and* me glaring at him.

"He's right." Now Jayat had to pitch in. "I was with Evvy on the road up from the seaport. She's been different today, and it only started after we left Oswin's pond. On the road she acted like any girl — all right, one who's *really* fond of sparkly rocks, but she was fun. She wasn't short-tempered or, or strange. Dedicate Rosethorn, you acted yesterday as if she behaves that way all the time, as far as I could tell. If she was normal then, today she was someone else."

If I ever got on my knees for anyone, I would have knelt right there. I would have knelt and begged these two not to help. I didn't want Rosethorn angrier with me than she already was. I'd messed up. They were complicating it.

"She was seized by the earth's power." Because Luvo stood on the floor beside Jayat, it seemed as though his voice came from nowhere. Everyone but Rosethorn glanced around, startled. Rosethorn looked straight at Luvo. "She traced the remains of the earth lines that Jayatin spoke of, seeking their remnants in the soil. Then she found new, greater lines." With a grunt Jayat set Luvo up on the steps so he could be seen.

I didn't dare move. Luvo scares me when he's like this, when he speaks with the age of his mountain within him. In Yanjing, his mountain supports huge glaciers. There are villages and forests on his flanks, and deep, ice-cold caverns in his depths. People worship him as a god.

Luvo didn't look at me. He was talking to the others. "She followed the earth lines into the heart of this island. She used their power to go far deeper than she could venture with only her own strength. In a chamber full of magma, she met the creatures that inhabit it, the children of the earth's heart. They captured her. They kept her for hours until Evumeimei escaped. She did so not only with her magic, but with all of the power she had collected over the course of the day, power that had clung to her as she examined the failed earth lines. She did it with *the power that made her act so strangely*. If she had not had it, she would have perished alone under the earth. I could not help her. I would have been devoured, had I followed her. You mages would not have survived the first thirty feet, even traveling as pure magic, as Evumeimei and I do. The force of this magic would have crushed you. It nearly crushed my young friend."

Something he had said itched my brain. He said the power clung to me. I sat on the step closest to my rump. My knees didn't want to keep me upright anymore. What was the idea that had caught my attention? Something about power clinging, and sticking?

I looked up. "I know why the plants and water have been going bad."

"I don't believe this!" Fusspot slammed his cup down, slopping tea on the table. "She gets her animate rock to plead her case, she plays the tottering invalid to get our sympathy —"

"Be still." Azaze spoke with a voice like ice. "Unlike you, she has an idea. You have only tests you wish to perform." She looked at me and twitched her fingers in a "come on" gesture.

I glanced at Rosethorn. She nodded.

I opened my mouth. Words, an avalanche of them, spilled onto my tongue. "In the gorge with all the dead trees, I felt the skin of the rocks was touched by bad air. There was poisonous stuff in it, chemicals that stuck to the rocks after it passed. Under the ground, the poison was all around the rocks on either side of the crack in the earth — it was left behind when the bad air passed through the crack." I started to cough. My throat was dry as chalk. Jayat went to the kitchen and brought me a cup of mint tea. I sipped it until my coughs stopped, while Jayat went to stand with the kitchen maids. "When I was in the big chamber with all the magma and the rock spirits, I got adopted by two. I named one Flare, and the other was Carnelian. They didn't have names of their own. They wanted me to play with them. They dragged me all over the place. Everywhere they went, Flare and Carnelian yanked me up into these cracks. They couldn't make themselves as thin as me because they were solid magma. They could melt part of the cracks, but they could only force them open so far. They want out of that chamber *really* bad. They keep saying it like it's their prayers — they want *out*. And they keep trying. In the chamber they were surrounded by wavy lines, like you see coming off of cobblestones on really hot days. I think those wavy lines were the poisoned air, and the poisoned air is the only part of them that can escape through the cracks." I finished my tea. "The last thing they did with me, I *think* they tried to jam all three of us straight through the top of Mount Grace."

My hands started to shake. I put my teacup next to Luvo so they wouldn't see, and tucked my hands in my armpits. "That was . . . bad. I got away, finally, and escaped through one of the cracks we had tried before. The stones in it were coated with poison. The stuff that's killing the water and plants comes out ahead of Flare and Carnelian. The rest of the magma spirits can't get out, not yet, but the poisons in their air can. If they followed Carnelian and Flare, they could kill this whole island." I opened my mouth to tell them more, but the word avalanche was over. Trembling, I waited for Myrrhtide to start on me again. I could feel sweat trickle down my back. My head pounded.

Fusspot didn't say a word. I looked up. He was pouring water into a bowl. Once it was full, he wet his finger and wrote signs all around its rim. Then he stared into the water, his pale eyes fixed. He was scrying in the bowl. He'd done so every night on the ship, communicating with Winding Circle, or trying to see what was going on around us. What was he trying to see now — Flare and Carnelian?

Rosethorn came to sit on the step next to me. She put an arm around my shoulders and held me close. She spoke in a whisper. "Are you sure of all this? No, never mind that. You are an appallingly truthful girl. Do you understand the meaning in what you have said?"

I shook my head. My poor stomach lurched.

"You describe the beginnings of a volcano. It makes sense of what's happening with the plants and water here," she explained. "Your friends looking for a way out — they will bring lava and gas with them in an explosion that may kill everyone on Mount Grace. Perhaps even all of Starns."

I shivered. Flare and Carnelian had such dreadful strength. Then there were the other spirits behind them, waiting. They might not search for a way out, but they would follow Carnelian and Flare. I was *sure* of it. "They *would* kill everyone, Rosethorn. That underground chamber is bigger than the lake. I don't know how deep it is. The power of them all . . ." I twisted to look at Luvo, though it hurt my bones to do it. "Why didn't you say we're looking at a volcano? I wouldn't have gone down there!" I kept my voice as quiet as Rosethorn's.

"I did not know." Luvo hung his head knob, not looking at us.

"But you were born in one!" I poked him with a finger.

"And I told you, who remembers his birth?" he asked. "I have not encountered a volcano in our travels. I did not know the early signs of an eruption. Rosethorn, are you *certain* that these signs pertain to such an occurrence?"

I put my hands to my head. Luvo asking Rosethorn to explain things a mountain should know — I felt as if my world had been upended.

"To pass the initiate's examinations, we're taught the basics of all the Living Circle disciplines, even when they don't match our powers. Evvy's story fits the facts. So does the spot die-off of plants, the acid water, and the vibrations and earth shocks. I had my suspicions — so did Myrrhtide — but this confirms it." As Rosethorn whispered, she laid a cool wrist on my forehead. Then she checked my heartbeat with the other. She frowned. "Not good. You're clammy, and your pulse is thin and rapid." She looked at Jayat. "She has the symptoms of shock. Has she eaten?"

"She couldn't, Dedicate Initiate." Jayat came over. No one else seemed to want to. It was as if we had something catching. "She threw up a lot, but she didn't eat anything first."

"I see. Thank you, Jayat." Rosethorn looked at me. "For those studies I mentioned, we had to read classic writings. In *The Book of Earth Magic*, a handful of mages wrote of spirits of molten stone found deep in the earth. They described what happened when they found a route to the surface. It was much like what you told us." She stood and shook out her robes. "I'm going to brew you some tea. Then you'll eat something. *Then* you'll tell us all about your explorations and discoveries with the stones here. We need to see how much time we have before this island blows up under us." She went upstairs.

"What can she possibly do?" Luvo stepped clumsily into my lap. "I do not understand why she rushes off in this manner. The new mountain will come. We will be consumed in molten lava. That is the cycle of birth and death in stone. There is nothing to be done."

His behavior today now made a lot more sense to me. I cuddled him close in my aching hands and kept my voice down. For some reason, Rosethorn didn't want everyone in the room to hear what we were talking about. "You

123

thought you were going to die, didn't you? That's why you curled up in a ball and didn't talk to Jayat. You just figured, uh-oh! Here comes the lava, I'm going to die, nothing to be done. Luvo, you bleater, you're not some rock stuck in the path of an avalanche, you know! We'll get on a ship and sail away from this!" I gripped him and tried to stand, only to have my knees go to jelly. I sat again. "All right, it may take us a while before we get to the ship."

Before I knew what he was up to, Oswin came over and picked us both up. Like Jayat the night before, he wasn't ready for Luvo. His knees bent under us. He grunted with the strain. His face turned a nice, dark ruby. As he staggered to carry us to the table where Azaze and Fusspot sat, I tried to distract him. "The emperor of Yanjing gave me a coat made of silk that was the same color as your face right now. You forgot about Luvo's weight, didn't you? You're very strong for an old man."

"I'm forty-five! That's not old!" Oswin slid us onto the bench at the elders' table.

"It certainly is not." Luvo almost sounded huffy as I put him on the table.

Azaze had been talking to Fusspot. Now she got up and looked at the people who had been witness to all this. "The rest of you, off to your homes. The council must gather immediately. Master Miller, Mistress Weaver, Master Carpenter, will you remain? I'll send an hostler for the smith, the chief herder, and the chief miner. Jayat. Fetch your mistress. Tell her I *insist*."

Jayat gulped. "Yes, Headwoman Azaze." He ran out of the inn.

Azaze went outside for a moment. When she came back, she sat down across the table from me, and looked me in the eyes. I don't *think* I flinched. It was hard. This tall, stern-looking old lady would do better as a queen than as the headwoman of an armpit little village snuggled to a mountain that was about to blow up.

"What do *you* think you saw down there, girl? Or did you just invent a tale to keep yourself out of trouble?" Azaze demanded.

If she spoke to everyone like that, I'd bet her children died of fear when they were small. "If I was doing that, I'd have said I got a face full of bad air, and it made me do strange stuff," I told her. "When I lie, I'm smart enough to keep it simple. That's where liars always go wrong. They get fancy. Then they forget the details. It's best to have a simple, basic lie that you don't have to worry about remembering."

Azaze's thin mouth twitched. I *think* she maybe smiled. "Your career to this point has made you an expert in lying, I take it."

I nodded, though it made my head spin. "Yes, Headwoman Azaze. But I never lie to Rosethorn. She, um, discourages it."

125

"Evvy and I have an understanding." Rosethorn had returned with packets of herbs and a mug. She grabbed the teakettle and poured hot water into the mug. "She tells me the truth, and I don't hang her in the first well we come to. It's a solution that works tolerably well for both of us."

I watched sadly as she tipped powders into the mug. It didn't help to know she was adding her magic with them. Her power just made the brew taste that much nastier.

"Is this Evvy such a handful? She seemed well enough last night." Azaze had a real smile on her face now. The village's miller, weaver, and carpenter, who sat with us, were out-and-out chuckling.

"As much as my student — her former teacher — Briar was a handful," said Rosethorn. "He and I had a similar understanding. Evvy, stop making faces. You will need a clear head tonight. You are drinking this, whether you like it or not."

"Not even honey?" I had to ask, though I could see she hadn't looked at the honeypot.

"Honey would just make the experience pleasant. I haven't forgiven you for racing off without a word." Rosethorn looked at me and her face softened, a little. "Honey would also give this tea nasty side effects. I'm sorry, but it's true. Drink it all, Evvy."

I took the mug. "You could try harder to make them taste good, you know."

She gave me a mocking smile. "Now, where would the fun be in that?" She turned to the maid who had been serving the elders. "Is there any egg-and-lemon soup left?"

The girl nodded.

"She'll need a cup of that to start, then a cup of the white bean soup. If she can eat more, the artichokes in oil," Rosethorn ordered.

I held my nose and gulped a mouthful of the tea. Even that way, I thought it would be a miracle if I kept the stuff down. It had the musty, greenish taste of cellar mold. Before I met Briar I had eaten vegetables stolen from cellars. I knew what that taste was. Wherever did she find the herbs for these drinks? I was always afraid to ask. She would tell me.

And yet the sweat on my face began to dry. My stomach settled after three more gulps of the stuff. My ears stopped ringing. My knees, ankles, elbows, and wrists felt like they were made of bone, not green twigs. My brain decided I was not on rocking ground, but a solid bench. My heart stopped hammering.

I put the mug down. "Not the sludge." With my eyes I begged Rosethorn not to say the dreaded words.

She looked into the mug, where soggy herb paste waited. Then she checked my forehead, and my pulse. "*Much* better." She threw the sludge on the open hearth fire. It roared up in flames. Everyone flinched with a gasp.

I looked at Rosethorn with admiration. What had she *put* in that tea?

The maid set artichokes and both soups in front of me. Remembering what had happened when Jayat showed me those dumplings, I ate slowly and carefully.

"How could you go under the earth if your body did not go?" While she had waited for Rosethorn to finish doctoring me, Azaze still had questions. "Can all mages do this?"

I shook my head. "Some can, some can't." I felt good enough to take out the rocks I had gathered that day and put them on the table. When I'd first come in, the smallest of them had felt too heavy for me to lift.

"Don't talk with your mouth full, Evvy." Rosethorn sat next to me, accepting a cup of normal tea from the maid. "My young friend will have water." Two of the other people Azaze had sent for arrived. The maids rushed to serve them.

I swallowed my beans so I could answer Azaze. "It's useful if you can do it, the traveling in your magic. It's how Luvo could see things on his mountain. It'd take him for-ever to walk over all of it. His mountain's *huge.*" I grinned at Luvo. "So he just goes around as his magic self."

"But how does his mountain do things with Luvo gone?" That was Myrrhtide, asking a normal question, for a change. He looked at my small pile of rocks and didn't even sniff.

"My mountain rejoices." Luvo walked over to stand in front of Myrrhtide, so that Myrrhtide would have to watch him as he spoke. "I do not rearrange its crystals and pillars, or redirect its streams and glaciers. I do not reshape it with avalanches, floods, or tremors. It can slumber in the sun and cold in peace. My mountain finds me too active a heart for its liking, Dedicate Initiate Myrrhtide."

"No wonder you get on so well with Evvy." Myrrhtide leaned back, though he kept his eyes on Luvo. "Being so wise, Master Luvo, I'm surprised you didn't warn us of what is happening under *this* mountain."

"Warn you? As I have said, I did not know." Luvo sat on his rounded stone rump, his head knob pointed up at Myrrhtide. "And what is the point of a warning? The volcano will be born, devouring all in its path. It will continue to destroy, or it will become land, and a mountain. The new eats the old. It is always so."

"But we're humans," said Myrrhtide. "We can flee. Provided we have time." He nodded to yet another village notable who came in the door.

"That's what we're going to work out, once the entire village council is here." We had forgotten that Azaze was listening. "Evvy — it is Evvy?"

I nodded. I was fishing stones from my other pocket and setting them on the table. Here was an odd, interesting bit of obsidian, like pumice in texture. Here was a fine-grained gray rock that had begun life far below the earth. There were other kinds of volcano rocks that had been high on Mount Grace.

Azaze snapped bony fingers under my nose to get my attention. I think she did it several times before Rosethorn kicked me gently.

"I could have kicked her myself, Dedicate Rosethorn," Azaze said. "Evvy, if we give you slate and chalk, can you draw maps? Where this chamber is compared to the village, and the lake, and the mountain? Where these cracks are?" Azaze turned a beaded ring on one of her fingers. "It will be easier for the council to follow what you're saying if you have even a crude map." She pointed to the table behind us.

I hadn't seen the big slate and the tray of colored chalks that lay on it. Someone must have brought them out while I was eating. I took some flatbread and walked over to the slate, thinking while I chewed. Drawing maps of places I had gone in my magic was something I had studied at Winding Circle. I sketched a view of the mountain and the lake from the side, as if I'd cut Starns in two.

I was concentrating so hard I didn't hear Oswin go out and return. I did notice when he plopped his saddlebag on the table next to me. "Here. Maybe this will help." He undid the straps and took out a leather tube. He pulled a roll of papers from the tube. He thumbed through them, muttering to himself. "Margret Island, no, Lore Island, Karl Island, Sustree, Sotat — ah!"

He selected a paper and spread it next to my slate. It was a really good map of all Starns. I whistled my respect. It had the usual things, like roads, towns, and rivers, but it also showed the old lines of power that Jayat and Tahar once used. There was even a trick of coloring that showed ridges and gorges.

"Will that help?" Oswin weighted the corners with plates and cups.

"A lot, thanks!" I said. "Where did you get this?"

"Oh, I did it. It's useful." Oswin told me.

I smiled at him as he put Luvo on the table next to me. "Useful for somebody who goes around fixing things?"

"And I guide people over the island for coin. If they pay me extra, I try not to get them lost."

"Did you draw all those maps?" I asked him.

"No, only the ones for this island and a handful of our neighbors. The others I bought. I wish I were traveled enough to have done the others myself." Oswin put the other maps away.

I had a feeling I'd touched a sore spot. I looked at Luvo. "How far under the mountain was I? I figure three and a half miles, but you'd know better than me."

"Three and three-quarter miles straight down, Evumeimei."

"But you weren't there, Master Luvo," commented Oswin. "You said you weren't."

"But I am in her mind now, Oswin. I can feel as she felt then. Having learned this measurement of yards, miles, and feet, I am better able to tell than she how far she has traveled under the earth. She is better at it than she was, but it is harder for meat creatures."

"*Meat* creatures?" Oswin asked.

"He means living things like people and animals. I *am* trying to think, you two." I worked carefully to finish the half-view of the chamber.

"Now a map of the area around the mountain?" Luvo suggested as I picked up another slate.

I nodded. "The one with the cracks in the earth. I don't know if Flare and Carnelian can split one wide enough for many of the spirits to escape. Even one could do a *lot* of damage." I felt a draft on my back and turned around.

10

Telling the Council

Jayat came in with the oldest woman I had ever seen. Maybe she was as old as Luvo. Her skin could have been smoked and stretched over her bones, it was so brown and tight. Her eyes were like black jet beads. She wore a small turban of a nasty, bright orange cloth. It didn't even match her pink and yellow plaid dress. That was tied at the waist with a brown sash, and she wore a ratty green shawl over the whole mess. She went barefoot, her toes more like roots than human feet. Her hands were knobby, too. She clung to Jayat with one and clutched a cane with the other. She looked right at me.

"Lakik help you if you lie, girl." Her scowl would frighten street dogs. Her voice crackled like grease in the pan. "If you do, every louse and flea I have taken off others will become your new friend." She glared at Azaze. "You summoned all the council for the rantings of a disobedient child? You sent Jayat to drag me out of my nice warm bed?"

"And over to the nice warm seat by the fire, Master." Jayat handled her as if she were made of eggs. Gently he helped the old crosspatch to a padded seat the kitchen girls had brought out. It was set beside the hearth. He didn't *seem* like he was dragging her.

If Azaze was frightened, she didn't look it. "Dedicate Initiate Rosethorn of Winding Circle, Dedicate Initiate Myrrhtide, this is our mage, Tahar Catwalker. Tahar, sit down before you fall down. The tea is made just as you like it. The girl whose tale has alarmed us is Evvy. Her companion — the little fellow, the green and purple crystal one — is Master Luvo. He is the heart of a mountain, but not locally, as I understand it."

Mage Tahar snorted. "Our mountains know better than to get up to such mischief." She squinted up at Rosethorn and Myrrhtide, who were bowing to her. "Stop that. Both of you have more power in your thumbs than I have in my whole body. We all know it. I can't say much for the temple's way of raising a child, if Jayat speaks true. Stealing horses, running all over without leave —"

"Oh, she's done worse." Rosethorn's face was straight when she said it. "Spying, fighting, stealing, insulting people of great rank . . . But how can you manage young girls these days? In this case, Mage Tahar, Evvy has done us a favor. Without her warning, we die. We might yet if this council does not act quickly."

"We'll see. Don't gawp like a girl at her first dance, Azaze. Let's get on with this." Tahar thumped her cane on the floor.

Jayat sat on a bench near Tahar's elbow. Azaze looked at the maids, who left, closing the door behind them. Now it was just us and the town council. Oswin propped the slates where everyone could see them when the time came.

Rosethorn stood in front of them to speak. "Myrrhtide and I came in response to your complaints with regard to the poisoning of your plants, streams, and ponds." She looked calm and beautiful, her hands clasped in front of her. These people wouldn't know she had been riding all day. "Evvy and her friend Luvo came by chance, except that the gods seldom leave these things to chance. Luvo is the heart of a mountain, traveling with us for a time. Evvy is my friend, a young stone mage, presently in training at Winding Circle."

I hung my head so she wouldn't see me blush at her calling me her friend.

Rosethorn told them what had happened that day, up to me riding off. Jayat took over, explaining how he caught up and stayed with me. Then I told my story to the council. I described the underground chamber, Flare and Carnelian, and the spirits underground. I explained the poisons on the stones under the dead spots, and my idea that the poisons were borne on air that escaped volcano spirits as they pushed toward the surface. About how the shocks were their attempts to escape that chamber. About how they were going to succeed, somewhere around Mount Grace, very soon.

Using the maps I had made, I showed them where Carnelian and Flare had come closest to the open air. Luvo told them where the chamber was while Rosethorn made me drink a second cup of her medicine tea. By then I was very tired. Even after I had the tea, the room seemed a *little* spin-y. I took a step away from the slates and lurched. I caught myself on the table. I had never had to talk to people like this before, drained of magic and my bones aching from exhaustion. I searched the grown-up faces for Rosethorn, but either I was too tired to pick her out, or she wasn't there.

"The volcano spirits will come out sooner or later," I told the village council. "It'll go better if they break through one of Mount Grace's sides facing the open sea. But the thickest stone they have to push through is that way. If they come through the top, or through the cracks, they'll dump lava and poisons on any villages around Mount Grace, maybe on the whole island. Maybe on the neighboring islands."

"That makes sense." Oswin looked up from his tea. "If we confine something that moves, like a stream, then give it a small path to escape, like a hole in a pipe or a dam, you know yourselves it's a lot stronger. And remember the volcano on Levit Island three years back? We could see the blast from here — that went through the top of the mountain. There wasn't a tree left standing on the whole island."

Softness settled around my shoulders. Rosethorn tucked a knitted blanket around me. Even as I grabbed it I recognized its opal colors. Lark had made it special for Rosethorn, knitting in signs of strength and healing and warmth for her.

"But she meant this for you." I tried to take it off. Rosethorn settled it back around my arms.

"She meant it for anyone who needs it. Right now you need it," she whispered very quietly in my ear. "You still need to convince these people, all right?"

The smith got up. "Azaze, you and these learned dedicates are paying heed to this nonsense? She makes up this faradiddle and expects us to swallow it? The wench is trying to duck a beating at her master's hands. I don't know how she worked the magic to get the rock to look as if it talks. Plainly she's talented if she can fool Winding Circle mages. That still doesn't mean honest country folk like us have to scramble for her nonsense." He looked at Myrrhtide and Rosethorn. "Forgive me, Dedicates. Your minds are plain addled with all that magical learning if you swallow this chit's tale."

Myrrhtide glared up at him. "I am not addled. I am no more likely to swallow anyone's 'tale,' as you call it, than I am likely to fly. I am a Dedicate Initiate of the Water temple of Winding Circle. I have studied at Lightsbridge university and at Swanswing university in Hatar. In that time I have studied the writings of some of the greatest earth, water, and fire mages ever born. What they record of the days before a volcano's eruption sounds very much like what Evvy and Luvo have told us since their return to this inn tonight."

So *that* was why Fusspot hadn't started yapping at me the first chance he got. He really *did* believe me. He even *said* he believed me.

Maybe I ought to try to be nicer to him.

Fusspot wasn't done with the smith. He thrust his teacup over in front of the man. "What do you see in my cup?"

The smith gave him a glare that would start a fire. "Tea, you pompous —"

"Master Smith!" Azaze's voice cracked like a whip.

Fusspot acted like he hadn't even heard. He'd never acted that way when *I'd* insulted him. If he had, I would have stopped. "What is my tea *doing*, Master Smith? Please note that I am not touching the cup."

The smith jammed his hands in his pockets. "It's shivering."

"As was my wash water," Myrrhtide said. "As is the well water. As is the water in the pots used for cooking and laundry. Before volcanoes loose their heavy fire,

Master Smith, the ground can tremble for days, constantly. This is why we addled mages keep written records from the past. So we can learn from the experience of others who have gone before."

For a moment, even though he's little and skinny, Fusspot seemed majestic. Like he was cloaked in the wisdom of those long-ago mages. Like he was worthy of respect, even as they had been.

"I don't understand this at all." The Master Herder was a woman. She was wringing her hands. "I know the herds have been odd for days, skittish, panicky — I thought it was so many earthquakes. I just don't understand, why us, why our mountain? Have we offended some god? We try to pay respect to all the ones we know of, but perhaps we missed one? Our mountains have always been so quiet."

"Nonsense." Luvo actually sounded cross. "I know that you meat creatures are exceedingly short-lived, but you are supposed to have minds, and memories, and eyes. You are supposed to use these things." He looked at me. "Are some breeds of human more stupid than others?"

"Luvo, it's been a long time since I've heard you be actually rude." Rosethorn kept her voice quiet but direct. "I don't understand what has upset you."

Luvo turned his head knob so his invisible eyes were on hers. "I have known you for three or so of your mortal years, Rosethorn. I have seen what happens in these situations in which you involve yourself and Evumeimei. For reasons which are unclear to me, you will insist on remaining in this place to reason with people who will not heed you. They will delay your departure until you, and thus Evumeimei, are in peril of your lives. How long until these volcano children find a way out, and lead all their kindred through it? A week? That is very little time. It may not give you enough chance to get out of range. If these meat creatures argue and deny and quibble as I saw those others do, back in Gyongxe, I am certain it is not enough time. Now that I see there is a chance that I — we — will survive this volcano, I do not wish the bleatings of human sheep to delay our escape. Perhaps I am a bad mountain. Perhaps I should resign myself and wait for the earth's cycle to take me. But I have grown attached to Evumeimei, and to you. I would like to see more of your world. I would like to see Lark and Briar again."

"We don't have to sit here and be insulted." This time it was the Master Miner who spoke. I knew he was the miner. Though his clothes were clean and his face well washed, grains of stone were worked into his wrinkles. I reached out to see what the stone grains were. It was like trying to take a deep breath, only to find your lungs won't open up. I hugged Lark's blanket around my shoulders, trying not to cry. How long would it take my power to come back?

"I have sons at home who will insult me for nothing." The miner was still talking. "Forgive my saying so, Master Luvo, though I don't mind telling you I feel funny, calling a little fellow like you 'Master.' But I've been in the mines all week. Nobody enjoys the ground-shakes, but we've weathered them. It just seems like Mount Grace is missing her lover more than usual. But she isn't the volcano sort. I've seen two of the volcanoes we have in these islands, Sharyno and Kieta. Our Mount Grace has never been that sort."

That made me perk up. "Never? Never?" I looked at Jayat and Tahar. "You know the spell for looking at a thing, right? The one where you tell it to show its nature? My book mage friends say it's like your ABCs, you all learn something like that."

"I know a curst sight more than my letters, you pepper-mouthed minx." Tahar glared at me for good measure. "My Jayat, too."

With Lark's strengthening blanket around me I could walk. "I'll be right back."

As I was climbing the stairs I heard Luvo say, "All of these islands are volcano-born. How can you not know that? The lines of power that your mages called on, they are but tributaries to great faults in the earth. Those faults lead to the furnaces in which everything was made."

In my room I got the rocks I had collected the day before: mica, obsidian, quartz, and feldspars. All had been shaped far below the earth, where they should have stayed. I carried them downstairs, my knees wobbling.

"It is a small undersea volcano, seven miles off your shore and one mile deep." Luvo was telling them about the vent we had found under the ocean. I could see the village councilors didn't believe him. I wasn't surprised. One thing I had noticed in my travels with Briar and Rosethorn. People took to them because their magic was ordinary. So Briar and Rosethorn talked to plants and played with them like pets. At the end of the day, they had dirt under their nails, stickers in their clothes, and a crop to show, like everyone else. Unless people witnessed it when they did some great magic, calling out huge thorny vines from a gravel slope, or turning a tiny tree into a giant one, they seemed like everyday people. They were the kind who got invited to meet daughters or say the blessing over the new grandbaby.

But Luvo was not like that. Luvo was not everyday. I wasn't everyday. I was Luvo's friend, and I had no liking for people. They were fine as long as they left me alone, of course. I preferred cats and rocks.

I put my stones on the table next to those I had gathered that day. Azaze and the carpenter moved aside so Tahar and Jayat could see them. "Ask the stones, Mage Tahar, Jayat. Stones don't lie or make up pretty stories. Ask them what their nature is, where they came from. *What* they came from. Don't ask me, I'm a lying chit trying to get out of being in trouble. Ask the stones how they got made."

I sat at the table where Luvo stood. Even with Lark's blanket around me, I guessed I had overdone things. I was feeling cranky. I'd been up at dawn to traipse all over their silly island. I had tried to see where their precious source of mage-strength had gone. Then look what had happened to me! Catch me warning people their stupid home was going to blow up again.

Now that Rosethorn and Myrrhtide knew the problem was nothing to do with plants or water, we could go home. Against volcano spirits, my magic and theirs was helpless. Our ship was waiting for us in Sustree. I didn't even care that it meant another week at sea. I'd have the new rocks I'd gathered here to entertain me. And maybe a view of the volcano when it finally exploded. That would be really interesting.

Jayat and Tahar drew spell designs on the floor. Their lips moved as they called on the rocks to show where they came from. I sighed. It was taking *forever*.

Then I had to smile at myself. I was spoiled. In the old days, in Chammur, magic never happened at a snap of the fingers. We waited for the mage to dance, shake rattles, burn herbs, or spin a prayer wheel a hundred times, until the mage was ready and the magic was done or failed.

It wasn't until I knew Rosethorn and Briar that magic turned into something at the speed of, "Here you go."

I smelled heating stone first. It's a dry smell, like the sun in the desert. Grains of dirt and dried leaf from the rocks I hadn't cleaned were baking. Then the leaves burned outright. I shook my head. In a *good* spell, the heat that the stones remembered would never escape the spell. If the leaf bits were burning, there would be scorch marks on the table, too. Azaze had better not blame me.

My pieces of mica started to crack. I wasn't bothered. I'd collect more on the way back to the ship.

A little volcano image appeared over each rock. Jayat looked up from the design on the floor. He was sweating. He made a swirling motion with his hand. The little volcanoes formed one big image, one big volcano that stood over six feet tall. Just as the single image came together, a blast of smoke and stones blew the mountain's side out. Everyone flinched, though the blast — the eruption, my books back home called it — went through them like a ghost, and vanished.

Tahar sighed. The image disappeared. The room seemed darker, though the lamps and the fire still burned. I went over and picked up a beautiful pink granite chunk I had found that morning. It would have burned anyone else. Just as I thought, it left a scorch mark on the table. My lovely mica was just ruined. They might have to scrape that off the wood.

The nervous herder gulped her tea before she spoke. "But — I don't understand. Where was the lake? Where was Mount Grace?"

"This happened thousands of centuries ago." Rosethorn rubbed her eyes. "Didn't you look at the trees? The only time you'll ever see leaves like that is captured in stone, just as you'll find animal and fish skeletons. They're the ancestors of your trees. The *distant* ancestors."

"But our lake." Just like her goats, the Herd Mistress wouldn't let go of something she had her teeth into.

"The place where the volcano erupted . . ." Tahar was hoarse.

Jayat poured her a cup of tea.

Once she finished drinking, Tahar went on. "Where the volcano blew out its side, *that* became our lake. The remains of the volcano became the spine of our Mount Grace." She looked at me. "The child found countless rocks here which were born in a volcano. If Dedicate Rosethorn is right, that volcano last erupted in the dawn of time. We sit on top of its sealed grave. That seal is about to come right off."

Rosethorn got to her feet and put an arm around me. "Well done, getting their own mages to show them. Very well done. Time for you to go to bed. There's more talking to do, but you're about to collapse. Don't even try to carry Luvo. I'll bring him when I come up. It's not as if he sleeps."

"Are you sure?" I know I was swaying where I stood. "I can go for a bit longer."

"Of course you can." I knew better than to believe her when she spoke all syrupy sweet like that. "Why, you can last just as long as it takes to go back up those steps. I'll bring the rest of your stones, too. Go on, Evvy. You know it will just annoy you to hear us negotiate with the locals. It usually does."

"It annoys you, too."

"Yes, but my vows say I have to be nice to people sometimes, for the good of my soul. You haven't taken vows. Scat."

Every now and then I like to do as I'm told, just to confuse people. This was one of those times. I climbed the stairs and fell into my bed. I don't think I even took off my sandals.

11

Helping Out

Magic, at least the kind Rosethorn and Briar and I have, is greedy stuff. It doesn't always need us to be awake or even conscious. We ambient mages, drawing on part of the everyday world, have it easier than book ones. Our power hunts when we're weak, looking for more. Our magical selves draw new power to replace what's gone. I was asleep, but my power wasn't. It went to the stone alphabet that Briar had given me. That was a collection of rocks, one for each letter of the alphabet. They were neatly laid out in pockets sewn in a quilted piece of cloth.

He used to tease me about it. "Other kids get a book or a scroll to learn their letters. I had to get you an alphabet made of stones, so your letters would make a dent in that stubborn head of yours."

He didn't fool me. He wanted me to have something nice of my own. Something that was all new. I never let on that I understood, of course. Briar would just start hitting the air like he was pushing me away. He'd say, "*Girls!* Always making a boo-hoo about stuff!"

Just so he knew I didn't forget, I showed him every new stone I added to the cloth pockets of my alphabet. And just so he didn't think I was sentimental, I told him all the magical uses for the new rocks. He'd moan and roll around, saying stones bored him. He'd also see how nice I kept my alphabet.

I have a mage kit, with rocks dedicated to spell work, like any stone mage. But my alphabet is where I store spare magic, in case of blizzards. Or in case I ran into something that milked me so dry I couldn't even call sparkle to quartz.

I didn't think of that as I slept. I didn't think at all. Instead my magic latched on to my alphabet. From agate to zircon, I drained it. In my sleep I felt my strength return.

Eventually I also felt a rude foot kick my bed. It was Rosethorn. "I wish I could let you sleep, but you've had a full day and two nights. We're running out of time, and half this village isn't even packed."

I sat up and moaned. I was stiff all over. "But I can pack us in two shakes of a goat's tail. Why did you even wait? You could have tied me to my horse and taken me down to the ship. You've done it before."

Rosethorn was pouring water in the basin. "And then what? Leave you there? Come wash your face." She

148

waited. Then she frowned. "You thought *we* would be leaving?"

I tossed away my blankets. Someone, I guessed her, had taken off my clothes and put me in my nightshirt. "Of course. What can you do about a mountain blowing up? Even *you* can't stop that one, Rosethorn." I was surprised she couldn't see the logic of it. "Fusspot won't be of any use, either. Plant and water mages can't stop moving lava. We should be at sea already."

"You would just leave everyone here to their own devices." Rosethorn said it, she didn't ask.

I was *ravenous*. Someone had left cheese, bread, and grape juice by my bed. I gulped down the juice. "What are they to me? They're not you or Briar or anyone we care about. It's *their* island, they have to solve getting off. They're lucky I could warn them." I stuffed bread into my mouth. It was a little dry. They must have left it for me yesterday.

Rosethorn finger-combed her hair. "You would abandon even the babies, Evvy? Even the cats?"

Her remark about the cats stung, especially around my eyes. After losing my cats in Gyongxe, I had avoided even the ship's cats on the voyage home. What was the use of getting attached when I would leave them when we got to Emelan? Lark had offered to let me have a kitten at Discipline, but what if it got sick and died, or was killed by a wagon, or the temple was attacked?

Just because I was afraid to have a cat didn't mean I stopped caring about them. It was mean of Rosethorn to hit me on my sore spot. "Cats die all the time," I made myself say. In my mind I could see the dead animals of Gyongxe. I couldn't save the animals on this island, either, any more than I could save the people. And I *like* animals. "The world remakes itself. We can't stop it. We'd be stupid to stay. It's time to save our skins."

Rosethorn sighed. "Lark was worried about this aspect of you. I'm not so fond of people myself, Evvy, but I took my vows for a reason. There are two classes of people in the world, the destroyers and the builders. I want to build, not destroy. You need to ask yourself who you're going to be. Deserting people like Jayat and Tahar, or Oswin and Azaze, who have worked hard to build a good village, is a step toward becoming a destroyer. In any event, you're not getting a vote. Myrrhtide is at the lake. He's reaching to every water mage around the Pebbled Sea. Anyone who's close enough will send ships to evacuate Starns. Azaze sent people to warn the other villages and Sustree. And *you* are going to Oswin's to help them pack. Oswin is trying to get the mountain villagers down, and Nory has her hands full with the children. So eat up and ride out there."

I'd been stuffing food in my face while she lectured. Builders and destroyers — was this the pap they fed people when they took their vows? And I'd always thought

Rosethorn was a sensible person. "We need to *go*," I repeated when I could talk.

"Then the quicker Nory gets the children ready, the quicker we can leave," Rosethorn told me.

I knew that tone of voice. When Rosethorn has her mind set, that was the end of any conversation. I grabbed my clothes. "Myrrhtide can really reach all the way to Sotat and Emelan in water? From here?"

Her smile was crooked. "Why do you think he came? It wasn't because I find his personality charming. I pray that Tuhengri of the winds and Runog of the deep send us enough ships to be of help." She picked up her mage's kit. "Wash your face and clean your teeth." She paused, a funny look on her face. "Might you talk your volcano friends into waiting until we get away?"

"Humans never cease to look for ways out of the circle." Luvo sat up on the windowsill, watching the dawn. "Behind the ones Evumeimei calls Flare and Carnelian are thousands who press forward. They hunger for their time of glory and transformation in the open air. It is what the stuff you call magma, or lava, is made for. If Flare and Carnelian do not lead them, they will find others to do so. Those spirits will not listen to Evumeimei."

Rosethorn shrugged. "I just thought I should ask." She looked at me. "Oswin's, Evvy. I mean it."

I can't say I dressed happily. I yanked my clothes on. If they hadn't been sewn by Lark, I would have ripped seams.

I jammed my feet into my sandals. People! Rosethorn would risk her life, and mine, and Luvo's, over these bleaters. What if we did get them off the island in a couple of days? There was no guarantee that we would get far enough away to be safe. I saw that old-time explosion that Tahar and Jayat raised from my stones. Those flying chunks of rock looked big enough to punch clean through ships. They would kill anyone they hit. From my books, I knew that volcanoes created earthquakes, and sometimes gadolgas, the killer waves. Gadolgas might swamp a ship overloaded with passengers and their belongings.

I'd rather dive into a volcano than drown, any day.

"How many people have left already, Luvo, did you see?" I asked.

"Quite a few. Those with carts and horses. They assembled and took the road at dawn. I watched them from this window." Luvo hesitated for a moment. "Evumeimei, many villagers came to those with wagons and begged them to take their children. I could see that there was room for at least one or two little ones. Still, many of those in the wagons refused. Some held off the others with sticks and whips."

I growled and put his cloth carry sling around my shoulders. Then I tucked him into it. "The rich only look after themselves. They don't care if the poor are left to die. Let's hurry Oswin's tribe along."

I took him down to the stables, saddled, and mounted my horse. We passed carts and riders on the road. They were all on their way out of the valley. I ignored them and looked at the land itself. Now that I had seen the first volcano in the vision spell, I spotted traces of the ancient crater it had left. It surrounded the lake, forming the rim of tall hills and the spire of Mount Grace. Many of Jayat's lines of power had been cracks in it. They led from the shallowest parts of the crater down into the great chamber where I had met Carnelian and Flare.

All this time the old volcano's remains had been asleep. Then magma began to fill that hollow again miles below the ground. All that power slowly building in the earth . . . It gave me the shivers.

Once I reached Oswin's, I found a patch of grass for my horse. I unsaddled it and left it to graze there. The door to the house stood wide open. A boy whose hair went in every direction but down was wrestling a wooden box across the yard. He was on his way to a rickety cart tied together with rope. "Don't . . . expect *me* . . ." He heaved his crate into the cart and stood there, panting. "To do anything for you. I promised Oswin I'd load this Lakik-blessed thing."

"Lakik don't bless things, unless it's with fleas or maggots." That's what Briar always said, and he'd gotten me in the habit. "I'm looking for Nory, anyway."

"I'll pray for you," he said. "She's inside, herding kids."

"Which one are you?" I asked.

He was already dashing around the house to the back. His hair bounced like storm-tossed branches as he ran. "Treak!" he called.

So that was furniture-breaking Treak. He didn't *look* crazy.

I banged on the open front door. Nobody answered. I heard yelling upstairs, so I followed the sound. There I found Nory and the girl she had called Meryem the last time I visited. They watched as four boys tore a room to pieces.

"I don't care if you can't find every toy," Nory told the boys as she clung to Meryem. "Even if you *don't* have everything you want in those bags I gave you, we leave at noon." She turned to me. "What do you want?" Her blue-gray eyes flashed dangerously. "If it's Oswin, he's helping the widow who lives by Bottdik Pond. Up the main road and turn by the split willow. There's only one way to turn, and one split willow." She walked down the hall, towing the howling Meryem. She must have realized I hadn't moved. She halted and glared at me. "Why are you still here?"

I sighed. "I was told to come make myself useful. If you want me to go away, fine, but Rosethorn sent me to help."

She cocked her head at me. "And you brought your toy rock for comfort?"

Luvo poked his head out of his sling. "I am of use in my own way."

If Nory was impressed, she hid it pretty well. "All right. Give Meryem a bath and dress her in clean clothes." She thrust the little girl into a room off the hall. "You have a tub in there. The water's probably only warm by now. She has clothes, and brushes for her hair, and soap, and towels."

"What good does a bath do?" I asked. "She'll only get dirty again on the road."

Nory propped her hands on her hips. "Meryem has bad dreams about soldiers killing her family some nights. She had the dreams last night. When she has the dreams, she has accidents. I cleaned her up as best as I could, but unless you want to carry her on *your* horse, you'll give her a bath."

I didn't want to carry a girl who'd wet herself with me. I guess that meant I'd have to wash her.

Nory frowned at Luvo. "I haven't the foggiest idea about what use you might be. You can't pack."

He said, "I can watch those boys and guide them in their choices of items to take. They obviously require supervision."

Nory smiled crookedly. "That they do. Suit yourself. Watch them all you like. If you actually watch things. I have a hundred questions, I suppose, but the other girls are probably fussing and there's Oswin's things to pack." She trotted up the stairs to the garret. I put Luvo on the floor and watched him go back to the room with the boys. Then I went into the bathroom with Meryem. She stood next to the large tub, scowling at me.

I scowled back. "Don't think you can out-stubborn me. My magic comes from rocks. I might as well be one myself as far as stubborn goes. Dirty clothes off and into the tub."

She broke to my left. I stepped back, close to the door, and grabbed her by her shift. Since she was dirty anyway, I dumped her into the tub, clothes and all. She thrashed and wailed as I pulled the shift off. Now both of us were soaked. I grabbed a handful of gloppy, homemade soap, and tried to put it in her hair. Meryem got in a lucky head butt. She jammed my hand up into my face.

By the time I had rinsed the soap from my burning eyes, she was gone. I cursed in every language I knew, then grabbed some towels. I promised myself I'd tie her up if I had to.

I followed Meryem's wet footprints down the stairs and out of the house. They were still clear in the dirt of the path to the dead pond. I ran, then. I was scared she might fall into the water. The acid water would burn her.

The sight of dead animals in the pond stopped her on its shore. When she saw me, she ran to the far side of the water and stuck her tongue out. I was thinking of a plan of attack when bubbles rose to the surface of the water. They popped with the stink of rotten eggs. Slowly I approached

Meryem. As I did, other bubbles burst. They smelled less like rotten eggs and more like other kinds of bad air.

Bad air.

"I'm not coming!" cried Meryem. "You're not my family! I'm not leaving! People always make me leave!"

"Maybe they're trying to save your life!" I didn't want to argue. I wanted to think. What might bubbles of bad air mean? If they were coming up, what was coming after them? "Go back to the house. Go back and wait! Go!" Bad air went hand in glove with Flare and Carnelian. How close to the surface were they? What if they were right behind these bubbles?

"OOOMMMM." The sound made the air quiver. "OOOUUUUUUUMMMMM."

Meryem shrieked. "What was that?"

That was Luvo, getting serious. The boys must have tried to play some trick on him. The sound would be even worse to them, trapped in the same house with Luvo.

A large bubble popped with a stink that made my throat close. I moved away from it. I couldn't let myself be distracted. "That sound is a warning that you'd better get back to the house *now!*"

She didn't make me repeat myself. She ran to Oswin's as fast as she could.

"Finish your bath and get dressed!" I yelled after her. Then I lay on a dry patch of ground, away from the mud. I put my hands flat on the earth and drew from the rocks all around me. Even though I had built myself up again with my stone alphabet, I wasn't as strong magically as I was before I had come to Moharrin. I needed whatever power I could gather. I could find magic in ordinary stones — they were the heart of my power. They wouldn't hold as much as ones I had fiddled with, but they could still help.

Today I was lucky. To my left was a pocket of feldspars, forged in that volcano. All of them held some of its ages-old strength. Rainbow, plain, and black moonstone, plain feldspar crystals and gaudy sunstone, I drank all of it in, then thanked the rocks. In the ground I searched out the heavy, dense granite, dark and stubborn basalt, and the cruel edges of gabbro. I spread my net wider for stones filled with holes: scoria and pumice. I needed them so the drag of the volcano spirits would pass *through* me instead of pulling *on* me.

Once I was armed, I glanced at the pond. It bubbled like a kettle boiling on the fire. "Don't wait any longer, Evvy," I told myself. I let my magical body fall out of my flesh one, seeping into the ground.

There I saw as clearly with my magical eyes as I could with my real ones. The power of the volcano spirits shone in tiny wisps from a crack on the bottom of the pond. I dove into it, following the power back down into the earth.

12

The Quartz Trap

It took me a long time to track the traces of their magic until I ran into Flare and Carnelian. When I had noticed those bubbles in the pond, then seen their power under it, I had been afraid they were close to the surface.

Both of them had kept their humanlike shape and seeming. I hoped that was a good thing.

Where were you? Flare circled me so fast I began to spin like a top. *We looked all over the chamber but you were gone! We thought you had left us with everyone* old.

Why did you go? We know you did. We didn't like *it.* Carnelian stared at me. The stone around us softened and dripped down the sides of the crack where we drifted.

You almost crushed me up there. Although we were deep underground, I somehow knew where Mount Grace was. I pointed to it. *I'm not like you. You have to see that. You nearly killed me. Of course I ran away. If you start trying to crush me against this roof here, I'll leave again, I promise.*

You're big and strong. I'm not. I have a right to preserve my life.

We couldn't crush anybody here. The roof is weak, can't you tell? There's more bounce. Flare pushed the stone over us with his arms. It didn't bounce, though parts of it melted away. *I think it bounces. If we push . . .*

The shimmering waves around him streamed into the thin crack in the stone. That was the poisoned air, I knew. It would speed to the surface far in advance of him, bubbling into the pond. Could it widen the crack and open the way for Carnelian and Flare?

I didn't think Nory would like it if a volcano, or even a slowly leaking lava flow, came up out of Oswin's pond.

Maybe if I help. Carnelian rose to put her shoulders against the crack. It widened under her pressure. More poisoned air rose into it.

I felt heat rise below us. I looked down. At the far end of the crack, where it entered the underground chamber, the others had noticed something was going on. A handful of them had swum up to stare at us. I had to get Flare and Carnelian out of here. The others might not follow if we moved quick enough. They weren't as curious as these two. I wished I could get Luvo down here with his big noise. Luvo could teach them!

Luvo. Teaching. I thought of the crystals I had seen, the ones whose strength I had borrowed. Something about Luvo teaching crystals . . .

That morning on the mountain, above the canyon of the dead trees. Luvo was telling Jayat about the new line of power. He was saying it might be a trap for a mage, because of all the quartz crystals around it. The crystals would grab power and reflect it inside themselves. They would be a maze for magic. I might have a trap for my new friends. Of course, it would only work if pride wasn't something common only to humans. Still, Luvo had pride. It was worth a try.

I know a game you might like. I looked back at the other lava spirits. *But it's a small game. The place to play it isn't very big. The three of us could play, but there isn't enough room for them.*

They won't follow. Flare didn't even look at them. *They only follow if it looks like we're getting out. Will this game let us get out?*

Flare and Carnelian stared at me, their black-rimmed eyes wide around the orange fire inside. If I'd had skin on, it would have crawled. They looked *hungry.*

It was so much easier to lie without a real face or body. I could see myself reflected in those flaming eye openings. I was a shimmering silver ghost shape of a girl, with nothing to give away what I thought.

No, it won't let you out! I don't know any *game that does* that! *This game makes you stronger, so maybe you can break through the peak one day, if you can't find another way out. But the way this game is played* is *a little scary.* I hesitated for a moment, then did the thing that Briar always called "setting the hook." You gave the person you lied to one last shove, so they would do what you wanted them to. *It's probably too hard.*

It's not *too hard!* Carnelian might be a spirit of a young volcano, but in some ways she wasn't much different from a human. *You'll see! Just tell us how it's played!*

I drifted toward Mount Grace. Flare came on one side of me, Carnelian on the other. *The game has one tricky part. See, I notice that when you touch the cold hard parts of the ground, it starts to melt.*

So? Flare sounded just like any other boy. *If it melts, it gets out of our way.*

Except you need to work with *that stuff for this game*, I explained. *There's a special form of it, called crystal. It's got flat sides all at angles to each other. Within the crystal, things bounce from side to side, and they get bigger as they bounce. Say you put power in the crystal, like the kind you two have. If you bounce around inside the crystal long enough, it'll make you stronger.*

Why didn't you say so? Flare swarmed ahead of me. *What's this crystal look like? Here we go shoving ourselves into cracks, when we could have been in these crystal things. . . .*

I was stupid then. I grabbed his fiery legs. For a moment my arms sank into him, becoming part of him. I felt myself start to melt into Flare. His body started to become mine. My heart roared like a furnace: I wanted to soar up through the earth and shoot straight into the sky. I panicked and struggled, fighting against his pull. Finally I yanked free.

That hadn't happened before. They had grabbed me and towed me all over Starns, and it hadn't bothered me.

Carnelian looked at me. I swear I saw her smirk. *We're stronger, aren't we? Not strong enough to break out, but soon.*

I glared at her. *Without my game you'll never break out. Flare!* I kept my hands to myself. *If you go into a batch of crystal like you are now, you'll melt it. You'll never get stronger that way!*

Flare came back. *Then how does it work?*

Wait. I sent my magic out, until it began to come back to me in chimes. It had struck that great bed of quartz under the canyon. *This way.* I led them toward it, then stopped far below the quartz, so they wouldn't melt the crystals. *The trick is, you have to break yourself up into tiny, tiny bits no bigger than this.* I showed them just a scrap of my finger. I had been calculating all the way. I had to scatter Flare and Carnelian in hundreds of tiny pieces throughout the bed of stones. Broken up, small, they wouldn't be hot enough to melt them. They would bounce inside each piece constantly. And they would get too dizzy to pull themselves together into whole creatures again. They would be occupied for a while, maybe forever.

It wasn't foolproof, but it was the best I could think of, in a hurry.

How will we get strong if we're all in pieces? Carnelian seemed to be the thinker.

Each piece *gets stronger, reflecting from the faces of the crystal.* I used my "everyone knows *that*, bleater" voice. *So all of you is strong, not just part. Then, when you find the way out, you're better than when you went in.*

I'm not sure. Flare darted back and forth. *Break ourselves up? It took me forever to become one separate person in the deep down under.*

In the core. Carnelian whispered it like it was the name of a temple. *In the core, where all of us are born.*

Well, we were in pieces there, and had to come together to make one person, before we came up to the pool, Flare said. *What if I* stay *in pieces this time? What if Carnelian stays in pieces?*

I thought of a core that was all volcano spirit, and shuddered so hard I nearly broke into pieces myself. *You won't stay apart, you two. How can it be a* game *if you stay apart? The game is that you get stronger. The winner is the one who puts herself together quickest, Carnelian or Flare.* I wasn't about to tell them the trick: that if they broke themselves up, and jumped into each piece of quartz, they wouldn't be strong enough to escape and put themselves back together.

What makes you think it will be Carnelian? Flare demanded. *I'm faster. I'm the one who wants to win and get out the most!*

You are not faster! Carnelian exclaimed. *And whose idea was it to break out in the first place? Mine!*

It was your idea, but I found the first crack. Flare broke into hundreds of tiny flames. All of them asked with his voice, *Where are these crystals?*

We'll see who wins this game! For someone who worried about breaking apart, Carnelian sure managed it in a hurry.

I led the way through the ground until we came up into the cold, hard bed of quartz crystals. Two fiery clouds shot past me. They split up like flocks of birds to dart into the stones. Bits of blue and orange fire tangled and sprang apart: pieces of Flare fighting over a particular crystal with pieces of Carnelian.

I watched for a time. I needed to see if they overheated the quartz. Thankfully, I hadn't been asleep the day I studied heat and stones at Winding Circle. A candle flame would not burn the stuff. Inside hundreds of crystals I saw flecks of Carnelian and Flare. First, they would have to see that I'd tricked them. Then, they'd have to find a way to escape each small mirror maze, where the only thing they could see on the inside was themselves. They might be trapped for weeks. Just to be sure, I wandered over that seam of quartz at least three times. They were bouncing inside.

It's hard*! Feel how hard! And cold! And it doesn't melt or burn like the walls of the chamber!* Carnelian's voices whispered, shivery with excitement.

It feels so different from the others! Remember the straight edges we could see, before they melted? This is what straight feels like, and flat! Flare's whispers actually sounded happy.

I hadn't thought of that. It never occurred to me this would be wonderful for them. Flare and Carnelian had only known the lava pool and the spirits, or the melting stone and earth that kept them from breaking free. They hadn't realized yet the quartz bed was a prison. Maybe it would keep them happy for a long time. Then I wouldn't have to feel bad about sticking them there. They were only kids like me, after all. It wasn't their fault they could destroy so much.

I finally began my swim up through the ground. It was hard. I was getting tired. It was more like a climb than a swim, actually, with me grabbing power from every stone I passed. Even after I'd drawn on my stone alphabet and the stones I'd found coming here, I wasn't as strong as I was normally. Borrowed magic or stored magic is never as good as what you have from day to day.

I slowed to look at a cluster of sunstones. How did they get the name sunstone? They hardly shone, and only glittered in spots. They *were* mostly orange.

Evumeimei, you are dazzled. Luvo's voice spilled over me like icy water. It woke me from my dazed state. He poured his strength into me as I dragged myself into my cold, real body.

No, I'm all right! Turning his power aside was like trying to kick an elephant.

Where have you been? Luvo wanted to know. *Norya is quite pleased that you frightened Meryem into taking her bath, but she says that you should have stayed with her.*

If I had stayed with Meryem, Nory might have had Flare and Carnelian eating the house. I opened my eyes and sat up, safe in my body. Luvo had come down to the pond to find me. I put a hand on his back. It was quicker to show Luvo what had happened than to tell him in words. I let him see it all as I had seen it.

For a long time he said not a word. I began to fear I had made him angry. Perhaps he thought it could have been him trapped in the quartz under the dead tree canyon. Then he began to glow, his crystals shining. Warmth spilled out of him. It was real *and* magical. The creakiness in my joints and the fog in my head vanished. I felt as if I could take Mount Grace apart stone by stone.

Delightful, Evumeimei, Luvo told me. *Most* splendid. *To divert them with the quartz bed is ingenious. They have not known crystal before. Whole, they would have destroyed it. In small pieces, they will be able to enjoy its facets, its resistance to heat. They can learn that it is the firstborn mineral of lava. They may even see that quartz crystals are the children of one of their kind. As such, they will want to get to know all of that bed of crystals.*

"Too bad the bed isn't larger." I could hardly breathe. "I wish it ran the length of the island and back. My biggest worry is that they might reach the end of the crystals somehow and break out."

Luvo got up and paced for a moment. The glow flowed after him like a scarf that connected us, still wrapping me in his approval. "I have an idea." He said it out loud, instead of in our magic. "It will take me a time, however. If you will remain to watch over me? I vexed the boys enough that I know they would consider tossing me in the water."

"Let them try," I assured him.

Luvo sat. His approving glow vanished, but I still felt all that wonderful warmth. I hugged it to me. Did Luvo's mountain feel like this when he lived inside it? He said the mountain was happy when he was gone, but I couldn't believe it really was.

I heard someone approach. It was one of Nory's boys. "Please tell 'im" — the boy pointed at Luvo, who had curled into a purple and green lump — "that we packed all our things and put 'em in the cart, and then we helped Nory and the little ones, and we carried what Nory told us to, all to the cart. If'n he asks. If'n he don't ask, don't tell him we're even alive. If he forgets us, that's fine. But we done like he bid. And Nory says if you want soup you ought to come, 'cause we're leavin' at sun high." He turned to go, then looked back at me. "He ever done you like that? With the noise, and the house shakin'?"

I nodded and tried not to giggle. "Several times."

"And you still be with 'im? You mages is god-touched. I aims to get as far from him as the sea'll put me!" He trotted back to the house.

I watched Luvo, thinking about those times in Yanjing that he had used his mountain voice on Briar and me. We had been awed and curious, not terrified. Well, maybe we had been a little terrified, the first few times. Or just *deeply* impressed. It's hard to tell the difference between so much awe and fear.

Luvo uncurled. "I have done a thing." He wobbled as he sat up. I felt pulses like earth shocks travel through me. They didn't pass through the ground, though they somehow moved in the *stones* in the ground. A long, groaning shock dragged at me. Another shock followed. It dumped Luvo and me on our sides. Another dragging shock came next, and a last bump that threw me and Luvo in the air. We landed with a thump.

The strange part was, we were the only two things that moved. Nothing else did. Not one piece of grit or stick.

What did you do? I cried in our magic as I grabbed on to a nearby tree and stared at Luvo. Aloud I said, "That was like an earthquake, but in the magic! And it bounced you, too!"

"Sooner or later Flare and Carnelian would have found the end of the quartz bed," he told me. "You said it yourself. So . . . I arranged for them never to find it."

I just stared at him. "How can you *arrange* that?"

Luvo stood on all fours and shook himself. His crystals jumped and settled inside his clear stone skin. It was enough to make a person ill. "I took one end of the bed and pulled it toward the other. Before I joined the ends, I gave one a half twist. I had the idea from a puzzle shown to me by a Gyongxe monk. Try it with a piece of paper. Once the two ends are joined, if one traces the paper's edge, one will find the circle has only one edge throughout its length. The circle is infinite. Flare and Carnelian will never find an end to it. They will pursue their reflections in each bit of quartz forever." Luvo hesitated. "Evumeimei, when you tricked them into entering the quartz bed, did you realize, that if they reassemble themselves, they would be far stronger? I do not absolve myself of blame. It will be worse if they escape my variation on your trap."

I hugged my tree. "It was the only thing I could think of in a hurry," I growled.

Luvo made a sound that was scarily like a sigh. "That is my excuse, too. We shall pray we are off Starns when — if — they do manage to free themselves. I fear they will destroy much more than this island should they escape."

I looked at him. "We didn't *mean* to make it worse."

"We bought time, Evumeimei," Luvo said. "We must warn the people of the neighboring islands to flee in any case. The measure of how great these children will be as a volcano is beyond our skills. We must hope that we have done enough, and go. Before Flare and Carnelian are too strong for our trap to hold them."

13

Oswin's Kids

Nory waited for us at the back door when we reached the house. "Do you believe I'll thank you for inspiring Meryem to bathe and dress? You were supposed to be *with* her."

I gave her my best glare. With my head spinning, I doubt it was very good. "I had something important to do, all right? If I hadn't, maybe none of us could have left here at all. And your darling Meryem might have gotten her toesies boiled."

The darling Meryem peered at me from behind Nory's skirts and giggled. I scowled at her, but not very hard. She was as cute as an amethyst once she was clean.

"There's nothing around here to boil her toes." Nory didn't look convinced.

"There would have been, had not Evumeimei acted quickly." Luvo walked over to Nory and sat on his rump so he could look up at her. "How are the boys?"

She had to back up and kneel to talk to him politely. It was interesting to see that she *wanted* to talk to him politely. "They're packed and in the cart. We're all ready to go." She glared over Luvo at me. "You can forget anything to eat."

My head ached and my hands shook. Her mention of food explained my wobbliness. I had overdone things, even with Luvo's approval magic to bolster me. I needed food. I'd hitch a ride in the wagon back to the inn, and get something there.

"If you're ready, why are we gabbling?" I picked up Luvo. "We're wasting time." This was the problem with meat people. They had to be talked into everything. I made myself forget the time I spent arguing Flare and Carnelian into doing things. Anyway, it was stones I was thinking of, calm and quiet stones.

"So I'm to believe you found some huge magic thing to do out by our pond." Nory led the way back through the house. "A pond so useless we can't even get decent-sized fish out of it."

"We can play in the water when the weather's hot." Meryem decided to hold on to my hand. I don't know why, but it made me feel funny. She kept looking up at me, too. Was there mud on my face? I had plenty of it on my clothes.

"Yes, Meryem, you play in it when you're hot." Nory stopped to shoulder a pack and pick up two carry sacks left in the hall. "Then you walk back here and track dirt in the house. And *you're* coated in pond mud and I have to give you a bath."

Meryem just grinned. "Treak gives us a bath some-times. And Lexa and Jesy and Deva. You aren't the only one. And they mop the floors sometimes. It isn't just you."

"Sometimes." Nory checked the pack's straps. "And sometimes they get silly and pour water all on the floors and get mud all over everything." She pushed the front door open. "Some help. Urda save me, did you kids pack up the entire *house*?"

Just like Nory, I was staring at the cart. It was piled with boxes and bags. I saw a crate with chickens and another with puppy noses sticking out of it. A dog was tied to the cart by a length of rope. From the look of her, she was the puppies' mother. Eleven people, boys and girls of different ages, stood around it, waiting for us. A pair of sorry-looking cart horses sagged in the shafts. They looked as if they expected nothing but bad out of life.

"You aren't taking *all* this with you?" Nory demanded. She had told the boys to pack only what would fit a *small* bag. I had even seen the small bags.

"You let *us* worry about what we take, Nory. You and the little ones can ride right here." The boy giving the orders was Treak, the one whose hair went every which-way. Now he patted a spot on the cart where Nory and the littlest children could sit. "Jesy can drive."

"Thanks, Treak." A wiry blonde girl with the thickest spectacles I had ever seen — Jesy — clambered onto the driver's seat. Nory settled Meryem and a small boy, then climbed up beside them. Another boy offered me the reins to the horse I had left with Treak earlier that morning. It was freshly combed and saddled. The boy held out his free hand, palm up.

He wanted *payment*? I asked, "What's your price? I don't have any money."

"A ride to the inn." He was a cheerful fellow, black as shadows, with ribs that showed against his skin. None of these kids was what I'd call plump. "I'll save myself a few blisters that way."

I slapped his open palm with mine to show we had a bargain. Then I mounted and pulled him up behind me. Once in the saddle, I rearranged Luvo in his sling and rode out ahead of the cart.

Traveling on horseback, I tend to forget the bumps in the road. I was halfway to the village when I heard a nasty-sounding rumble and thump behind me. I glanced back. The cart's front wheel had gone into a deep rut. There was another bump as it came out, followed by the crunch of breaking wood. The little ones screamed. The other kids shouted. The dog barked; the puppies replied. The chickens shrieked. I turned my horse so my rider and I could look.

"Oh, ringworms," the boy whispered. He dismounted to help. The cart leaned to one side, the rear left wheel bent in under the box. The left front wheel was also bent. The axle was broken. The cart was going nowhere.

"Hog puke, dog dung, and navy snot!" Treak jumped up and down in the road. *Now* he looked like someone who could break furniture in a rage. "Lakik's curses twelve times on the scum swiller who fixed this last!"

"Oswin did." Tears rolled down Meryem's face. "Don't you yell at Oswin, Treak! I'll cut you!" From somewhere she had gotten a small dagger. She held it like she knew how to use it.

Pirate kids, I thought, and sighed.

Nory took the knife away like she'd had a lot of practice. "Kill Treak later, Meryem. Get down carefully." She and the driver, Jesy, climbed down and helped the children get off.

As some of the kids cried and others asked what they would do now, I made a mistake. I let my weariness and my need for food run my mouth. "I knew this was a bad idea! Carrying all these things, for what? Those ships will be packed! Surely Oswin told you that. It's why you had orders just to bring a *few* things, not all this." I waved my hands at the cart. "When the volcano explodes, you'll still *be* here with all this *junk* —"

"It is not junk!" Nory stared up at me. Her eyes looked like blue-gray ice in the winter sun. "What do you know? I bet you've never done without in your life! I'll bet you never had to run from anywhere with just the rags on your back! Every one of us has left our *whole lives* behind more than once, so don't you preach! We have to save what we can!"

I ground my teeth. "And if they don't let you bring it on the ships?" She had a nerve, talking that way to me. She didn't know the first thing about what I'd had to do.

Meryem grabbed a beat-up looking thing that maybe was a doll once. "I have to have Dolly. Dolly's my family."

My gut twisted. "They'll let you take one dolly, Meryem. It's crates and bags and trunks of stuff I'm not sure about."

Luvo raised up in his sling so we were touching. *You crossed five lands with your cats,* he said so only I could hear. *You wouldn't let anyone separate you.*

"If we can't take it, then we'll sort it out on the docks, not a moment before! You don't tell us to give up our home and our treasures, too!" Nory was crying. "Treak, stop running around or I'll hit you, I swear! Find a blacksmith. Not the Master Blacksmith, we can't afford him. Maybe his apprentice will fix this rattletrap."

It wasn't my job to tell her the blacksmith had left before dawn. I dismounted and gave my horse's reins to Treak so he could ride for help. Then I put Luvo beside the road. I helped the kids stack their things, including the crated animals, on the grass, out of the way. Meryem seemed to think she and her dreadful doll were supposed to help me. Everywhere I turned, I tripped over her. When

we stopped for a drink of water, Nory shoved an egg turnover at each of us.

"The rock says you'll be ill if you don't eat, Evvy. I
didn't ask you to help," Nory told me.

I devoured the turnover. I never refuse food, even food
grudgingly offered. Pride is something rich folk can afford.
Nory gave Meryem and me another egg turnover each.
Then we split one stuffed with chicken spiced with carda-
mom. I gobbled it, too. The headache that squeezed my
temples loosened. "He's not a rock. His name is Luvo. He's
as close to a god as any of us will ever get."

"He says you bought us time with a trick you played
on the volcano spirits," Nory remarked.

"Heibei, take this bad luck and bury it," I said.

Nory thumped me in the arm. "What's that supposed
to mean?"

"Don't hit Evvy." Meryem was licking her fingers.
"You don't hit me."

"I like you. I don't like Evvy. What's hay-bay?"

I sighed and rolled my eyes, which would have gotten
me a tweak of the ear if Rosethorn had been around.
"Heibei's the god of luck back home in Yanjing. I asked
him for help. He's a good god, not undependable, like your
Lakik. It's bad luck to say a thing is taken care of, even
when it's Luvo saying it." I wasn't as sure as Luvo that it
would take time for Carnelian and Flare to see they'd been
tricked. I decided to keep that notion to myself. "I'll feel

better when we're on ships and well away from this island."

"Your rescuers are here!" Jayat drove up in a cart that was some less rickety than the first one. The new one already held two trunks — his and Tahar's, I would have guessed. "You kids start loading up, all right?"

Meryem was the first to start loading the cart. The other kids scrambled to help.

Treak, behind Jayat, dismounted from my horse and tied it to a tree branch. Up the road came two of the inn's hostlers. They had a rig they could use to tow the broken cart into the village.

Jayat went to Nory. "Why didn't you have Oswin check that thing before he left?"

"He did. He's the one who fixed it so it would go." Nory could pout very prettily, I saw. She also knew how to use her beautiful eyes on poor Jayat. "I believed him. Even though I knew he was half out of his mind, thinking about every little old widow on the mountain. I should have seen his mind wasn't on the job." Nory grabbed a seabag and lugged it over to Jayat's cart. "Evvy's rock says we have more time."

Jayat looked around. "Luvo? How can this be?"

Luvo started to explain about Flare, Carnelian, and the quartz trap. I couldn't bear to sit still anymore. From the sun's position, I knew we weren't leaving that night. I untied my horse.

"I'll see the rest of you at the inn." I wanted a look at Oswin's map again. "Luvo, are you coming?"

"I will stay with the cart, Evumeimei. If there is a shock, I can steady the rocks under it, and reduce the effect on the wheels."

Jayat looked at him with appreciation. "Thanks, old man. That's kind of you."

"What's your rush, *Evumeimei*?" Nory's eyes glittered. "Or don't you like to be around us poor homeless waifs?"

"Nory!" Jayat looked shocked at the way she spoke to me.

"Nory's mean to Evvy." Meryem perched on top of the cart with the luggage, her doll tucked in her sash. "Nory thinks Evvy doesn't like us."

"I need to replenish my magic." I didn't enjoy the way Meryem's words made me feel. Meryem thought I *did* like them. It's no good liking people, not when they're probably going to get killed. I had learned that the hard way. "You think Luvo and I know more about the volcano spirits by accident? We found them under your pond. We set a trap for them deep in the ground. Now I have to strengthen myself again. You don't need me to get to the village. Luvo just said he can help you." To build myself up this time, I wanted Oswin's map with the lines of power sketched on them. It was still on a table at the inn when we had left that morning.

When no one else said anything, I mounted my horse and rode off. It occurred to me that if I left the animal in the stables, someone might take it. That wouldn't do. Just outside the village, I dismounted and led the horse into a clearing beside a stream. The clearing was shielded from view by trees. There I removed the saddle. I tethered the horse where it could graze and drink safely, once I'd checked that the water was free of acid. When the horse lipped my shirt, I stroked its muzzle and sighed.

"I suppose we ought to be better acquainted." I had tried so hard, since Gyongxe, not to get to know any animals well. The only exception was the dog, Little Bear, who had been at Discipline. Mostly I had blamed him because he wasn't a cat, which seemed unfair, now that I thought of it. I checked the inner rim of the saddle. There was the horse's name, "Spark." A look under the horse's belly told me Spark was a mare. "Hello, Spark. I'm Evvy. You probably knew that already. I need you to wait quietly here. We're going to do some more running about. I'll try to bring you some treats when I come back." I thought, And if they won't let me bring you aboard my ship, I get to leave you here to die.

She made a happy horse noise and bumped me with her nose. I hesitated, then gave her a rub with some handfuls of dry leaves. After I wiped my eyes — they were watering — I went on into Moharrin.

Some carts stood in the open space in front of the inn, but not many. I bet that those who could afford good carts had left already, rushing to get places on the ships. People waited in the courtyard with their bundles and their horses, donkeys, or mules, if they had them. I also saw dogs, sheep, goats, and baskets and crates with cats or birds. I turned away. I wasn't the one to say that they probably wouldn't be allowed to take their creatures along. The inn's servants were carrying boxes out to pack into the carts. They were too busy to do more than nod to me and dodge the children who played in the yard. Why hadn't these people taken the road already? Were they waiting on someone? Tahar, maybe, or Azaze.

Inside the inn's public room, I found Azaze folding blankets as she supervised the maids sealing food in crocks.

"Not that one, the lid is cracked! The first bump and we'll have fish brine all over us! Firouze, pack that basket tighter — we aren't going on a picnic." Azaze cast a quick dark eye my way. "Evvy, you were supposed to be helping Oswin's children."

"They're on their way, with Jayat and *two* of your stable boys and Luvo," I told her. "If they have any more help they won't get here at all. Have you seen Rosethorn?"

Azaze looked down that beak of a nose at me. "Do I hear snippiness from you, girl?" She inspected me and sniffed. "Sit down." She began to pull things from jars and baskets onto a plate. "One thing I have learned about mages in my years, you have to eat when you are working. What did you do out there?"

I scowled at her. "What makes you think I did any work? And I had two and a half turnovers."

Azaze set the plate on a table with one hand. She thrust me onto the bench in front of it with the other. "You're trembling, you're pale, and your mouth is pinched. Whatever magic you worked, those turnovers weren't enough to bring you back."

"They weren't very big," I admitted. She'd given me bread stuffed with ground lamb and cheese — travel food. I began to eat while she poured me a cup of mint tea.

"No one has seen your Rosethorn," Azaze said. "Myrrhtide is still in the lake. He's working magic, too. I've had a lad taking food out to him, for all the boy thinks I'm crackbrained to do it. He hasn't seen as many mages collapse as I have. I hope whatever you did was important."

"I thought so." I waited to say it until my mouth wasn't full.

"That's what matters. I'm getting back to work — I have my account books to pack up — but if you need anything, Firouze over there will get it for you." The maid she pointed to nodded at me. I waved and kept eating. Maybe I *was* still hungry. I cleaned the plate.

I was right about the map. It was still on the table where we'd left it last night. Once I was done, I knelt on the bench and studied it. I memorized the old paths for the land's strength. They followed the cracks that led to that huge chamber under the mountain. The old paths might have been erased in the earthquakes, but only so new ones could open up.

If I was to build my power again, I had to find those new cracks and tap their strength. Or, better yet, I could find one of the *big* veins that fed the small ones. I touched a thick red line that showed a main fault. I doubted the local mages had dared to tap these. One of them ran straight under the Makray River, all the way up to Lake Hobin. I could reach the place where the river poured out of the lake easily. Why bother with little cracks when I could go to a stronger source?

Somebody plopped down next to me. "What's that?"

It was Meryem. Oswin's children had arrived at last. "It's a map," I said. "Leave it alone. Oswin will cook you in a stew if you touch it."

She actually laughed at me.

Rosethorn leaned over my shoulder and inspected the map. "Luvo says you and he trapped those two would-be volcano creatures in a bed of quartz." Her pale skin was smutched, and so was her robe. She looked like she had been working hard. She slid onto the bench with a sigh.

I picked up Meryem and pushed her toward the door. "Shoo," I told her. Once she was out of the inn, I looked at Rosethorn. "Yes. I got them to break themselves up into a lot of tiny pieces, really tiny ones, and put each into a quartz crystal. There's a big vein of them under the dead tree canyon. And Luvo turned the whole vein into some weird circle. Carnelian and Flare will think they're traveling in a straight line, getting stronger, when they're just going around and around."

"But the solution is only a temporary one?" Rosethorn could always sense a flaw in my plans. A kitchen maid set a plate of food down in front of her. "Thank you. Mila and the Green Man bless you and yours."

The maid curtsied and hurried away.

I sighed. "Yes. They'll escape sooner or later, and get back to volcano-making." I stopped. Rosethorn was too polite to talk with her mouth full. Instead she raised her eyebrows, waiting for me to go on. I leaned closer so she would be the only one to hear me. "Bouncing around in the quartz...If they can pull themselves together, they'll be a lot stronger. I should have worked it out, but Rosethorn, I thought they were going to pop out of the pond right by Oswin's house. Luvo made it harder for them to escape the quartz, but that's all he could do. We've just bought a little more time. Myrrhtide has to tell the ships and the mages to get people off the neighboring islands, too. *Now*."

Rosethorn swallowed. "You and Luvo made it worse." She said it *very* quietly.

I was sweating. "Maybe. Kanzan the Merciful smile on me, I hope not."

"Don't waste a plea on your Kanzan now," said Rosethorn. "You might require her more later, when they're about to hang us all. What are you going to do?"

"I'll collect all the power I can hold," I promised. "Luvo can get some of the people outside started on their way to the ships. He was really inspiring for Oswin's boys."

Rosethorn's mouth quivered. She had seen Luvo inspire people before. "Then go collect more power," she told me. "I shall be inspiring the slow movers, too. I want to be on the road out of here at dawn tomorrow."

I heard the thumps of Luvo's feet on the wooden floor. I turned to look at him and said, "I'm going to find one of the big veins of earth strength that's on the map, the one that runs under the river. Do you want to come?"

His magic brushed me. He knew I was nearly drained again. "I do not care to explore the greater strength of the earth's fire, Evumeimei, not unless I must. I tested my own courage this morning in my dealings with Carnelian and Flare."

I never thought of that. He hadn't seemed worried at all. I had told him they were broken up into harmless pieces. He had acted as if he believed me. A lump formed in my throat. He had trusted me to make certain that it was safe for him to go near the two volcano spirits.

"And I wish to spend some time in solitude, if we do not plan to travel on right away."

"We do not." Rosethorn sighed. "There's too much to organize yet. Don't you remember how it went in Gyongxe? People are so much harder to get moving than we plan for."

"Then I will take my solitude. Evumeimei can find me by the shore of the lake if I am needed." Luvo turned and walked away.

"Are you all right?" I called after him.

He looked back at me. "Yes. I am also covered in dirt and spilled honey. Nory tells me this is a normal consequence of being near young humans. I do not care for it, and I wish to be clean and quiet."

Rosethorn put her head in her hands. "We both understand, all too well. Go, with my prayer that no one sees you."

Before I left I went upstairs to collect my stone alphabet. If I was right, I would be able to stuff each piece of it full of power. I couldn't pass up that chance. On my way out of the inn I stopped at the stable to collect feed and treats for Spark. She was going to do a lot of work in the next few days. I could thank her, at least.

Burdened like a mule, I left the courtyard. Only when I heard Nory yell, "Meryem! Where's Meryem!" did I realize I had company.

I looked around. She trotted beside me, clutching the Dreadful Doll. "What do you want?"

"I want to go with you and see magic," she told me.

"You're not going to see magic," I said. "I'm going to ride the horse and sit on the ground."

"When do you do magic?" asked Meryem.

"Later."

"Can I watch?"

"You won't see anything. The kind of magic I do, nobody can see."

"Then how do you know it's magic?" Meryem wanted to know.

"How do you know you ate supper?"

"My belly tells me."

"My magic tells me I'm using it," I said.

"But I want to see it."

"The only magic I have that people see is stones." I held up the cloth roll with my alphabet. "And you see magic like that all the time." I bent down — I almost dropped the bag of oats — and picked up a stone from the road. "It's here, too. My magic is in every stone." It was actually a nice piece of feldspar. I studied it for a moment, and found a bit of power inside me. I drew it through the feldspar. It caught inside the crystal, making it shimmer and glow.

Meryem gasped.

I handed the glowing stone to her. "Now go back to Nory." I lifted my foot and gave her a push on the bum. Treak was coming for her, a scowl on his face. "Hurry, before Treak catches you."

Meryem looked up and saw him. She squeaked and ran to the inn, clutching the feldspar I gave her.

Spark was waiting right where I had left her. I gave her a nose bag of oats while I saddled her again. Once I was done, I stopped to look at my hands. They were trembling. I was scared. Telling Rosethorn what I'd done with Flare and Carnelian had made me see how bad it could get. Each bit of their strength would grow as it bounced from facet to facet in the crystals. But what choice did I have? They had been under the pond. Might they have shoved their way out? I had no way to know. What I'd had was all those kids, as well as Nory and Luvo, in the house nearby. Luvo couldn't even come near the chamber under Mount Grace with me. The power of the volcano spirits was the power that gave birth to him; it could destroy him. He could get near it only after Flare and Carnelian broke themselves up into hundreds of tiny pieces.

I couldn't risk it. I couldn't have risked them escaping that pond to kill Luvo and the others.

But Luvo and I had only bought days for Moharrin and the other villages around Mount Grace. If the quartz held out. If Carnelian and Flare didn't get so strong in it that they melted each crystal, if they didn't break out, if the volcano spirits didn't find new leaders to bring them up into the air . . .

"Ifs just make your head hurt, Evvy," Briar told me often. "They're probably bad for your teeth, too. Concentrate on 'will,' as in 'I will do this,' or 'I will do that.' It saves you head- and toothaches, take it from me."

I wished Briar was here. He made cold-sweat fear seem like a small problem I could kick in the bum. And he always made me laugh as he did it.

14

Oswin

I mounted Spark and guided her onto the road, trotting through Moharrin. I waved at the people who called out to me, but kept going. Not everyone was waiting to get out of there. Spark and I passed a stream of horses, donkeys, and carts already bound for Sustree. There were even some people on foot.

We left them all behind. When we turned off the main road, we followed the trail to the place where the river flowed out of Lake Hobin. Up here, where the river flowed from the lake, it was rapids. Once I got to the rocky bank, I found a place where Spark and me could halt. I watered her and gave her some carrots, then tethered her.

Finally, I settled myself. The river had shifted. I could see the former bed. It was marked with dried slime and dead creatures who had not been able to follow it. Rocks along the original banks had tumbled from their places. The old stones were cross. They were used to water sliding over them. They did not care for this new life in the sun.

"Luck of the circle, lads," I told them. "One day you're under water, the next you're not."

"You talk like a dedicate," Oswin said. I jumped. I hadn't even heard him ride up. "Are you a novice?"

"What are *you* doing? Are you following me?" I asked.

"Absolutely." Oswin swung down from his swaybacked horse and took off the saddle, like I'd removed Spark's. "You looked like you were going to do something mage-like. One more of those times when I might learn something useful. Your Rosethorn is badgering people to get packed and get their carts in line. Word got out that Luvo said we might have a few more days, so our people act as if they have forever. I've done all I can for the moment, so I followed you."

I didn't feel like arguing. He'd get bored fast enough. People always do. "Don't make any noise, then. I need to find the new line of strength and draw all of it I can."

"Why?"

"Why? Because I might *need* it," I said, testy. "I'm not restocked from yesterday, all right? Because I'm a squirrel who stores up nuts of power for the winter. Why." I closed my eyes and sent my quivery magical self down into the ground. I searched out the fizzing rocks that showed me where the old line of power had been. Then I spread out and down, seeking the new one. Just as I thought, it was under the changed riverbed, a seam in the granite that shot straight down. It blazed white-hot with the earth's pure strength.

I soaked it up like the rays of the sun after a long winter. I bathed in it, drank it, filled my skin with it. The more I gathered, the more was offered to me. Streams of it poured through me to those things I was connected to, my stone alphabet and my mage kit. We brimmed over with power.

I let myself follow the big fault where the power flowed away from the mountain. It ran along the Makray. It made the river's bed. I flew in my magical body down to the place where the river met the sea. There I fell deeper into the earth to get away from the salt water. Down I moved through sand and basalt. The ocean's floor rose high over me. Far from Starns, fire warmed my body. I had found a vein of magma that rose into the ocean floor. It carried power with it. I followed it, curious to see where this thin pipe of molten rock and magic went. It opened into a hole in the ocean floor, at the bottom of a small crater. All around me strange, goggle-eyed creatures with rippling flaps of skin raced away. They were used to lava, it seemed, but not to magical people popping out along with it. The touch of the water made me shiver. It didn't like me. I darted back into the small lava pipe.

Back I swam into the vent and along the fault. I found other cracks like the one that opened into the crater — like the one Luvo had shown me, that day we reached Starns. There were tiny volcanoes, some no bigger than my head, all around the Battle Islands. And the faults in the sea, big ones and little ones, were roads under the skin of the earth. They could lead me to other islands, or even the shores that surrounded the Pebbled Sea. It was amazing! I could travel back to Emelan this way. I was so fast in magical form, not weighed down by my meat body and a need for a ship. No more dealing with people, no more being hungry or cold . . .

I was drifting, dreaming of freedom, when all the world — or at least my part of it — shuddered. The seam where I traveled *squeezed.* Volcano spirits from deep within the heart of the world roared. Heat rose to press my skin. Magma was moving up into the fault. If I didn't leave, it might catch me. I didn't want to be there, far below the sea, when that happened. I didn't think I could survive it.

I raced back to my body, covering dozens of miles under the earth, skidding between layers of basalt. Up I flew from under the sea, plunging into the fault that led under the Makray River with relief.

I tried to slip into my body, and stopped. It was too small! My magical self was bigger than usual, built up with all the power I had taken from the earth. I had trained myself to hold my magic in a certain way. All that romping under the sea had interfered with my control over it. Kanzan and Mohun, couldn't anything ever be *simple?*

I ordered myself, Evvy, stop — calm down. Be steady, drag yourself together. You're a tight little ball of you.

I pulled myself inward. I didn't want to lose any of the power I gathered, but I needed to concentrate it.

When I was packed together as tightly as I could manage, I tried once more to slip into my real skin. This time it worked.

I opened my eyes. It was trying to straighten my legs that made me groan. I was horribly stiff. Oswin offered me kibbeh patties. I grabbed one and bit down. The beef and wheat were greasy, but good, though someone had overdone the cinnamon. "Nory cooked these?" I asked.

Oswin grinned. "She always puts in too much cinnamon. Tell her, if you want your nose bitten off. She likes cinnamon." He gave me a flask. It held good, cool mint tea. I looked at him as I drank. He had made himself comfortable while I was away. He'd brought his saddlebags over. One was open. There was a pad of paper sheets stitched together, an ink brush, and an ink bottle. He must have been writing. I sniffed food in the other cloth bundles I could see in the bag. I also spotted books around the food bundles. Oswin used the other saddlebag as a backrest.

I looked around. Rocks had fallen into the riverbed from the heights across from us, making fresh changes in the rapids. A crack had opened in the riverbed. That had dropped the bottom another thirty feet. The lake was booming down into the new channel, throwing up a fine, cool spray. Moharrin had a new waterfall.

"There was a shock?" I asked. I offered the flask to him, but he shook his head.

"More like a long shiver, but a hard one. Some trees fell." There were shadows in Oswin's blue eyes. It must have been a scary shock.

"Why didn't you go? I must have been entranced for a while," I said.

"Go back to see Nory try to get the axle fixed on that cart?" he inquired. "The smith's apprentice might have done it — he's sweet on her — but he left with the smith. She'll be furious, which means she'll be bullying someone else into fixing it. I'd offer, but I doubt she'd even let me try a second time. She knows I'd probably just botch it again. I feel bad I couldn't get her and the kids a decent cart."

"You do lots of other things for them," I told him. "You give them a home."

Oswin spat on the ground beside him. "It won't do them much good if it and they get buried in ash and lava. What were you doing away from your body? I wouldn't think gathering power would take so long." He offered me some dried figs.

I ate those, too. "I was exploring the fault under the river on out to the sea." I looked over at the granite marker nearby. It had fallen over. I called to it. Slowly, pulling against the soil, it straightened. I tugged on the surrounding rocks. They rolled into place, bracing the marker until it stood firm again.

Oswin swallowed hard. "I'm used to a bit more fuss when people work magic."

I shrugged.

"Maybe *you* know the answer to this, since you're the stone mage," Oswin began. "What are they, these lines? Big *and* small? Tahar and Jayat don't know what they are, apart from the fact that they carry power. They only know they can use them." Oswin drew his knees up to his chest like a boy and wrapped his arms around them. His eyes were blazing with curiosity. "They never say where the power comes from, or why they find it in these places, and not in others. When the lines moved, Tahar and Jayat were at a complete loss. They couldn't find new ones."

"But that's silly," I told him. "Why didn't they just do a spell for feeling power, and sweep across the ground? The big faults didn't move far. They couldn't. Look. The lines — they're faults, or seams in the earth's stone cloak. The faults reach down. Miles, some of them. Way below us, the world is full of molten rock — lava. Well, Luvo and my stone mage teachers call it magma inside the world, lava when it's out in the air. It's heat, it's pressure — it would mash us flat in the blink of an eye — it's light, it's the elements that make up every stone, every mineral, every metal and every gem ever was."

"How do you know?" Oswin asked me.

"What?" I was confused.

"How do you know that's what's in it?"

I blinked. "Well, when one of my teachers was called away, I sneaked a look at the books for the advanced students. But I would have known anyway, after this. I can feel them. The — the makings of gold, and iron, and sulfur. Like healer mages would know if a woman's unborn baby is a boy or a girl or dead or a mage."

Oswin shook his head. "I'm surprised you bother with us human beings at all. You must live in a dream world, if every stone and crystal speaks to you like that."

He'd finally startled me. How could he know that, and him not a mage? "People are all right." I sounded like a liar even to myself.

Oswin smiled at me. I wondered how much he saw, and how much he missed. Suddenly what Jayat had said, that Oswin fixed things without magic, made a lot more sense. "All people, or some people?" he asked.

"I don't know. I haven't met all people," I replied. Maybe I should have let the volcano spirits squeeze me instead of escaping up to this.

I think he took pity on me. "You were telling me about what's far below the surface stone," he reminded me.

"Underneath. Um — that's right." I drank some more mint tea. "It's all amazing hot. Aside from volcanoes, the only openings to it are those faults. And they move. The faults shift. But these big ones, the earth doesn't erase them, like it might the little ones. The big ones the

198

earth needs. They're like the belt in your breeches, to pull in tight when you lose weight, or to let out when you gain it."

Oswin looked at his stomach. "It's not *that* big. My belly."

I shook my head. "They say girls are vain. Every man I've ever met was just as bad. Anyway, the earth line *here* is one of the big faults under the island. It's part of a web of faults under the Pebbled Sea. They feed the other volcanoes around here, and the earthquakes. And the smaller faults split off from the big ones, like, I don't know, fingers from the hand."

"A network, you say," murmured Oswin. "Throughout the Pebbled Sea."

"And the lands around them. The world adjusts itself all the time." It was getting cool as the sun passed behind the mountain. I got to my knees, wincing.

Then I felt it, far in the distance. "Oswin, grab the horses. We've got another shock coming, and it's going to be bad."

The volcano spirits in the hollow chamber were moving. They were hunting for Carnelian and Flare, miles below us. Their movement sent power rolling from the chamber, out through the faults. I wasn't going to ask myself how I knew, when they were so far down. Instead I lurched to saddle my horse. Oswin did the same, then strapped his saddlebags in place.

"Let's go on the road," I told him. "But don't mount up. We have a little bit of a wait."

"Is that so?" He soothed his horse. "You can tell even though it's not right away? No one mentioned you were a seer."

I glared at him. "I can feel them moving, that's how. There's a whole lot of them. They're looking for Flare and Carnelian."

Oswin led his horse into the roadbed. The spirits were deep under the river, pressing against the armor of stone between us and them. The earth shook. Spark wrenched against her bridle. I clung to her as stones began to rattle and move. Oswin had taken off his tunic and wrapped it around his horse's eyes. Even so, he still had to cling to the animal's bridle to keep him from running. Boulders crashed in the riverbed. I heard trees toppling. My teeth clacked together so hard they hurt. The spirits smashed against the sides of the fault, calling to Flare and Carnelian. I bit my lip. Could their bellows reach all the way to the quartz trap?

Slowly the great mass of them split. Most rolled on down the fault to the sea, hoping to find Carnelian and Flare out that way. The others returned to the chamber under the mountain. The ground quieted, and settled.

I looked at Oswin. "The sooner we get everyone out of here, the safer they'll be. It's bad to expect anything with that much power to follow a timetable."

15

Arguments

When Oswin and I returned to the courtyard at the inn, we found a mess. People clustered around a soaking wet Myrrhtide, shouting at him. Others were carrying their things back *into* their houses. Azaze came out of the inn, thrusting men and women aside. Oswin shoved in to stand beside her as they cleared a space around Myrrhtide.

Azaze held a poker. She looked like she was ready to use it on someone. "Dubyine, how dare you speak to a guest this way?"

A big woman armed with a ladle faced Azaze. "How *dare* I, Azaze? How dare you and these outsiders take *us* for green kids? There's gonna be no volcano! First they say, it's coming any time now! Then they say, a couple more days. *I'm* not fool enough to be taken by such a trick! They're going to loot the town when we go. They already got rid of the richer folk, but they're not getting what little *we* have!"

"*Trick?!*" Myrrhtide's face was garnet-colored, he was so furious. "I am a Dedicate Initiate of Winding Circle temple, and you call me a common *thief*?"

He'd better calm down, I thought, or he'll have a heart attack. From the look of his neck and temples, a whole lot of Myrrhtide's veins were about to explode.

"Dedicate Initiate, do not trouble yourself with this rabble." Azaze put her free hand on Myrrhtide's arm. "They aren't worth your time. I assure you, though, I will make them worth *mine*."

"You and who else, Azaze?" Dubyine smirked at her. "You and Oswin here? I don't think that's enough."

"I'm just wondering, Dubyine. Did you notice the earthquake we just had? What do you think that was? A whisper from the goddess?" Oswin sounded as friendly as if she offered him cake, not a bashing with a ladle.

"We've had a hundred earthquakes this year. Maybe you and Azaze are fools, but I know a thing or two. These false dedicates won't help themselves to *my* little bits of things." Dubyine gave Myrrhtide a small, mean smile. "Though I'll turn a blind eye for half of the proceeds."

"You *dare*!" Myrrhtide's eyes bulged from his head. "To say such a thing to me — *me* —" His mouth opened and closed.

Yep, I told myself. Heart attack for sure.

"I have spent this entire day immersed in that lake." Myrrhtide's voice shook. "I have sent calls to every quarter of the compass, requesting ships to save the people of this island. *This* is how you thank me? Threats? Bribes? The council of Winding Circle will hear of this! They will remember, and you can whistle for it when you need our help again!"

"We don't believe you're *from* Winding Circle, mate." Several men closed in behind Dubyine. The one who spoke gave me goose bumps. When I saw him I started to send heat into the rocks around the courtyard. I called them, wriggling them from the ground. I might need them for weapons. If ever someone's looks screamed "pirate," it was this man's. There were tattoos on his arms — he didn't have sleeves — and a big scar on his face. "And now you've rid us of our richer folk and their fighting servants," he said to Azaze, "we see no reason why we should let you take *any* of the profit."

"Karove, you've always been a greedy fool." Azaze nodded to someone behind the man Karove and his friends.

The master miner and some other people walked out of the shadows. They looked just as hard as Dubyine, Karove, and the others. In their hands they carried staffs or clubs. What *they* might have done next I don't know. They didn't get the chance to do it. The ground under Dubyine and Karove sprouted vines. Rosethorn was nearby. From the thorns on the vines, I guessed she wasn't in a good mood. Little springs of water spurted from the ground under the feet of the pirate-looking men. In a blink of an eye they were up to their ankles in mud. That was Myrrhtide's work. The men sloshed and slipped, falling. The miner and his friends stepped in to take their weapons away.

I drew the heat from my stones and let them settle into the ground again. I didn't wait to hear Azaze and Oswin apologize to Myrrhtide. I went inside. When I found the maids, I asked them to fix some hot food and tea for Myrrhtide and Rosethorn. Then I climbed upstairs. The maids wouldn't go near Myrrhtide's bags. I took out a clean robe and some underclothes, and spread them on his cot. I fetched clean towels for him, too. Then I went to my room.

I heard a boy's voice as I approached: Treak's. "So have you seen these volcano kids Oswin was talking about?"

"I have seen them as small pieces only. I cannot see them as whole beings, any more than I can visit the chamber where they and their kindred live." Poor Luvo. After visiting the lake he must have gone to my room for some more quiet. "They are part of the force that gave birth to me. Their power is the same as mine. If I draw too close to them, my existence will end. I will melt."

I walked in. Not only was Treak there with Luvo, so was Meryem. Worse, they had my chunks of granite out, the ones I kept for an emergency supply of strength.

"What are you doing with those?" I demanded. "They're magic. Luvo, why did you let them meddle with my magic things?"

"To keep them from meddling with things which might do them harm, Evumeimei," said Luvo. "They cannot release the power from these, as you know quite well."

"We're not deaf," said Treak, "we can answer for ourselves. We're hiding from Nory. She wants to make a drag sled from blankets and branches. I told her wait till Oswin comes back. He'll pull together some way to cart the rest of our things."

"She says that's lazy." Meryem was putting my granite cubes in their wooden box. I was impressed that she remembered the right spot for each cube. "She says that if more people did for themselves Oswin wouldn't work so hard."

"Well, Oswin's the only one of us who can get the grown-ups to help." Treak was trying to juggle two of my crystal spheres.

I snatched them from the air before he dropped them. "Leave my things alone!"

"You're as touchy as Nory," Treak said. "Who cares about stupid old rocks anyway?"

I almost said, Who cares about stupid old humans, but I didn't. Instead I ground my teeth and gave Luvo a very obvious look.

"Master Luvo's different." Treak waved a hand at Luvo. "He's a god or a spirit or something. The rules are different for them. But regular old rocks just sit there. They don't have a brain. They can't speak. They can't hear."

"You show your ignorance, young meat creature." Luvo was sitting on a wooden chair. He settled a little, and the seat bowed with his weight. I kept an eye on the seat. If Luvo forgot and settled again, the chair might break. "Rocks and crystals have memories far longer than yours. It was their memory, called forth by Tahar and Jayat, that told us of the first volcano here. Rosethorn can tell you of the prints of ancient animals and plants carried within stones. They can tell you of the changes in the earth and of the sea. You dwell here for a speck of time, but stones have the memory of thousands, millions of humans."

"Stones can tell you about light and heat and water," I broke in. "Look here." I took the cloth roll of my alphabet from my back. Carefully I untied it, opening it up on the bed. I drew out my favorite stone. "See this? It's an opal. The colors work because the crystals are arranged at different angles in the stone. Crystals bend light. Crystals know more about light than you could ever dream of." Meryem bent over the opal, her mouth open. I hesitated, then let her hold it. "Some stones will keep heat for a long time. Others you can heat and heat and heat and nothing happens. Some will tell you all about the weight you need to press stone together so its layers blend. Some will say how long they took to move from the bottom of the sea to the top of the mountain. How is any of that boring?"

Treak shrugged. "If you have to ask me that, then you can't understand my answer. Meryem, it's just a *rock*."

"It's a *beautiful* rock. It's the most beautifullest rock I ever saw." Meryem gave the opal back to me. "I have a beautiful rock of my very own. There's green and blue in it."

"It sounds pretty." I looked at Treak. "Just because you don't understand, don't pick on Meryem." I took out the stone that looks like shards of blue ice crystals trapped in white ice. I showed it to Meryem. "No, I'll hold it. It's really fragile. It's called kyanite."

"Lemme see." Treak grabbed for it. He broke off the long spar that stuck out of one end. He looked at the slender length of kyanite, then at me, shocked. "I didn't mean —"

He was wearing a red shirt. The imperial soldiers wore red tunics. For a moment Treak looked a little like one of them. They had smashed their way into my room to capture me, and broken the stones I was keeping there. "No wonder the thing you're best at is breaking furniture! Get out!" I yanked the stone from his hand. I didn't even care that it cut him.

"You mages think you're so great! You think even your dung is magic!" Treak reached for the basin. I think he meant to throw it at me.

Meryem seized his arm. "Stop it, Treak!" She looked at me. "He doesn't mean it, Evvy! I can fix your rock, honest! Oswin makes this special glue. I can put your rock together!"

I couldn't stand that look in Meryem's eyes. She looked like a kitten climbing out of a stream. "The rock's fine — it just lost a piece. Take Meryem to Nory, Treak. Before you really make me mad."

He towed Meryem to my door. Then he looked back at me. "I hope your volcano spirits *eat* you. I hope you get *lost* under Mount Grace!"

I answered before I thought. "It would be better than being around people like you!"

Treak towed Meryem out of the room.

"It is but one piece of kyanite, Evumeimei."

"I'm just being a meat creature, Luvo. Give me a time."

Now I could cry as I sat on the bed. He had handled this piece of my new life — the life with no hunger, beatings, or cold — as if it was a cheap toy. I tried to fit the kyanite pieces together. It was useless. Once the inner bonds that held it were broken, no magic could fix this delicate chunk of crystals.

Cloth rustled behind me. Rosethorn walked in. "I think Meryem feels you meant her."

"I'll set it right later." I had handled too much power that day. I'd bent my magic around too many new ideas. My mage self was up to it, because I was still alive, but my

208

body was still meat. It was weary meat at that. "I'm so tired, Rosethorn."

"Sleep, then. Don't wait too long to set things right with her. Unless you really would rather live with the volcano spirits." Rosethorn looked me over and sighed. "I'll bring your supper up later."

If I lived in lava, I wouldn't need supper, I thought. I lay down on my cot. I didn't even realize that I was still holding my kyanite as I went to sleep.

Luvo woke me when he stuck his nose in my eye. His crystals were glowing with a soft purple light that filled our room.

"What is it?" I whispered because I could see Rosethorn's sleeping body in the next cot.

Luvo said quietly, "I am disturbed by the movement of the earth that approaches now. It is —"

"Ten miles out." It was a big shaker, coming at us in a giant wave. "Rosethorn!" I called.

She sat up instantly. "Wha? 'S better be good."

"Quake coming," I said. "We have to be outside for this one." At least I was still wearing clothes.

We grabbed our mage kits. I stuffed my alphabet into mine. Then I settled my sling and put Luvo in it.

Rosethorn was scrambling into her robe. "I'll wake Myrrhtide, you wake the kitchen staff. They're the only people who sleep here. Send one of them to rouse Azaze and her husbands. Have the others wake everyone in the courtyard."

I did as I was told. All of us fled the inn. Most of the villagers who meant to go in the morning were camped just outside. By the time we came out, they were awake. They hung on to their animals or their children, waiting nervously. Many of them prayed. Rosethorn and Myrrhtide prayed with them. I guess they were supposed to, under the circumstances.

The earth surged from down deep, miles of stones groaning and rocking. Roof slates fell from the inn. Inside wood and mortar crashed. The horses protested; dogs howled. People screamed. A crack opened under the stable; half of the building collapsed into it with a roar.

At last everything was quiet again. People got up and went to see what damage there was in the rest of the village.

Azaze went to look at the stable. "Splendid. Just *splendid*. I had this wreck rebuilt four months ago, and now look! It's ruined! I can't afford an entirely new stable!"

"Evumeimei," Luvo whispered, "we must talk."

I chewed my lower lip. I knew a trick that only worked with stones that were of the same kind. It would prove really useful just now. "All right, but I need to do something first." I picked up my kit. "Let's find some privacy."

The half-moon gave me enough light to find the inn's kitchen garden. It was messed up from the earthquake. Mostly that meant the night was filled with the scents of crushed basil, oregano, and fennel. I put Luvo on an upended bucket so we could talk face-to-face when it got to be time. Then I took a chunk of quartz from my kit. It was no bigger than my palm. The important thing was that it was a collection of crystals, kin in spirit to the ones where I had left Carnelian and Flare. I let myself fall into its cracks and splits. In it I drifted, keeping a seed of thought in my head: the picture of Carnelian and Flare in the crystal trap.

And there it was, as if I stood only a few yards away. Waves of heat rose around me, rippling through the earth. Something weird had happened to the bed of quartz. It had been raised, twisted, and fused together into a great loop, just as Luvo had said. Inside its thousands of pieces I saw bits of carnelian and blue color, a spot of each to a crystal, all spinning. They moved so fast, each bit in its own little prison, that they looked as if they flowed *through* the quartz, instead of being stuck in one place. And the bed itself quivered in the earth, making the dirt and stones around it shake.

How long before their volcano friends found them? What if they felt that quivering and came to see what made it? And what would happen once they freed their guides?

My imagination showed me a scary picture. In it, the whole island of Starns shot into the sky, riding a huge column of molten lava.

"Heibei, this is a bad time to frown at me," I whispered. I pulled my mind from my crystals and put the clump away. Then I looked at Luvo. "We made a mistake. I thought if we could get Flare and Carnelian out of the way, the danger would be over. But it's not."

"The earthquakes that have come since we trapped them are not normal earthquakes." Luvo kept his voice down. "They feel more like the waves of the ocean, but far below the earth's stone shell."

"It's the others," I told Luvo. "The ones Flare and Carnelian said never had the nerve to do anything. I think they were wrong. The others want Flare and Carnelian to *lead* them out. Now they're hunting for them. They won't stop till they find them and *everyone* gets to break out into the open."

Luvo began to pace. I leaned back and waited, closing my eyes. My head ached ferociously.

Luvo halted. "I will build shields between the lower depths and the trap we have made for Carnelian and Flare. Obsidian drawn from the riverbed, I think. The obsidian will show the other spirits their own faces, nothing else. It will reflect, not reveal."

"Granite to back it, though," I suggested. "If the volcano spirits get close enough, they'll melt the obsidian.

Granite will slow them down. What do you want me to do?"

"Guard me as you ride to the ships," Luvo ordered. "Azaze and Tahar will wait no longer. Dawn is just a short time away. Pick me up."

When we came out from behind the inn, I saw that Luvo was right. Everyone was up and moving. No one had gone back to sleep. Tahar was bundled up in a hooded robe. She sat on the seat of her little cart, screeching orders. Jayat stood at the head of the pony that drew the cart. It looked like he was going to walk.

Oswin waited with Nory, Treak, and his other foster-kids. He carried a huge pack on his shoulders as if it weighed nothing, and a pair of kittens in a basket on one hip. If he was worried, he didn't look it. His head was cocked. He stared into the distance, his lips moving silently. Nory was fastening small cloth packs onto the backs of the little children. They rode the tired-looking ponies who had been harnessed to the cart before it collapsed. When Nory saw me, she gave me a glare that would have peeled paint. Treak and the older kids did the same. I went to saddle Spark.

Once I'd taken care of that, I placed Luvo in his sling and hung it from the saddle horn. He was as still as dead rock. The best part of his mind and power had gone into the earth. I strapped my saddlebags into place. Rosethorn had cared for her own horse. She was talking quietly with Azaze and Myrrhtide.

"I don't care if we have more days, perhaps!" Tahar's old voice was crystal clear above all of the others. She was talking to one of the village women. "Perhapses never got fields plowed or wood chopped, you brainless nit! Will you wait for earthquakes to pull your house down, or the volcano to burn it? We're leaving! The rock may be great among his kind, but he himself admits there's a chance the spirits will escape the trap. Jayat, stop ogling Norya. Move this collection of splinters!"

Oswin turned to look at the old mage. "What about Dubyine, Karove, and their people? They went back to Snake Hollow. Should we send word that we're leaving?"

Azaze snorted. "Let them stay and loot until the volcano cooks them."

Tahar leaned to the cart's side and spat on the ground. "That for Dubyine and her stinking crew. May they eat ash cakes and drink molten stone."

For all that everyone said that Tahar wasn't much of a mage, I saw lots of people grab amulets and press them to their lips. Either they didn't want to take a chance, or they feared Tahar's ill-speaking. As far as I was concerned, Dubyine and Karove had called Rosethorn a thief. That settled it for me. I hoped Tahar's curse took.

16

Mage Stuff

With everyone awake, the cooks fixed breakfast. When it was done, there was enough predawn light to see by. It was time to go. Carts and animals moved forward along the road, *finally*. I joined the line at the end, with the herd animals and the kids who watched them. It wasn't the fanciest place in the caravan. That's why I was shocked when Myrrhtide rode back and fell in beside me. "How are you feeling?"

I gaped at him. He *never* asked how I felt. "I know it's kind of dark, but you have to be able to tell you're talking to me."

"I know who I am speaking to. Your health is important, young woman. Right now you and Luvo may be our best protection from a tomb made of lava." When I stared at him, shocked, Myrrhtide snorted. "What? Because I spent the last day in the lake I'm too preoccupied to understand the obvious? Rosethorn and I can do very little against a volcano. You are all the help we have."

"You don't think we messed up, letting people know that we'd bought some extra time?" I asked. "I thought you'd be saying I don't have any right to call myself a mage."

Myrrhtide rubbed his eyes. "The first thing every mage should learn is that magic makes fools of us. *Now* you may call yourself a mage. You have learned the most important lesson. Tell me, then — if you *did* trap our young volcano children, why do we rush along today?"

I have no idea why it spilled out of me. Maybe it was that Myrrhtide had said that I might still call myself a mage, when I had fumbled things so badly. Rosethorn was busy. I could see her up ahead. She was growing vines to pull fallen trees from the road so we could get through. And Myrrhtide was actually listening to me.

He took me back over my tale. He asked questions to clear things up in his own mind. "Luvo didn't believe these other spirits were a problem?"

I shook my head. "He can see what I do, because our magics join in spots. He thought they were just stupid and didn't care. We believed if we trapped Flare and Carnelian, that would be enough." Six miles out and ten miles down, I felt the next squeeze coming. I looked around. We were passing a tall series of granite slabs. On our other side was a slope that led to the river.

I gulped. I didn't have Luvo to help me with this one. "Would you ask Rosethorn something for me? Could she lay vines over the shakier parts of the stone on our left? There's a tremor coming. I'll hold the stone back here if she can do that. Tell everyone we're gonna get a hard shake. It's coming fast."

Myrrhtide rode up along our draggledy parade, passing on the warning. I dismounted from Spark and passed her reins to somebody. Then I called up all that power I had collected the afternoon before, greeting the rock on my left as I walked over to it. This granite was lava that had cooled slowly enough for bits of quartz and feldspar to form in it. Water and plants had done some damage here. So had quarrymen, who had taken away stone for buyers around the Pebbled Sea.

Hold strong, I told the unsteady slabs. Can you feel these youngsters rushing around?

I heard the whisper of stone laughter. Then the volcano spirits rolled under us in a fiery tide. They were returning to Mount Grace far beneath the river. They bellowed for Flare and Carnelian as they traveled. They had been searching under the Pebbled Sea, with no luck. Now they plunged into the hollow chamber, discouraged.

The ground calmed. The granite boulders under my magic settled back into their beds, complaining. They had wanted to move. Another time, I promised them. Maybe even today.

That cheered them up. I knew it would.

I looked ahead. Apart from some tumbled bundles and people knocked from their feet, everything seemed to be all right. On we went. Eventually people started to fall behind, especially the older ones, and the kids.

Rosethorn rode back to me. She had a baby in a sling on her chest, and a one-legged boy riding behind her. "You look comfortable, on your nice strong horse, by yourself."

I scowled at her. "In Gyongxe you let me ride."

"In Gyongxe you had flayed feet. And I did make you get off the horse before you got flayed." She raised her eyebrows. "Are you too worn-out from playing with the nice volcano?"

She knew I wasn't. I gave Spark up to Meryem and two of Oswin's small boys. I even carried a baby. He wet himself, and me. For good measure he burped sour milk on my shoulder. By then the road had come down close to the river. I gave the baby back to his mother to be changed. Then I happily took off my boots and walked into the icy water. Cold doesn't bother me that much. And the smell of water and wet stone was much better than the smell of dirty baby.

I was gathering blue moonstones on the river bottom when the volcano spirits stirred in the big chamber under the mountain. It was strange. The more time I spent listening for them, the more I knew what they were doing. Now the ones who had gone out were rousing up the ones who had stayed behind. They started to whirl around, deep below the earth. The walls of the chamber began to melt, making the room bigger.

"Shake!" I yelled to the people on the road. "Shake, a big one! Shake!"

They scrambled to grab the horses and get out of the carts. I dared not move. I threw my power against the huge slope of loose, quarried rock beside the road. Even a tiny shiver would send tons of granite on top of everyone there. Next I sucked the river boulders' weight into me. I needed to be sure I wouldn't tumble when the earth began to kick. Once I was fixed in place, I spread my magic thin, covering as much loose rock as I could. Then I jammed it down, locking thousands of stone fragments in place. They shifted, trying to cut through my power.

Heat rose from the big chamber. The volcano spirits were hungry. They wanted Flare and Carnelian. I sent that hunger back to them as echoes. They felt battered by their own feelings. Confused, they backed deeper into the chamber. Knowing they were being monkeyed with, the earth spirits roared their fury. The ground under everything buckled and rolled.

Then, for the first time, I heard their voices. They wanted Flare and Carnelian.

They are near! one of them shouted. *We need them to lead us!*

We need them to lead us out! We need them to take us into glory and fire! another cried, one that sounded female.

They are the leaders, the guides! Where are they? That one seemed older.

Where are the ones who will free us of the prison and the shadows? From the sound of that voice, the spirit had been waiting to get out for a very long time.

Where are the ones who will guide us to freedom? And that one was my age, or sounded that way, at least.

Find them! Find them! They all joined in that cry, shouting it over and over.

The shake and the spirits' screaming seemed to go on forever. I held down the rocks on the slope until I thought I would melt. I was so full of heat and power I wanted to rip the earth in two and bare its heart. I wanted to shake the world to pieces.

The earthquake eased and stopped. The volcano spirits traveled out of the chamber to the north, leaving the big chamber half full. They sensed that Carnelian and Flare were someplace close. And now I understood their need. Luvo and I would never be able to hide Carnelian and Flare from the other volcano spirits forever.

Those two volcano kids had it all wrong. They'd understood only part of the story.

I pulled myself back to my body. Once more I brought a lot of power with me. And I needed it, to keep the unstable rock from burying the refugees. For the second time my magical body was too big for my real one. I swore in my home language of Zhanzou and dragged myself in here, tucked myself in there. Finally I jammed myself back into my skin.

I came around to discover I was drenched. Myrrhtide stood beside me in the river. He'd put his arm around my chest so he could hold my head above water.

"Uh-oh." My voice came out as a croak. "I guess I fell down."

He raised his eyebrows. "Most of you did. Your feet and legs are as stiff as stone."

I sighed. "Thanks for keeping me from drowning." I looked at his face. Fusspot actually showed whisker stubble, when he'd shaved every day. There were black circles under his eyes. "You should create a spell so your whiskers come off in water. Think how much time you'd save. You'd make a fortune peddling it to people. Even ladies would want it, so they'd never have to get their bodies plucked again."

"Shaving — *or* plucking — is the *last* thing on my mind," Myrrhtide said drily. "Will you tell me what was on *yours*? You nearly drowned. I couldn't carry you out. You felt like you weighed several tons."

"Oh. Right." I released the magics that settled my feet and stood on my own. "I borrowed the stones' weight so the shake wouldn't knock me down. It never dawned on me I'd need to be stiff all over."

"Why didn't you wade to the bank and do whatever you had to?" asked Myrrhtide.

I blinked at him. Heat came to my cheeks — not magic heat. I felt like a real village fool. "I didn't think of it. I just wanted to lock down that scree up beside the road, quick, before the next tremor struck."

"Ah." He said it like *he* would have gotten to dry land first. Probably he would have, too. "Then the exercise is valuable, if you learned from it. Now, if you'll excuse me, I need to check with my fellow water mages —"

He never finished. Miles off, in the direction of Moharrin, we heard something explode. Myrrhtide and I raced up the riverbank to the road. Everyone was nervous and unable to see a thing. We had come down the other side of the ring of tall hills that surrounded the lake. The cliffs along the road helped to block our view of Mount Grace.

There was only one thing to do. All of the climbers started up a solid stone cliff just a little ways back. I outdistanced everyone, fast. Well, they weren't stone mages who could cling to flat rock. When I got to the top, I had a clear sight of the mountain. She towered over the forest that surrounded the lake.

High on Mount Grace's eastern side, a thick plume of light gray smoke rose. It climbed rapidly in the sky, billowing.

Do not panic, I told myself. I couldn't have said it aloud if I had wanted to. My mouth had gone sticky dry.

Panic is bad. I reached for that plume with my power, telling myself, *A volcano spirit couldn't have escaped without you knowing, Evumeimei Dingzai! Every spirit in that chamber would be shouting the news!*

I felt nothing. There was no drop of molten rock anywhere near that fat column of smoke. I couldn't even find rock ash in it.

When I got back to the road, I begged some water from the inn servants. Then I went to find the mages. Azaze, Oswin, Tahar, and Rosethorn all gathered around Luvo, who was still in his sling on Spark.

Other adults listened nearby as Luvo talked. "It is steam and air only. It has been thrust through cracks in the mountain by the movement of volcano spirits." Of course Luvo would know. He could ask even distant stones to tell him what was going on. I had to be close to them to hear what they said. "One of those cracks passed through an underground spring. The water was heated far past boiling. The explosion was steam bursting through a crack in the mountainside."

Tahar gave the most wicked chuckle I have ever heard. "Dubyine, Karove, and their pack will gallop past soon enough. They whine about poverty, but they have the best horses on Starns. Master Luvo, they'll complain your magery was at fault, saying they *maybe* had a few more days. Don't tell them they're running from a teapot that boiled over."

"You didn't believe we had extra time!" I said it before I thought. Then I winced as the adults turned to look at me.

"I may be only a hedgewitch, but I understand enough about the world to know that its power is greater than I am. You mages who draw on it, whose magic comes from things outside you, you think you control it. Maybe when it's weaving or iron-making or pottery you can. I wouldn't know. But stone, or the green world, or water? You no more control those things than I control where my great-great-grandson burps." Tahar grinned evilly at me. "You're shocked that the volcano won't come and go as you predict it will. *I'm* surprised you're silly enough to think it. That goes double for you, Master Rock. Now, let's move on, before those spirits come to bump us all into the river."

I stood aside and let them pass me. Why Heibei hadn't made that one a great mage I don't know. She had the attitude for it. And she had told me the same thing that Myrrhtide and Rosethorn, in their own ways, were trying to tell me. It wasn't that mages didn't make mistakes. It was that they learned from them.

What could I learn?

Rosethorn stopped. "Did you amuse yourself in the river?"

I fished in my pocket and offered her a blue moonstone. "Want one?"

Rosethorn cupped my chin in her hand, looking me over. "The gods were watching over me when you got in trouble back at Winding Circle. All the same, Evvy, don't kill yourself with this. Don't try to hold back the tides. Briar will never forgive me if I let you die while he's away."

I smiled at her. "I'm not going to die. I bet it hurts."

She let me go. "Imp." She walked over to a cart and took charge of a baby.

Oswin came to me leading Spark. Once I took Luvo and his sling, Oswin gave Spark to a couple of kids. They climbed into the saddle with relief. I figured Oswin would wander off — he looked distracted — but he didn't. Although he carried that immense pack, he walked like it was filled with feathers. His hands were tucked in his pockets. He gazed off into nowhere, his lips moving silently.

Since Oswin didn't seem to want to talk, I turned to Luvo. *How did the shield building go?* I asked in our magics. *Will it fool the volcano spirits? Will it keep them from finding Carnelian and Flare?*

The shield is made, he said, *granite on one side, obsidian facing outward. It will reflect only the volcano spirits, should they find it. I do not know how long it will hold. The volcano spirits might come too close, and melt it, or enough of them may decide to ram it. Has Myrrhtide said if more ships have arrived in the seaport?*

I didn't ask, I replied.

"Question," Oswin interrupted.

I was so fixed on Luvo that Oswin's voice made me jump. We both stared at him.

He didn't realize he'd startled me. "You said Flare and Carnelian wanted to play when you first met them. They wanted to show you things, and they wanted you to help them escape."

"Ye-e-ess." I wasn't sure what he was getting at. I didn't want him springing any word traps on me.

"What if you went back to them now, and said you want to go out with them?" Oswin asked. "What if you told them you'd found them the perfect spot to do it? An easy spot? Then you led them to it — away from Starns?"

I stopped dead in my tracks and stared at him. Luvo stood up on his back legs inside his sling to get a better look at Oswin.

It seemed like Oswin was used to reactions like ours. "No, wait, listen a moment. You said they want to come out. They never insisted on *where*, did they? In fact, Mount Grace was their last resort. Some old faker of their own kind sold them that old wheeze. You know, the one that if they struggle and fight through tons of solid rock, they'd be *worthy* to break into the open air." Oswin said "worthy" like it was a very bad word. "Flare and Carnelian were smart. *They're* looking for faults that will take them close to the surface, so they can save their strength until the last

226

moment. You know they'll break free eventually. Why not do it where they won't kill thousands of people and make whole islands unlivable?"

"I have never heard of such a thing in all my millennia, Oswin Forest," Luvo said flatly.

Oswin looked at Luvo and shrugged. "You led me to believe you came along with Evvy for new experiences. This would be one of them."

"You propose to tamper with the great cycle of birth," Luvo told him with a little outraged thunder in his voice. "Mountains enter life in this manner. There is always the struggle, violence, destruction, fire. Things die, things are born, the old is buried in the rush of the new. So it has been from the very beginning of this world."

Again Oswin shrugged. "Once, if a baby started to come out backwards, the choice was to see if it could be born that way alive, to bring it out that way and risk the mother's death, or to try to turn it and risk the *baby's* death. Then a midwife learned how to turn the baby in the womb. More babies and mothers live because nature never minds a little extra help."

"How did you find that out?" I asked, curious. I'd never met a man who could talk midwifery.

"Jayat hasn't been around to help Tahar for long," Oswin explained. "Before that she was without an apprentice for a couple of years. I helped her. We are talking about volcanoes, Evvy."

227

"Blasphemy." Luvo was rocking from side to side. His weight shifts made him hard for me to balance.

"I'm not proposing an end to the process through which mountains are born. This is just a new wrinkle." Oswin was being very patient. "Could many stone mages even do it?"

"Evumeimei's skills *are* unusual," Luvo said, distracted from his crankiness. "I believe the fact that her first instructors were green mages influenced her power. Her magic follows more flexible channels than those of the stone mages I have encountered."

"I am standing right here," I told them. "I can speak for myself."

"I was wondering about how Evvy does things. Most stone mages I've encountered seem very, very *settled*," Oswin commented. "They only deal with their immediate circle of stones and learning. Certainly they aren't flexible. I never heard that a mage's first teachers have an effect on how their magic works, though."

They would remember me eventually. In the meantime, the refugees were drawing away. Luvo calmed down as I started walking, and Oswin caught up. He and Luvo kept talking about first teachers. I turned Oswin's idea over in my head. Hadn't Rosethorn mentioned something similar? She'd been joking, but Oswin wasn't.

Flare and Carnelian didn't *know* I had tricked them. If they did, their anger would be enough to blow the quartz trap to pieces. They might suspect. If I showed up before they broke out, though, if I set them free, I could convince them it really was just a game.

Worse, I didn't know if I could keep them from the surface. They were big before they went into the quartz. If they were bigger when they came out, I might not be able to control them.

I might die.

The road crested a high point in the ground. Below us was the long line of refugees. Rosethorn was riding back, a little boy behind her, a little girl in front of her. She looked tired and thin.

I promised Briar I would take care of Rosethorn.

I interrupted Oswin and Luvo. "Where do I take Flare and Carnelian? I can't just drag them any old where. They'll come straight back here."

Oswin grinned. "All of those roads that lead away from Mount Grace, and you can't think of something that's a better place than this?"

"I don't know any roads for *volcanoes*." I didn't feel like playing games! Then I bit my lip. The cracks. The cracks, that led to the faults deep in the ground. The seams in the earth. Where might *they* take me?

In my mind's eye I saw black, cold depths at the foot of a stone cliff. Strange sea creatures danced in cold salt water. They swirled around an opening that spurted clouds of hot water.

"Luvo . . ." I whispered.

"I saw." Of course he saw; I was holding him. "Is it far enough from human dwellings?"

"Is what far enough?" Now we had confused Oswin.

"I'm not sure," I said. "It's seven miles. We need Myrrhtide."

Oswin, Luvo, and I worked our way down the riverbank. Myrrhtide was in the water again, his habit kilted up around his waist. He walked along the river bottom as easily as I walked on the road. He didn't slip or slide like I did.

I stared in awe. Fishes darted around and between his feet, some of them big ones. Now and then one would leap in the air and hit broadside, splashing him. His pale lashes were marked with water drops. Water beads sparkled on his short red hair. He looked . . . happy.

Maybe our voyage would have been more fun if we had just towed Myrrhtide behind the ship on a rope.

"Excuse us — are you working on something?" Oswin could be *very* polite.

"No. Evvy, if your face freezes like that, you will frighten small animals. Is something the matter?" Myrrhtide asked gently.

Kanzan bless me, with fish nibbling at his toes, Myrrhtide was actually *decent*. "Back on the ship, when I banged you in the face, did you know where we were?" I inquired.

He bridled, as if I'd suggested he didn't know how to do his sums. "We were directly over the Ditlo Trench, the deepest such trench in the Pebbled Sea. It measures ten thousand feet at its greatest depth. Not one of the biggest trenches — there is a deeper one at the heart of the Syth, and another off the Bight of Fire that is said to be nearly twice that. At the one in the Bight of Fire there are creatures, completely bleached of color, who give off their own light — never mind." Myrrhtide bent to scratch a catfish on the chin. "I fail to see why an offshore formation like the trench would be of interest to anyone just now."

"Evumeimei, you would have to do this alone," Luvo said unhappily. "I can send you strength, perhaps. You know I dare not bring my essence too close to that of Flare and Carnelian."

"There's a spell that Tahar and Jayat know. Sometimes Tahar does something risky and needs Jayat to observe or to lend her strength, but not to get too entangled with her. Jayat uses it, too. That way she can tell him what to do when she's too weak to work magic herself. It might not serve you, of course, Master Luvo. We could ask." Oswin's eyes were shining. I began to see why Jayat spoke of him like he did. This man lived to work out things, even when he couldn't do them himself. Why hadn't *he* been born a great mage?

On the other hand, the idea of Oswin with the power to try some of his ideas was a little scary.

"Jayat!" Oswin's bellow nearly split my skull. "Come here, we need to ask you a question!"

"Will someone *please* tell me what that trench has to do with anything? We are running from a *volcano*, may I remind you?" Myrrhtide sloshed out of the river. He yelped as he stepped on something pointy on the riverbank. I set Luvo down and went to help him.

"Here. You can brace yourself on me and put your own sandals on, or brace yourself on me and *I'll* put your sandals on. Either way, step on that rock right behind you. No sticks to hurt your feet then." I pointed to the rock. "Or you can go back in the river. Your fishes miss you." It was true. They swirled in the shallowest water they could manage, right where Myrrhtide had climbed out.

He frowned at me. "Why are you being helpful?" He stepped on the stone slab and unhooked his sandals from his belt.

I took his footwear. "Because I found out you're not such a crosspatch. It's funny, the way you learn how decent people are, when things get bad." I knelt and undid the knot in his laces. When I had a sandal free, Myrrhtide braced a hand on my shoulder and lifted up a foot. I put it on and laced it for him.

"All right, young lady. What are you up to?" Myrrhtide asked suspiciously.

"Nothing bad," I told him as I did up the other sandal. "Mila and Green Man willing, and maybe Heibei too, it could even be good." Silk moths began twirling in my belly. Stop that, I told them. I haven't even *done* anything yet.

I stood up and smiled at Myrrhtide. "There you are. All shod and ready to visit the emperor."

He smiled, too, and tightened his grip on my shoulder. "Good. Very good. Now let's see what you and your friends are cooking up. And try to take care of yourself. You are starting to grow on me."

17

Stone Clothes

When Rosethorn saw us trailing the refugees and talking, she rode back to see what was going on. We told her what we planned.

"Absolutely not." Her mouth settled into a hard line. "Tamper with the volcano spirits a second time? Particularly when they might be getting *more* powerful? I won't hear of it."

"But if she can lead them away from Starns, the island will be safe." Oswin shifted from foot to foot, he was so excited.

"Oswin Forest, she is *my* charge. I am responsible for Evvy getting off this island alive," Rosethorn told him. "You have no guarantee that she would survive leading Carnelian and Flare out to sea. Even if they did not kill her for trapping them, what of the other volcano spirits? If Luvo won't face them, why should Evvy?"

"Her power is not the same as theirs, Rosethorn," said Luvo. "If Evumeimei keeps her distance from any groups of volcano spirits, she ought to be safe."

"'Ought to' trims no trees, Luvo," Rosethorn snapped.

They were still arguing two hours later. We had come out onto the flat, where the river made the long, slow turn toward Sustree. Tahar, Myrrhtide, Jayat, and even Azaze had joined in the discussion.

I lost patience. The longer I put off actually trying Oswin's idea, the better the chances were that Flare and Carnelian would escape on their own. I wouldn't give a wooden coin for our lives then. I had to get to work *now*.

I looked around for a place to stop and saw a good one. Leaving the others, I lugged my packs to some trees that shaded a cluster of boulders. The stones were stable granite. They were perfect for my needs.

Luvo came to watch me make the place comfortable as people went by. "What if Carnelian and Flare will not believe you? They may well deceive you into relaxing your guard, then turn against you. Evumeimei, you trapped them. What if they claim they accept you are their friend, then lure you into a trap of *their* devising? They are volcano spirits, not meat people. They have no faces or eyes that you may read."

I asked the rocks to shift, to make a seat that wasn't so lumpy. "Maybe they were pure spirits when I first met them. But once they got to know me, they started shaping themselves more like people. Copying me. They acted more human, too. I'll give my magic self a look that's more like human me somehow. I'll shape it with stones. If they copy me in this new way of looking, I'll know they still admire me. Stop ill-wishing, Luvo! I have to make this work!"

"I do not do anything that might be termed a wish for good or ill," Luvo said. "Neither do I want you to end your days as charcoal."

"I don't plan to do that, trust me," I told him.

Meryem came running over. She was dusty from top to toe, her *and* the Dreadful Doll. She carried it in a cloth sling now, just like the one I used to carry Luvo. Someone had also made a small pouch for her to wear around her neck. She kept the feldspar piece I gave her in that. I could tell because I saw the stone shining through the pouch. "Why did you stop? You look like you're making camp. You can't stop here, Evvy. We're running away from the volcano, remember?"

Heibei, this is *not* funny, I told the god. "Meryem, go with the others. Find Nory. I'm doing something."

"No!" The little tyrant stamped a foot at me. "You can't do it here, Evvy. You *can't*. Do it on the ship. The mountain is going to blow up, don't you know *anything*?"

The longer she stood there jabbering, the more likely it was that someone would come to find her. They might try to stop me, too.

"Meryem, I don't want you with me, all right? I'm a mage, not a nursemaid. Me and my rocks have important things to do, right now, so *go away*."

She blinked at me, her lip trembling. "I thought you were my friend."

"I'm not! I'm a busy mage, and I need quiet right now!" I snapped.

She had tears in her eyes, but what was I supposed to do? If Rosethorn noticed I was missing before I left my body, she'd find a way to stop me. If everyone got killed because Flare and Carnelian escaped, it wouldn't help that I'd been nice to Meryem. I'd wasted too much time already. The ground was quivering under my feet.

"Go on, go!" I added for good measure.

Meryem ran away. She vanished into the group of kids at the side of the refugee caravan.

"For a human, that was hard speaking," Luvo said.

"I'm in a hurry, Luvo. I'll make it up to her later, if we have a later." From one of my packs I took out my Zhanzou jacket. It was the only clothing I'd kept from home, but not because I missed Yanjing fashions. The plain black jacket had eight pockets in it. There were four outside — two over my chest, two over my hips — and two inside. I wore it when I needed to keep stones close to my body.

It was time to put my mage kit to use. I opened it up and considered my choices. I had to squint as I removed the stones. The magical glare from the spells on them always half-blinded me. First I showed Luvo the onyx globe. "This doesn't just hold power. The spells on it will ground me and help keep me in myself. They'll also deflect anything bad Flare, or Carnelian, or their friends might throw at me. I hope they will, anyway."

Luvo didn't seem impressed. "Volcano spirits will annihilate your globe. What else have you?"

"Rutilated quartz, to increase my effectiveness," I explained. Luvo clicked at me. It was not a sound of approval. I put the crystal in a pocket anyway and went on. "Jade for wisdom and protection. Sardonyx for courage."

"I doubt yours would ever fail, but that at least may accomplish what you wish for it."

"Rockwater for strength and perseverance."

"As if you ever required either of these things, Evumeimei."

"Malachite for protection from peril." I was getting cross.

"A moon cut from it would not be enough to guard you from Carnelian and Flare."

"You're not *helping*," I told him. "Garnet for strength and vigor."

"Piffle, all of it."

"You learned that word from Rosethorn."

"These stones are useless," Luvo argued. "Worse than useless if you rely on such toys instead of your own power."

I glared at him. "I *am* relying on my own power. It's the power of the spells I made and stored in these 'toys,' you stubborn chunk of rock!"

"This is folly, Evumeimei. Let these meat people flee this island. Let us make our escape with them. Oswin does not understand the immensity of power held by just one of these spirits. Beings like Flare and Carnelian and their kindred are the agents that make and unmake the surface of the entire earth."

"You worry so because you can't imagine tricking the forces that gave birth to you. I understand. But look here. The force that made *me* sold me for a handful of coppers. I'm not as awed. If I get in over my head, I'll just run away." He doesn't understand, I thought. I put Carnelian and Flare in a trap that ended up making them stronger. I have to limit the damage I did. I *don't* want to be one of Rosethorn's destroyers, even by accident.

I patted Luvo on his head knob, which I knew he hated. Then I made myself comfortable and closed my eyes.

The fault that ran under the Makray, up under the lake and Mount Grace, was warm. I gathered power from it as I raced through the ground in my magical body. I headed for Moharrin and the quartz trap. Travel was so much *faster* without my meat self. Of course, I couldn't haul anything useful when I moved like this. I paid a price in exhaustion when I returned to my real body. Still, if I'd had to go to the trap by foot or horse, I would have given up before I even tried. I probably would have reached the trap too late for us all.

A new earth shock picked me up. It threw me from the place where the river left the lake all the way to the far end. The volcano spirits were traveling in a fault just three miles from Carnelian and Flare. With my senses spread wide through the ground I could feel them. They rooted in the fault like pigs hunting truffles. I jammed myself through the ground past them. My claim to be Flare and Carnelian's friend wouldn't sound good if I didn't set them free.

I smacked into Luvo's black obsidian wall. It curved above, below, and to either side of me, a glossy black shield in the earth. A sparkling ghost floated in it: me. Flare and Carnelian were on the other side. I'd kept careful track of their location. They were just three hundred yards beyond this wall, with its granite back. The volcano spirits would only see this — at least until it began to melt.

I flowed through the cool black shield. Behind it was the thick granite slab Luvo had set there. That was guaranteed to slow the volcano spirits more than easily melted obsidian. From it, and from the earth around it, I collected what I needed for my new appearance. I made a girl shell from crystals and minerals, fitting them around me. I built a stone tunic of olivine and fashioned green tourmaline leggings. Black tourmaline served me for hair and eyebrows. I shaped rose quartz into a mouth. Black garnets worked as my eyes, and gold feldspar became my skin. By the time I reached the quartz trap, I was an Evvy made of magic and stone.

I had come in time, barely.

Tiny lightnings sparked around the quartz. They melted the earth and cracked the crystals themselves. Several dozen drops of blue and carnelian-colored fire broke free. They flowed together to join with others of their color. I didn't wait to see how big those combined drops had to get before they began to think on their own — though I *was* curious.

Would you release all the pieces of my friends? I asked the quartz crystals. *I think they've overstayed their welcome, don't you?*

It is our pleasure, said the biggest crystal. She sounded like an unhappy housekeeper. *Just look at how they've ruined our order!*

Your guests have been very *rude.* That crystal was one of the smallest, but it was also very old. *No matter how many times they were asked to settle, and find their places, they just wouldn't listen.*

I felt bad. I knew crystals loved organization. It's their nature. *I'm sorry. I didn't mean for it to turn out so badly for you.*

Oh, no. We have benefited immensely. The thing the mountain did to keep them here, when he united both ends of our vein? asked the friendliest of them.

Oh, that was splendid, the housekeeper said.

It was too exciting. The grumpy old one was determined to be unhappy. *There's been altogether too much excitement going on around here of late.*

The thing the mountain did, the friendly one said firmly, *it made quite a few of us better able to resist heat. That was good.*

And many of us have stolen power from your rude friends, the housekeeper crystal added.

But we will still be happy if they never return, the old one told me. *They do not know how to behave. Not like you.*

The crystals split. Out squirted hundreds of drops of indigo and reddish-brown fire. They formed a single, mixed-color pool in the soil, the big drops calling to the small ones that had already escaped.

I waited. The pool sloshed and stirred. The rocks and earth around it softened and shifted. At last the blue drops slid to one side, the carnelian-colored ones to the other. Slowly Carnelian and Flare took on the shapes they'd held when I saw them last. There was one difference. This time, they were taller than me by a head.

They looked down at me. The soil melted and drooled around them.

18

Luvo Thunders

I threw out my hands. *Flare, Carnelian, hello! I'm so sorry!* I talked like Briar did when he courted a rich lady while stealing her bracelet. He didn't steal anymore, but he taught me the approach for emergencies. *Maybe the quartz is a toy* my *people manage better. Are you tired? Were you bored? I was so busy helping my friends that this is the first chance I got to check on you! Honestly, I thought you would have solved it* long *ago.*

You trapped us! Flare raised a fist. *You wanted to seal us up so we couldn't get out!*

I grinned at him. *Why? I'm your friend.*

Maybe the others got you to do it. To stop us from having fun. Carnelian crossed her arms. *They never want to have fun.*

When would they do that? I asked. *I don't go near them, remember? Now, stop being silly. Shall I tell you how the quartz toy works? Or do you want the other game I have for you?*

That was no toy! Bits of flame escaped Flare. *It was a trap! You tricked us into it!* He grabbed for me.

I flowed just out of his reach. *Then why did I set you free? Honestly, Flare, if you're going to be like this, maybe you're not* ready *to be out. In the world above, we understand things like quartz toys.*

Flare split in two. He shot at me from both sides. I dropped down through the soil, then flew up, putting the granite between us. He must have flown straight at it. I felt the ground and the stone shiver when he struck the two-foot-thick shield.

I backed up until I felt heat behind me. I turned. Carnelian had flowed through the ground, past the shield, to follow me. She'd also reshaped herself, so that some of her flames had the shape of clothing. She couldn't make herself stone clothes, though, not when rocks melted within a few feet of her.

What kinds of games do you have? She smoothed a hand over her front, shaping the flames into a tunic of blue fire. *And what* was *the trick of the quartz toy?*

I folded my arms over my chest, like I was thinking. *It made you and Flare larger. Don't you like that? You would have broken out soon. I'm curious — is Flare your brother? Do you come from the same flames, or the same pool? Were you part of one thing, that you're so close?*

Carnelian shrugged. *At first I was in the core, with the others. We were all one. Then I came to know I was me.*

244

Separate. I chose to go in another direction from the others. I flowed away. After a time, I looked around. The only other one who swam in a direction, being separate, was Flare. So I kept swimming, and he kept swimming. Both of us, being separate. One day we swam side by side. We didn't even know we wanted to be out *then. We just didn't want to swim like the others.*

I arranged my stone clothes so I could sit cross-legged. *How long did it take you to get here? To the hollow under the mountain?*

Again Carnelian shrugged. She tried to sit as I did. The best she could manage was to blend her legs together. You have to understand legs to create a proper tailor's seat. When I saw she wasn't going to attack, I spread some power in the earth, above and below me, and on the other side of the shield at my back. When Flare returned, he wouldn't take me by surprise.

Once Carnelian was settled as much like me as she could manage, she answered my question. *We don't understand things like how long it took us to leave the core and come to the chamber. The older ones, the ones who have been here since the last big escape —*

The last big escape? I asked, curious. *When? Where? Excuse me, but we've never really talked.*

Carnelian shook her head. Her black flame hair drifted with the motion. *Here, of course. Thousands of volcano people got out in that escape. They took huge amounts of cold earth and stone up into the air with them. And some remained behind to tell us newer ones the story when we came, in the great chamber below. They said it was glorious. The thousands broke into the air. They soared out in freedom from this world. It was cold, where they went. They roared. And they died, of course.*

Well, that stinks, I said, feeling bad for them.

Stinks? Carnelian cocked her head. *What is that?*

I can't explain. Only it's not right, to get outside and then die. I noticed Flare was approaching. His power was hot and shifty. He was still angry, then, but he had it under some control. I drew strength from the stones around me, just in case.

Here comes Flare. He feels better now that he has melted rock, Carnelian said, pleased.

I wondered how Carnelian knew what he'd been doing. That must be some part of their magic.

What else is there? she went on. *We go, we soar into the air and burn in its glory. What more could there be?*

Flare came roaring through the earth, headed straight for me. I was about to jump clean out of the ground when he whirled away from me and spun around Carnelian. *You're starting to look like* her. He didn't sound happy about it. *You're shaping yourself like her. It's just rocks, what she has on her outside. I could melt them all with a breath. Maybe I should.* He opened his mouth as he looked at me. His tongue and teeth were made of flames.

You've had enough stone for the moment. Carnelian unfurled her legs from their knot, stretched out her arms, and wrapped all four limbs around Flare. *I was telling her about getting out. She doesn't understand. She doesn't think it's wonderful, to be outside and to die.*

They were half-melted together. Carnelian's blue tunic mixed with Flare's shoulders and chest. His black flame hair wound around her arms and legs. *Do you have something better?* Flare wanted to know. *At least when we leap outside, we turn into something new. We will become something none of the others have been.*

But Carnelian says others have *done this before.* I put a bit of needle into my voice. *A lot of them, right here. They blew the whole crown of this island apart.* I shrugged. *And that was* ages *ago. Nobody cares now. Nobody cares about old stories. They only care about new ones.*

Well, we *don't care about what* your *people care about.* Flare opened his mouth. His tongue shot forward. It was a long spout of flame, green and pink mingled with orange. It flicked the air a thumb's width from my nose. I felt the gold feldspar on the tip of my magical nose melt. I hid a shudder. I *never* wanted to see that again.

Tricks, I said. *If that's the best you can do . . .*

An earth shock rolled into us from just a few miles away. It drove me back against the shield, pressing me into the obsidian. It mashed Carnelian and Flare into one creature. With the shock came a bellow so loud I thought it would tear me to shreds.

As I pulled away from the shield, Flare said, *It's the others. They're . . . over that way. Hundreds of them.* He separated himself from Carnelian.

More sound blasted through the earth. The rocks that made my girl body dropped off. I couldn't hang onto them and my magical self at the same time.

They want *to talk to us?* Carnelian was as astonished as Flare. *They say we are to lead them?*

They turned toward the sound of their kinfolk. That's when I got scared. And when I get scared, I'm the first to admit it, I turn nasty.

Lead them where? I demanded scornfully. *Around and around and around? You couldn't even get out of a quartz toy.*

Lucky for me I realized what a bleater I was. I moved as soon as I said it. Flare turned on me. He opened his mouth and shouted. Except there was no sound, only ripples of heat. Everything between Flare and where I had been melted as that heat passed through.

I meant that in a helpful *way! A useful way!* I scrambled to tell them.

I don't. Flare came at me, stretching out, a snake of fire in the ground. Soil and fast-melting rocks went to soup as he raced for my throat, his blazing hands grabbing for me.

248

I darted away. Reaching Carnelian I said, *I can show you a way out. It's a lot easier than the mountain.* Then I ran, because Flare was coming.

Your quartz wasn't a toy. It was a trap, Flare growled. *You are a cheat. I'm going to melt you. Then I'll coat the quartz "toy" with you.*

People in my world escape those toys every day, Flare. And *we escape things like the mountain. Well,* I *did.* I turned on the persuasion. *But there's another way out that's* made *for only a pair like you and Carnelian. I found it by accident on my way here.*

Flare opened his mouth. Heat billowed from him, turning solid earth to smoke. I couldn't move fast enough. Pain *shot* through me, pain I thought I couldn't feel in that shape. I rolled into a tiny ball, fighting the agony. I was terrified that if I gave in to it, I'd lose control of my magic. I'd turn to smoke just as that soil had done, and be lost forever.

You will stop. Luvo's voice boomed from every pebble, every stone, and especially from the huge obsidian and granite shields. It shivered the soil. *You will stop, or I will crush you so deep, it will be forever before you rise this high again. Hurt Evumeimei once more and I will see to it that you forget your soul.*

I stretched out. Carefully I remade my magical eyes. Flare and Carnelian had curled up. I didn't blame them. I felt like paste. Luvo's voice was that big in the ground. He sounded like the mountain he was at home, a mountain far bigger than Mount Grace.

Rain luck on us, Heibei, I prayed. Don't let them find out Luvo has no power over them!

Evvy, who's that? Carnelian whispered.

You do not have the right to address Evumeimei, thundered Luvo. *You have not earned the right to address* anyone.

I shivered everywhere, in every grain of stone that filled me. Carnelian and Flare shrank even more.

He's not as bad as he feels, I whispered.

Who are you, Big Voice? Flare didn't sound as nasty as he had just a few moments ago, but he wasn't as wary as Carnelian. *And who's Evumei — whatsit?*

SHE *is Evumeimei. You are not so much as a drop in the earth's veins.*

Luvo's bellow flattened *me*, and my magical body wasn't entirely real. It drove Flare and Carnelian deep into the earth, hundreds of yards below where we'd been. I let myself drop to follow them.

I *had* to find out how he did that.

When I caught up to the volcano kids, they were slowly stretching themselves out, making themselves big again.

What was *that?* Carnelian kept her voice quiet, in case he might hear. *Where did it come from? How does it know you? Can it hear us? Can it find us?*

Flare just looked around nervously, as if Luvo might appear out of the rock. With a magma vein warming my magical feet, giving us all new strength, I knew Luvo couldn't come near this place. Still, after what he had just done, I had to think about exactly what Luvo meant when he said he was helpless. Apparently he and I had two different meanings for that word. I couldn't do *anything* when *I* was helpless, but Luvo could . . . thunder through the earth.

"It" is a "he," I explained. *His name is Luvo. Well, that's part of his name. The only part I can pronounce, anyway. He's a mountain. He makes the mountain you're trying to break through look like that piece of granite I put between us.* I was doing some *really* fast thinking now. *He's my friend, but I have to tell you, he doesn't like the idea of you and your friends blasting this mountain apart just so you can get out. I don't think he'll let you do it.*

The earth moaned. The others were calling, Carnelian and Flare's people.

We can't just stop. Flare sounded shaky. *They want us to do something for them. I can feel it.*

He may be a mountain, but he isn't this *mountain,* Carnelian said. *He can't stop us. We're going to go out.* She didn't sound much more confident than Flare did, but I had the feeling that didn't matter with Carnelian. If she wanted to do something, she would try it even if she wasn't certain she could succeed.

He can talk to the other mountains around here. I was still thinking as fast as I could. *If they all get together, they can do something. Trust me. I know mountains. They don't want you to blow them into gravel. Now me, I've been trapped. I know what it's like to want out. And I know a way — an easier way. There's a crack in the world. You won't have to break through anything. The door's already open.*

They drifted in the fault where we'd come to a stop, looking at each other. I shut up. There's a time to talk, and a time to keep still. Sometimes I even know which is which.

Finally they seemed to agree.

Flare asked, *And where might we find this crack?*

19

Melting

Once I explained about the crack in the world some miles beyond the hollow chamber, Flare and Carnelian rushed off to tell the others. Luvo had terrified them. They wanted to get away from him, *now*.

Me, I took hardly a moment to feel smug. For one thing, they might yet wake up and guess I could be lying like an emperor. They weren't stupid, after all, only not very experienced.

For another, I wanted to have a word with Luvo. I sensed him in the earth hundreds of yards above me. He must have reached down as close to the volcano kids as he dared. As quick as mercury on a warm dish, I rose through stone and packed clay. I stopped, drifting, when I felt Luvo's power around me.

LUVO! I shrieked. He wasn't the only one who could bellow.

Evumeimei? He was confused and worried. *Why have*

you left Carnelian and Flare? Are you hurt? Did they escape you?

They're convincing their idiot friends to come with us. You said you couldn't do anything down there! Thanks for saving my life, but you lied *to me!*

He was quiet for a moment. When he answered, he sounded even more puzzled, though less worried. *I cannot do anything so far from myself.*

Then what was that? *You nearly blew us all apart! You — you almost made us into fish paste, only we weren't fish!*

Now he waited even longer. This time, when he spoke, he spoke as he'd heard Lark talk when she handled the very stupid, or the crazy. *I was* talking.

Talking! You pounded with your voice! They were cowering! Flare was ready to turn to drops again! Who else do you talk to like that? I asked.

Other mountains. Glaciers. Faults in the earth. Things that vex me.

I shook my head. Possibly Luvo didn't know the voice he uses with the great, ancient parts of the world might overpower younger ones. Finally, I said, *It was something. Maybe it was talk to you, but it had weight. You helped me out of a very bad spot. Um. Thank you, again. You convinced Carnelian and Flare they want to try the underwater volcano. They'll do anything to get away from you.*

You are welcome, Evumeimei. That is good news.

The earth beneath us slammed upward, as if a giant punched it. Stone, clay, and water shot through us. I sent part of my magic out. Way down I felt a huge fist of melted stone push up. Flare and Carnelian's friends jammed in the thousands into the huge chamber under Mount Grace. The walls were melting, making the thing expand. Far over my head stones cried out as they split. Chunks broke away to fall and shatter after rolling for hundreds of feet.

I'd better go! I shouted to Luvo. I flew through the ground. I collected strength and fashioned spells as I went, adding pieces of granite for good measure. Then I pulled power and granite alike around me into a thick, tight ball.

WHAM! The slam happened again. It shoved my ball into a pancake. I was mixed in with the magic, spells, and granite. I yanked myself together into one central ball. Quickly I dragged my protection spells into a thick shell around that. Finally I added the granite shell once more. While I worked, the world shook. I felt cracks open in stone and dirt up where open air touched the ground. Bits of stone shot into that air, thrown from new chimneys in the mountainside. A few more jumps like that and the volcano spirits would spill through cracks in Mount Grace.

Let's go, I thought. I put a lot of magic behind it.

My granite ball slammed through the earth, into a tunnel that led down. It dropped, and so did I. I clung to every particle of the stone. If I'd had a real mouth, a real throat, and real lungs, I'd have been screaming as I dropped straight into a chimney full of magma.

Volcano spirits grabbed my stone sphere. They passed me down the pipe. Even granite has limits. My shell began to melt. The heat from the volcano spirits sizzled along my magical skin. It burned.

I was spreading out. My granite shield dissolved. My muscles felt like warm honey, my bones like melting butter. I fought to stay whole, but it was so hard.

I drifted in the heat. I thought I smelled power burning. That was silly, because magic doesn't burn. Slowly I descended into the birth chamber of stones. Evumeimei Dingzai was turning to smoke. My life was sizzling out. Any memory of what I did there melted. I wanted to hang on to the memories of my life as they dissolved, but I couldn't think why. Instead I gave them up, happiness by happiness. I floated in the great power of the earth. . . .

She's flowing into the river! That sounded like a girl. I ought to know her voice, I thought in a dreamy way.

A boy said, *I have her head — you grab her tail. Who knew she could get all liquid like us?*

I ought to know the boy's voice, too.

Don't let her drip! the girl ordered.

Blue and carnelian-colored hands dragged me along, out of the heat and the power. Legs, or tails, or something, wrapped around parts of me. They pulled me along.

Carnelian and Flare yanked me into cold stuff. It had hard lumps in it. They rolled me up, shoving my liquid pieces into a tighter shape. I squirmed and wriggled, fighting to get back to that hot river. I was going to float in the heart of everything. I would be reborn with the stones.

A chunk of diamond dug into my side.

Diamond. I curled myself up around it. How could I forget diamonds? Diamonds were so hard it was almost impossible to cut them, impossible to break or crush them. I could only *ask* one to break for me. It would do so only if it wanted to. I'd never find a diamond in all that molten stone. I'd never find *any* rocks in it. And I'd never find a single crystal.

What had I been thinking?

I uncurled myself and looked around. Flare and Carnelian, shaped like they wore clothes, sat on either side of me in the earth. They had saved me. They had pulled me out of there.

The others said they had a rock that acted like one of us, Flare told me. *You're lucky we thought that sounded weird enough to be you.*

They say they'll go, Carnelian said. *They say they'll follow us out. They were so excited they shook the earth. Are you fit to take us there now?*

I wanted to be melted some more. . . . The warmth pulled on me. I shook it off and ran my magical fingers through the diamond, soaking up its strength. *I can do it,* I replied. I was thinking, You saved my life. And now I'm going to lead you out into the cold, cold ocean to die.

It's either the ocean or the open air, Evumeimei, I told myself. Slowly I pulled every last bit of me back into my normal shape. They're going to die anyway, because they want to get out of the earth. And if they get into the air here, they're going to kill a lot of people and animals, too. They maybe did already, them and their friends.

What about *my* friends in the air above? That scared me. The last shake was such a bad one, and it had cracked the surface in so many places. How much ash, underground water, mud flow, and flying rock was set in motion? I had to get the volcano spirits out to sea, before they split the island like a melon.

We'd have to take the fault that lay under the Makray River. And we'd have to go deep, really deep. So deep the refugees on the road next to it would be safe.

I didn't even know if I could bear traveling so deep under the earth, but I would have to. Fat lot of good it would be, for me to lure the volcano spirits away from the quartz trap and Mount Grace, and have them escape right under everyone I wanted to protect.

I can show you the way, through the deepest cracks of the earth, I told Carnelian and Flare. *But I'm afraid to travel with your friends. I'm afraid I'll melt again. I have to stay away from them.*

Of course you're staying away from them! Flare got larger for a moment. We're *leading them, not* you*!*

Which way is the crack you want to travel? Carnelian watched me, waiting. I had a feeling she would wait forever. Her patience scared me a lot more than Flare's temper. If I ran away, I had a feeling that wherever I went, Carnelian would find me and take revenge.

I sent out a tiny burst of magic. It was nothing like what I'd entered the earth with. It showed me the chamber under Mount Grace. I described the part of it that opened onto the fault under the Makray River to Flare and Carnelian.

Gather the others, Flare, said Carnelian. *Tell them to assemble at that entrance. I will take Evvy there around the room of the melting together, outside, so there is no danger. She leads us, and we lead them.*

That's a good plan. Flare sounded happy. *We'll get away from Evvy's monster. And the ones who stay behind when we go? They can tell all the ones who haven't come up from the core yet that we led everyone to glory!*

He raced away through the crack in the ground. Stones melted in his path.

This way. Carnelian pointed down. *If you're feeling strong enough.*

No, but I have a way to fix that. I pulled my magical fingers through the diamond again. All of its inner surfaces vibrated, passing their power to me. When I had drawn every bit of magic from it that I could, I looked around. There was another diamond, a smaller one. Quickly I gathered its power. This was real luck. With these two stones I was nearly at full strength. I needed to be.

Carnelian dropped through the earth, straight down. I followed her. *So do you like mashing all together like that and losing yourself? It doesn't sound very good to me. No wonder you want to go out so bad.* I lied. It *was* good. When I'd turned into a ribbon of hot syrup, it had felt *wonderful.* I had been the essence of every rock in the world, free of my meat body. I'd been all the other volcano spirits, and they had been me. Evvy was lost. Instead I had just been a glorious part of everything. I wondered if I had felt like that before I was born, inside my mother.

I don't know, Carnelian replied carelessly. *Once we grow that little kernel that says we are one creature, separate from the others, we can't ignore it. We can't forget ourselves all the way. We can't stop being curious about things, either. We keep leaving the pool to look for new things, things that don't melt away when we come close.* We dropped through the biggest chunk of basalt I had ever seen. *Sometimes we go back to the pool and join it, Flare and me, because it makes us happy. We can't lose ourselves, but it's still fun. What do you do for fun?*

I was trying to describe eating and walking — I wasn't doing very well — when we popped into a huge crack in the ground. Far above I sensed the wet coldness of the stones at the bottom of the Makray River. Just above, far off, I saw and felt the volcano spirits. I had never entered the chamber under Mount Grace this way. I turned to inspect the heavy rock sides of the fault. They opened out down below. They shivered from the pressure of the earth and all the shocks that had come through. I hoped the fault would hold steady as we traveled, but I was out of choices. We had to go this way. More people could live through earthquakes than the mess caused by volcanoes: fire, mudslides, floods, moving lava, and falling ash so thick it suffocated. And I was truly impressed by how deep down the fault ran into the earth. I could keep the spirits well away from the river, that was certain.

I glanced at the chamber's entrance again. At first it was a small orange circle. Suddenly I realized the circle was getting bigger.

Flare raced down the fault toward us. *Go! Go! They're coming. Evvy, if they catch up, you'll melt again. Show us the way!*

I turned and dropped down the side of the fault, plunging into the earth. I was thrilled to find magic along those sides, left over from the power of the earth shocks and the passage of the volcano spirits. It fizzed and popped inside my skin, mixed with fire and the strength of stones. My magic belonged here, and it didn't belong. *I* didn't belong, unless I melted.

Don't think about melting, I ordered myself. Don't think about trading your meat life for this liquid one!

The lower I dropped, the slower I went. I had to draw the volcano spirits down, away from the surface and my human friends. I knew that. But I was starting to feel a little . . . smooshed. There was so much *weight* on top of me. True, I could draw on the magic in the stone for strength. But the water, the soil, and the clay were dull, and sullen. I had never had so much weight on me. It didn't matter that my body was magic, a thing of power, that could pass through it all. The island had its own great substance. It rested on me.

Come on! Flare shouted in my ear. *The others will see you. They'll think you're showing us the way!*

I glared at him. *Don't yell at me. Doesn't the weight bother you?*

What weight? Flare asked.

The island, I said. *The whole island is pressing down on us. Doesn't it make you feel crushed?*

Carnelian laughed. *That tiny bit of pressure? You've never been in the core. All the world presses on you there. It's why so few of us make it this close to the skin. Most can't fight the core.*

If Evvy meant pressure, she should have said so, Flare announced. *And I don't feel any.*

Flare's not sensitive to pressure like me, Carnelian explained. *He's one of the ones that's more sensitive to heat.*

Since you melted so fast, you must be sensitive to both. Don't ever go to the core, that's my advice.

Has the monster ever been to the core? asked Flare. *Does the weight bother him?*

I looked at Flare and smiled. He was still afraid of Luvo. He thought Luvo might be watching. *The core parts and lets him pass through,* I bragged.

Flare sped up until he was beside me. He wanted me to protect him from Luvo.

I never saw the core do anything like that, Carnelian said as we moved on.

The core's a big place, isn't it? You couldn't see everything at once. I tried to sound strong, but the earth was so heavy. I pulled magic from the walls of the fault. I couldn't even take the time to gather a new granite shell. The volcano spirits would catch up and swamp me again if I did. *Don't worry about Luvo. Just stick to leading your friends out into the open, and you'll be fine.*

She's right, Flare, Carnelian told him. *The others depend on us to bring them out.* Carnelian and Flare looked back. Far behind us came the other volcano spirits in a billow of heat that toasted my toes. I didn't want them any closer. Carnelian reassured Flare, *She's just showing us a way past her monster friend.*

And I know an easier way than through the top of the mountain. I didn't want them forgetting that my way was easy. I was scared they would get bored and try to find another way out.

On we flew, far below Starns Island. If I'd had lungs I would have been panting, the island was so crushing. The fault was huge, but it felt *tiny*. Worse, I felt like it was getting smaller all the time. The walls trembled with all those tons of cliffs, fields, rivers, hills, and lakes on top of them. If they slipped, how much of the earth's might would they release? Enough to split the island? The fault was the seam. This one was set to rip. . . .

Slowly, so slowly I didn't notice at first, the weight changed. It eased. The fault was rising. I knew I ought to sink deeper into it, but the change felt so *good*. Suddenly a huge amount of pressure vanished. I sent power up, enough to feel the shape of the world overhead. We were three miles deep, no more. We had passed out from under tall cliffs. The fault had entered the shallows of the sea.

Stop! I heard a volcano spirit cry. *Where do we go?*

We came this way before! someone else called. *While we searched for you!*

Be quiet! Carnelian shouted back to them. *Are we your leaders or not? We told you, we know a way out! A way that will leave us the strength to fly when we have broken through!*

More *of us will fly free this way!* Flare whirled in a circle before the distant spirits, a fiery beacon. *You said you trusted us, so* trust *us!* He told me softly, *And we had better be able to trust* you, *Evvy. If not, we will twine around you until you are nothing but smoke.*

Don't threaten me, Flare, I warned him. *I'll tell Luvo on you.*

He glared at me for a moment. Then he blazed white-hot, sending heat clean through me. It felt . . . nasty. I pulled away from him.

Carnelian rammed him from the side. *Steamhead! Do you* want *her friend to come for us?*

The others were roiling where they waited a hundred yards back. They were getting restless. *Come on, you two. Stop frisking,* I ordered. *We have a long way to go still. Your friends will come to see what's going on if you don't move. Do you want them to find out you're listening to a whosawhatsit like me?*

That was enough to calm them. We went forward. I led them along the quivering fault. We were away from the river, after all. My friends were out of the way if steam or even ash and stone escaped the ocean floor. And I was free of the weight of Starns.

It never occurred to me that the sea might be even worse.

20

The Sea

Overhead I felt her weight grow as we flowed under the waves, a mile, then two miles from shore. I had thought the island was bad. At least when we were under it, everything on top of us was filled with stones. This was something like the voyage to Starns. I was burdened with miles of stoneless water.

Don't be silly, I told myself. You're wrapped in stone. You're miles under stone. Well — only three miles down, now. But still, that's plenty of stone. A little while ago you were burdened with stone.

But now the power of the sea lay on me. Normally, the magic in water touched me not at all. Stone and water were too different in the usual way of things. Maybe I was changed, after melting and spending so long in my magical body. Perhaps it was because I was in stone that had carried the sea for time out of mind.

Possibly it was because this sea knew I was there.

What are you, hiding far below with those other hot worms? Not rock, but rock in your veins, the sea hissed, its voice slithering down into the fault. I looked at Flare and Carnelian. They didn't seem to hear that creepy, cold voice. *Rock in the power that runs through* you. The voice dripped down through the tiny cracks that ran to the salty water. *I'll draw you up, small silvery rock worm. I'll draw you into my aqua embrace and float you between tides. You will never touch so much as a flake of quartz in your life. Won't that be amusing? Come up, come up. I will have you in time. No rock thing fights me forever.*

When do we get there? That was Flare, and he whined. I hate whiners. *We've been traveling forever,* he went on.

It's not forever, I snapped. *Be quiet and keep moving.* I shouldn't have silenced him. The minute he went quiet, the sea was at me again. I clung to the wall of the fault, drinking up its magic as I slid along. I wanted it to make me feel stronger.

Do you know how many rocks I have worn down, little silvery worm? the sea asked. *I have rolled over specks of stone that lie on my belly. I rub them until they are tinier still, wearing them down to dust. I thrust them against the boulders underneath, scouring the boulders until they are smaller and smaller and smaller. Piece by piece, limestone, obsidian, marble, it must all surrender to me. You are just another stone for the grinding. In time, your hot companions will be more stones for my grinding.*

I was slowing down. So much malice . . . The sea had so much hate for anything that was not part of it.

Hot pain seared my arm. Carnelian had grabbed me!

Ow! I yanked free. *Are you trying to cook me or something? Don't do that!*

You were hardly moving! Carnelian accused. *How much longer, Evvy? Maybe you're lost. If there was a way out here, why didn't the other spirits find it before? They said they came this way to search for us.*

There's a way out — we have to turn soon. Stop complaining! I told her. *If you want something you have to work for it! I didn't say the trip was a quick one, don't try to tell me I did!*

Flare got behind me, shielding me from the view of the volcano spirits. *Stop shouting, Evvy. I think you lied to us, like you lied about your "toy."*

I'm no liar. How much longer did I have to bear this? I should have seen anything made of fire would have no patience, even if it was also stone! *Grow up. There are no easy answers in the outer world. We have a ways to go.*

Maybe we should try to get out here. *There's a crack.* Flare rammed himself up into a hairline fault. It ended a hundred yards up in a slab of granite. The fault widened a little, then stuck. He rammed again.

Carnelian waited until Flare backed up. Then she jammed herself into the fault with him. The volcano spirits rushed forward. They thought we'd reached our destination.

You want to do that? I yelled. *Fine! But the place I talked about is miles on!* They weren't listening. I was furious. We were only two miles offshore. It wasn't far enough to spare the island.

Come on, I pleaded. *That isn't the way. It isn't far now.* When they popped out of the fault, I grabbed their hands, ignoring the pain. *Tell the others you were just trying your strength or something — ow!* I had to let go, but at least I'd gotten their attention. Flare hesitated, then motioned for the volcano spirits to stop.

I looked at my hands. Their form had melted a little. I pressed them against the sides of the big fault, taking in more of its strength. It was shaking harder than ever. I looked back. The volcano spirits were slamming around, hitting first one side, then the other. I had to get them moving again, before they started an earthquake.

They're bored, said Flare. *They want to get to this place. So do we, right, Carnelian?*

No — *I* didn't have to get them moving. I wasn't their leader.

I shuddered and drank as much power as I could bear. *Have you told them how amazing this new place is?* I asked. *You'll have black clouds all around as you come out, and black smoke. You won't have to break the earth open at all! Since you won't tire yourselves breaking through stone to get free, you'll be able to fly high!*

Carnelian and Flare went back to tell the others. They stopped attacking the sides of the fault. When I saw Carnelian and Flare returning to me, I flew on ahead, showing them the way.

Their concentration was broken, though. The volcano spirits roared behind us, growling and grumbling. They were whining, too! I didn't have to speak lava to recognize the sound of complaints. The fault developed branches, and each new branch distracted everyone who wasn't me. Wheedling and pleading, I brought them along another mile. It was work, all the time with the sea laughing at me.

They say, if we're going to swim, they want to do it melting together. Carnelian was spending too much time in a girl shape: She actually pouted, her lower lip stuck out and everything. *They say when we go around melted together, at least they can taste Flare and me, and feel bold like Flare and me. They can be excited like Flare and me in the melting together. In the fault they just run along. There's nothing new.*

Flare leaned against the side of the fault. It melted away from his shape, the stone quivering like a jelly. *I felt something give back there. Back where we were, before you dragged us here. There was a lot of the cold stuff in the way, a lot to melt and draw off our strength, but if we got the others to do the shoving —*

So you can jump into the air and die? I would have gladly smacked their heads together, if I hadn't cared about my hands. *If you don't fail? You don't even know how much stone is on top of you! I do! No one has broken through it in thousands of my years. That's so long the only way we even know it happened once is because there is a record in the stones themselves. How many times do I have to tell you, there is a crack that comes all the way down here. You'll be able to leave without exhausting yourself in breaking through. The only problem is, a little travel and you start bleating like sheep!*

They stared at me.

What's bleating? Carnelian asked.

What's sheep? That was Flare.

We stared at each other, just hovering.

Pathetic. We were half a mile below the bottom of the sea. Her voice was even louder in my mind this time. *The silvery worm tries to bribe melted rocks. Give up, worm. Give yourself over to me. I will have you in time. I will have them in time. You will be exhausted, they will be dead. I will grind and scour you all to nothing. I never, ever tire.*

The edges of my magical body were blurring. I was losing my grip on myself, on my concentration.

The volcano spirits came roaring up.

Enough. We're going to try here. Flare slammed into the side of the fault, where a deep crack reached up. That wasn't even a fault, just a hollow. Carnelian and a huge ball of the others flew after him, striking the hollow with a roar. More cracks appeared there. Other volcano spirits rippled forward.

I came to my senses. *No! Not here, this isn't it!*

They ignored me. Flare and Carnelian fell back among the volcano spirits. In one huge surge they struck the roof of the fault again.

WHAM! All around me the seafloor shook. There was a slow, grinding, growling crunch. The walls of the fault slid, one to my left, the other to my right. Overhead the sea gasped, feeling its belly lift.

At least you aren't nattering at me anymore, I told her.

WHAM!

The volcano spirits punched the fault again. Once more the walls slid, two inches to my left, an inch to my right.

Earthquake. A few inches in a fault was an earthquake.

I had to get back to my humans. The ground under their feet would be buckling. What if there was a gadolga — a tidal wave — headed for Sustree? I had to reach them.

We were three miles offshore. It would have to be enough. There was nothing else I could do. I was tired, scared, and I couldn't make the volcano kids listen. I'd done my best. And at least I wouldn't have to sit around and watch them shoot out of the ground and die.

*   *   *

I thought it would be easy to get back to my real body. It was, what? Four miles as the goose flew? One mile from the shore.

But I was so tired.

You are half the size you were when you crossed my borders, silvery worm, the sea taunted. *Why bother going back? You wished to melt. Stay and be ground to a speck instead.*

Don't you ever tire of the sound of your own voice? I whispered. It wasn't very good, but it was the best I could manage. I felt as small as a pebble when I found land that wasn't under salt water. Instantly I leaped to the earth's surface. It was wonderful to shed the weight of water and earth together.

Once there, Luvo's magic was a huge beacon in my eyes. I flew to him, drawing on his strength. He wrapped me around like a good father, taking me into his depths. If my magical body could have cried, I would have wept. I felt so safe in his heart. I was surrounded by his power. He was layered like a tree with centuries of stone life. Here was fire, water, sun, patience, resolve, wrath, wisdom, anything I could ever want.

I knew then that I wanted to be Luvo someday. I don't know how, but I can strive to be more like him.

The patience will need a lot of work.

Evumeimei, there is a thing, Luvo said in my mind. *I fear you will not like it.*

Something about his tone worried me. I didn't want to leave the good place he had made, but I did. I popped into the body I had left and fought to open my eyes. From the sun's position, I'd been gone three hours. I was in Sustree, tied to my horse with ropes. Obviously Rosethorn had found me.

From the look of things, we had just arrived. The docks were a mess. People were trying to get onto the ships. Men and women with weapons were making the refugees leave things: wagons and animals, mostly. Children screamed for their pets. Adults argued and shouted at the guards, who told them there wasn't enough room. The animals just looked confused. Rosethorn, Myrrhtide, Azaze, Oswin, and the other village leaders were trying to get people aboard the vessels. Tahar was aboard one small ship. I could see her seated by the rail, grim-faced. Jayat was still on the dock, helping Azaze.

Nory was right beside me. She hung on to my knee so tight it hurt. She'd already pulled me half out of the saddle.

"Stop that!" I smacked at her, or tried to. My arm was too numb to work. "What's the matter? Why aren't you helping?"

She glared at me. She had pulled me down so far our eyes were on the same level. One more tug and I'd be hanging off the saddle. "Awake, are you? I'm here because I wanted to be around when you opened your eyes."

"Why?" I asked.

"So I could do this."

Even if I could have moved, I wouldn't have been fast enough to escape the hard slap she landed on my cheek. Then she slapped me again. She was crying. "While you were playing mage, Meryem decided you would like her again if she gave you a pretty rock she left at home. She went back. I'm not allowed to find her. I'm needed to look after the others. So she's dead in all these shakes, or she's hurt, or she's going to starve. All because you're a pig who's mean to little girls!"

Then she punched me in the eye and walked off.

Meryem. Meryem had gone back to Oswin's house. And the volcano was going to come through the ocean floor only three miles out. That wasn't good enough if a small girl was left on the island. She would be out there while ash and rock bombs fell and set the forests afire.

21

Panic

I was struggling to get free of my ropes when I heard Rosethorn say, "Hold still, Evvy." My ropes were hemp, of course. At Rosethorn's command, they came untied. Azaze caught me before I fell off Spark.

"Oswin isn't to know one of his children is missing," Azaze told me quietly. "Understand, girl? We can't go back for her, and Oswin has twelve others who need him. It's a sorrowful thing but true. In the rush he won't be able to count them. Not a word, or I swear, you'll travel in the bilge — or not at all."

"She won't talk. Evvy understands reality." Rosethorn looked as bleak as slate. "We have been here before, haven't we, Evvy?"

I nodded and sat on the ground. Puffs of ash rose around me. We *had* been here before. I hadn't wanted to be in this position ever again.

"We've work to do. Try to get yourself moving, girl." Azaze bustled off.

"Myrrhtide put our packs on that ship over there, the *Brown Gull*. Try to be aboard when the captain weighs anchor. For now, when you can walk, start helping to get some of these people seen to." Rosethorn looked at me. "Did you do it, at least? Lead them away?"

"I don't know." My voice cracked. Rosethorn passed a water bottle to me. I think I drank half of it. I sounded better when I spoke again. "I got them away, but only three miles out. I was exhausted. I couldn't drag them any farther. They got bored. They're trying to smash their way through the ocean floor." I hung my head. "Maybe they'll stay there, or move on. Or maybe they'll come back, to the places they know."

Rosethorn rested her hand on my head. "Evvy, you were foolish to take on volcanoes in the first place. It was like wrestling Luvo."

I was going to cry, I just knew it. "Rosethorn, it's my fault Meryem ran away. I said mean things to her."

"I know. She told Nory, who told me." Rosethorn's voice was quiet. If she condemned me, I didn't hear it. I couldn't look at her, so I couldn't see it in her face if she felt that way.

"If she dies here, it'll be my fault," I said.

"And you will have to learn to live with that, Evvy," Rosethorn told me. "I never said the first steps on the road to becoming a destroyer wouldn't hurt. I would imagine it would bother you less, over time."

I broke down and cried, then. Rosethorn sighed. "Perhaps that was hard. I am, sometimes. But Evvy, six-year-olds are tender plants. The slightest frost kills them. I cannot blame you, not really. In the years when you should have learned to be with people, you were scrabbling to survive all alone. But you haven't learned to go easy with the defenseless, something I'd hoped Briar and I would have taught you by now. I can only pray you will remember this, and not get worse. Oh, Mila save us — I have to go break that up. Come help me when you can." She strode off along one of the docks. Two men were fighting over a bag of something. It ripped in two. The seed in it sprouted and fell to the dock as living plants.

"Now you have nothing to quarrel about!" Rosethorn informed them angrily. "Get on that ship!"

I massaged my cramped leg muscles, trying to get my body moving. Ash drifted onto everything from the crack that had opened on Mount Grace. It lay in a light powder over people's faces, the animals, the ships. It made me sneeze constantly.

"Do you need a hand up?" Oswin had come over. He helped me to my feet. "Listen, Evvy, don't blame yourself about Meryem. I should have kept an eye on her." His face was pale and strained. "I knew what had happened. When Meryem's upset, she heads for home."

So much for not telling him. "You're not angry with me?" I couldn't look at him.

278

"You didn't order Meryem to go back." He steadied me. "Nory's blaming herself. She's wrong, too. This is a mess." He looked around. He was right — it *was* a mess. One ship was riding low in the water at the dock. It was overloaded. Sailors tossed goods overboard, while passengers screamed in rage. Didn't they see that furniture would do no good if they drowned?

"Where *is* Nory?" I looked around. I didn't want to get punched again. I also wasn't sure what Nory might do to me next. Kill me, maybe.

"Helping Treak get the children aboard our ship. That one over there, with the sun on its prow." Oswin walked over to a family with a wagon. He helped them take bundles out of it. "You should get aboard your ship, Evvy. Myrrhtide wants to set sail. He says the shakes are setting up strong currents in the sea. Once we're out there, he can use his magic and those currents to help us move quicker. And the captains have winds tied up in knots. They're going to set them free to get us away from here."

"Not southeast." I unsaddled my horse, Spark, who had been waiting for me all this time. We were going to have to leave my patient little mare. Would she be clever enough to get away from the shore? Would she go far enough? I slapped her on the rump when I had all of her tack off and watched her run. "Oswin, did you hear me?"

Oswin turned to look at me. "Huh? What did you say?"

"I said, tell them not to go southeast," I called. "A volcano is coming up underwater there. That's what caused the quake a little while ago."

"Southeast — got it." Oswin stared at the ship where Tahar sat. Treak stood beside her, jumping up and down. He waved to Oswin. The other children were with him. Some of them were crying. The others looked miserable, furious, or both. The boy who had ridden with me on Spark was hanging on to two of them, who fought his grip. Oswin walked toward the ship, his eyes searching the faces at the rail. "Treak, where's Nory?"

My belly flip-flopped. I knew where she was. And if *Nory* had gone missing . . . I looked around for Jayat. A moment ago he'd been standing with Azaze. Now Azaze and the guards were moving the last of the villagers onto the ships. I couldn't see Jayat anywhere.

Oswin turned and strode down the dock, his face grim. Ash streaks made him look like a Qidao shaman had painted him for war. His eyes blazed turquoise, blind with the ideas in his head. He looked half crazy.

Azaze moved in to cut him off. "Where are you going?"

"Nory's out there," he said hurriedly. "She went after Meryem. They —"

"And what of your other eleven children?" she demanded. Once again I thought Azaze should have been born as a

queen. Right now Moharrin needed a queen, not a head-woman. Only a queen could stop Oswin if they wanted to keep him. "You are all they have, Oswin Forest. You saved them from starvation yourself. *You* stepped in and interfered with the destiny the gods chose for them. If you abandon them now, the gods will surely strike all of you down as payment for your abandonment of your duty."

"You can't know that." Oswin's voice was as hard as diamond and as soft as chalk.

"I know that the gods watch when you replace their plans with one of your own," Azaze's voice was sure. "You had best make good on your new plan if you interfere in theirs. You can't just decide you're tired of your new plan, or that one part of it is more important than the rest. What will happen to those children when we get to wher-ever we're going? I'll do my best, but I can't control them. The only one who could ever do that is *you*."

"Azaze —" Oswin reached out to Azaze. His hand shook. "They're my children, too."

Azaze's face was iron hard. "But they are only two of your children, and they are out of your reach. Treak obeys only *you*, Oswin. You're the only person I know who can grind lenses so that Jesy can see. Deva calls you 'Papa.' And —"

A boy's voice rang out clear over a sudden quiet at the docks. "Oswin, are you leaving us?"

Oswin's shoulders drooped. He looked back at the ship where the other children waited. "No. It's all right, Natan. I'll be there in a moment."

Azaze took one of his hands. "I am sorry, my boy."

"They have my idiot Jayat with them, or Norya does, at least!" Tahar screeched from the ship. "That's more luck than they deserve!" She looked and sounded furious, but there were wet streaks under her eyes.

I'm wasting time, I thought as Oswin got back to work. *I need Luvo.*

He stood with Rosethorn and Myrrhtide, on the dock. Enough of the refugees were on the ships that they had decided it was time to do magic. Rosethorn twisted and knotted strands of hemp. She was using spells to strengthen the ropes and sails of the ships. Myrrhtide whispered over chains set with water-magic stones: jade, pearls, beryl, aquamarines. They were too busy to notice anything else, including me.

I knelt beside Luvo. Through our magic I told him, *Take care of Rosethorn. Make sure she gets home safe. I have to go back into the fault.*

Luvo reared up onto his hindquarters. I couldn't see his eyes bulge. If he'd had them, though, they'd have popped from his head. *You will do no such thing. What would it accomplish? You are as weak as a flake of mica. Three miles is enough if these meat creatures hurry.*

I didn't have time to say it fast. I gave it to him all in a rush, as pictures and feelings. I showed him Meryem, Jayat, and Nory all headed inland. That three miles weren't enough, if the volcano was a big one. That the volcano spirits could get bored or frustrated. They could return to the cracks under Starns if they couldn't break out where they were. That if the volcano was big enough, it would set the forests on fire.

How it was my fault for losing my temper with Meryem, and with Carnelian and Flare under the sea. How I should have been patient, and made the volcano spirits keep going. How after Gyongxe, I just couldn't bear for more animals or people to die if I had a chance to save them.

How the great fault under our feet was slipping little by little. Sooner or later it would slip a lot.

I know all this. Luvo sounded testy. *Evumeimei, I have never done so much rushing in all my days as I have done in my time with you. Now I must rush some more. I do not welcome it.*

I don't want you to rush! I cried. *I want you to leave with Rosethorn and tell her what happened to me!*

For a moment he was as silent as only a stone can be. Then he said, *Take this part of my strength.* He set a *huge* ball of magical fire inside me. For a moment I thought *I* might explode like a volcano. *Find the diamonds ten miles down. Gather their power. Then try to deal with Flare and Carnelian again.*

That was all he said. I struggled with what he'd given me, trying to arrange it so it stopped choking me. When I could speak, I asked, *Luvo? Luvo?*

He was gone. Just . . . gone.

I opened my real eyes. Luvo was a purple and green lump on the dock. He looked like a rock. Rosethorn and Myrrhtide hadn't noticed anything. They were deep inside their own spells. I tucked my friend in Rosethorn's mage kit. My hands shook. He weighed no more than an ordinary rock of his size. Then I walked away. I used empty wagons as shields. No one noticed I was going in the wrong direction.

They'd think I was already on the ship. Once they knew I wasn't there, they wouldn't turn back. They had to save the most people. And Rosethorn wouldn't return alone. They would need her to keep the sails and the ropes in one piece. Captains hoarded the winds they bought against emergencies, since they paid a lot of money for them. If they freed all of the winds at once, they wouldn't risk losing everything if a hemp rope or a sail gave way. For that they needed a plant mage with the ships. Rosethorn knew it.

I hoped she would understand why I had left. I thought she might. I wanted her to know that I meant to build and not destroy, at least when it came to meat creatures.

Anyway, I was out of time.

I ran in the direction that Spark had taken. She was cropping grass outside the village. "Silly horse," I said as I slipped a bridle on her. I had found it in the street. "You were supposed to head into the hills."

She didn't like it when I climbed onto her bare back. She tried to nip me. I tugged her head around and kicked her sides. "We're in a hurry, Spark. Stop playing."

We galloped up the hill behind the town. I wanted to get farther from any gadolgas that might flood the town, but the gods decided my stopping place. A big shake rolled in. It knocked me off Spark's back. I clung to the rein as the poor thing neighed and reared.

When I got her calmed down, I took off the bridle. "Now go. Away from the sea, knothead. Heibei watch over you."

This time she went, headed up into the hills. Even horses learn.

No more time, no more time. Who knew what the volcano kids were doing now? They hadn't escaped the earth, or the quakes would have stopped. They were still ramming themselves into the fault.

I lay flat on the ground, sucking more strength from the granite all around. Accidentally or guided there by the gods, I had found a good place. I thought then that I should say good-bye to my body, just in case. I wasn't sure I would be able to come back to it. The fault was really unstable. My chances were good that the volcano spirits would overwhelm and melt me.

So I thanked my strong arms, that helped me to climb and lift and fight. I thanked my hands. They had led me to Briar and my magic, by itching to handle and polish stones, and by accidentally waking the power in them. I thanked my legs, with the muscles that could hike and kick. I thanked my poor feet. They had carried me so far. They'd had such awful punishment from the emperor's soldiers. I thanked my belly and guts, for putting up with the bad food I gave them when I couldn't find anything else. I thanked my bones, my skin, my mouth, my nose.

Maybe that was how I could survive the volcano spirits. Carnelian said she and Flare could still remember who they were during the melting together. My stone magic wanted to melt like all stone did. I had to remember my meat self, my human body. I had to remember what made me Evvy.

Holding tight to Luvo's strength and the power I drew from the nearby stones, I rolled into a ball of magic and dropped through the shivering earth. I had to get to those diamonds. I needed as much magic as I could stand. All around me every stone and every grain of dirt was moving. Every bit of water had spread to make the soil damp. Ponds and streams leaked out and down, turning the ground into mud. This was part of a big earthquake, when the ground seemed to turn to water. Houses would collapse, their walls sinking and cracking. The sides of the hills and mountains would slide.

I would not slide with them. I was two miles down, three, and still dropping. The ground's shivering made it easier. The movement shook power free of the stone. I gobbled it all as I passed. I could hear the thunder of the volcano spirits who had stayed behind under Mount Grace. Their voices boomed through the faults. They were wondering if they should have left, too. They were asking if they ought to find Carnelian and Flare now, and follow them out.

The earth bucked around me. Each time Flare, Carnelian, and the others rammed the fault, they shook it. Stuck as it was, the fault trapped the power of their blows, storing it.

I turned some gathered magic to speed. If the fault came unstuck in a big way, the earthquake that followed would make these little ones seem like the shake of a lamb's tail.

It scared me to think of disasters, but disasters were coming no matter what. They might be big gadolga waves. They might be earthquakes. If the volcano broke through too close to Starns, it would bring earthquakes, fire, and ash. And a volcano here wouldn't be a disaster just for the island, but for the nearby Battle Islands, too.

How lucky are you, Evumeimei, I thought. You go from Gyongxe's human war to nature's war on Starns. At least you know it isn't you. This stuff has always begun by the time you get there.

Seven miles, eight. I felt the diamonds now. They sang to my magic, a chorus of nightingales. Luvo had found a bed of them, each one a dull star filled with the earth's power. If I'd trapped Carnelian and Flare here, instead of the bed of quartz, I never could have controlled them.

Now I bounced from stone to stone. I rippled over faces so hard my power skidded on them. Doing so, I breathed in the strength from the hearth of the world.

But it was Luvo's power in me that mattered here. It sang to the diamonds. Luvo's strength called up sparks and flares of power, drinking it in. Drop by drop, I was flooded with magic that was harder than that of any stone I'd ever felt. It was the strongest in any rock that existed. It would guard me in the heat, it would make me strong. Each surface in that diamond bed gave up a stream of magic that wound through Luvo's and mine. When I was ready to burst, I leaped free.

Lines of power showed in my vision. I could see the fault lines all around me, silvery gray fire tinged with red. They vibrated with the strain that the shakes were putting on them. In the distance, I saw the hollow chamber under Mount Grace. The volcano spirits who were still there boiled and leaped. Some of them raced through the earth, following the path Flare, Carnelian, and I had taken out to sea. Others were so excited that they pounded the highest part of the chamber, smashing into the peak of Mount Grace. Some jammed into cracks in the mountain's shoulders. They turned groundwater into steam and anything that would burn into ash. Both escaped into the air over the mountain. Those volcano spirits couldn't get out of the mountain — not yet. How many more shakes would it take before those cracks opened and let them out?

I screamed and flew through the ground, seeking the quickest path to the place where I had left Flare and Carnelian. I had to let them and their friends out! They had to go where *I* chose. They would *not* escape through all the places *they* were trying to open up. They'd learn the truth — that *out* was cold, slow, and not at all exciting. They would be free, even if it wasn't what they had dreamed. Who gets exactly what they dream in life, anyway?

The sea hissed when it felt me reach the ground below it. *Silvery rock worm, you are so much bigger now! So much more to seek and grind to sand! You should have stayed in the dry places, where you were safe!*

I'm in a hurry, and I have no time for you, Great One. I covered myself with the faces of diamonds.

Where are you? she demanded. *You cannot vanish, not in my own realm — where have you gone?*

I let the sea cast around, searching blindly for me. Over my head, my reach so much greater with the power of Luvo and diamonds in me, I felt other magics that I knew. The ships were sailing. Rosethorn, Myrrhtide, and Luvo were in them.

Thump.

The earth around me thudded, like someone had struck the giant, loose head of a drum. The fault shook a little, not a lot. I half-hesitated, afraid this small shake might knock the fault loose, but it held. I kept moving. I was flying so quick I soared past Flare, Carnelian, and their friends. Feeling silly, I had to come back around to get them.

Again! Again! Flare yelled.

Flare, it's not working. *Look at it,* Carnelian ordered.

Carnelian and Flare had hammered the crack in the fault where I'd left them. They had melted away slabs of rock and tons of earth. They had gone just a little crazy. Though they weren't even a mile closer to the surface, they were still at it. The volcano spirits crowded in behind them. I was squeezed between rock and magma. Since I was decked out with so much power, I felt hot and too big for the space that held me.

Do you think you can hide from me down there, silvery worm? whispered the sea. *I will come to you in time. I will scour away all this rock that shields you. I will beat it down to helpless specks that float on my tides. I will turn your hot friends to cold stone and treat them the same. And then I will have you. I have everything in the end. You will be cold. Miniscule. Helpless.* Mine.

I began to gasp, though I couldn't breathe in this shape. I was too hot. I was trapped. The weight and the heat were making me smaller, making my edges runny. If I didn't stop this, I would melt again!

I gathered the diamond magic into a human shape, so Flare and Carnelian would know me. Then I slammed through the crowd of volcano spirits, cutting my way through. They pulled back. They had never seen anything like me before, not with all the power I had to shield me. I scared them. They didn't know that I would eventually melt if they swamped me again. I didn't wait for them to work it out. Instead I darted into the open space they'd left around Carnelian and Flare.

For some reason Carnelian and Flare still kept the humanlike shapes they had taken after they had met me. That was my good luck. I grabbed each of them by an ear.

Stop that! Flare yanked against my grip. I poured diamond into it to make sure he couldn't get loose. *We're trying to get* out*!*

That hurts*!* Carnelian wriggled and squirmed. I used more diamond on my hold on her, too. *Evvy? Is it you? Or the monster with the big voice? You shiver like him!*

I glanced down at myself. Now my magical body looked as if it was made of ice — or diamond. *What are you on about, shivering? It's me, not Luvo. I'm tired of being reasonable. If you won't mind common sense, then you just have to do what I tell you. This* isn't *the way.* I dragged them out

of the hollow they had made, through the crowd of volcano spirits. They got out of our way. Seemingly they
feared anything that could tow their precious leaders along
like naughty children. If they had children, and if they
towed them by whatever passed for ears.

I hauled Carnelian and Flare along the fault, in the
way *I* wanted to go. They fought me with all their
strength. They *were* really strong, but Luvo's power, all
that I'd collected, and the diamond magic together made
me stronger — for now.

Where are you taking us? Flare dug at me. He ripped at
my arms with claws made of fire. They slid off my diamond armor, leaving scratches in it. The magic was tough,
but Flare was still a creature from the earth's heart. Even a
diamond was in trouble there. *We're not going back down!*

You're going out the way I told you to! I snapped. *I'm tired
of fussing with you and finding ways to keep you busy and
out of my hair. You're a danger to my friends. You can't be
trusted to do things so you don't kill everything in sight. If
you're so determined to die, fine. You'll do it where you don't
murder everything else for miles around.*

Why do you care? Carnelian wasn't fighting me as hard
as Flare. Instead she twined her arms around the one I
used to grip her ear. Her warmth burned even through my
diamond armor. *Everything's all temporary anyway,* she
said. *You touch it — well, we touch it, and it disappears. It's
not like it's important.*

That sounded like Luvo and me calling people and animals "meat creatures." It scorched me almost as much as Carnelian's hold. *It's important to them,* I said. *And in my right shape* I'm *one of those temporary things.*

Carnelian tried to pull me to a halt. *One of* them?

I dragged her onward.

Flare hauled against me, trying to wrench away. *How can you have* any *power over us? How can you be here or touch us? This is* our *world!*

Is the monster a temporary thing, too? Carnelian's voice was very soft and scary. *Are you saying we ran from the likes of that?*

For the first time I was more scared of Carnelian than Flare. I sped up. *No. Luvo isn't like me at all. You're lucky you listened to him.*

I wonder. Flare was suspicious now, too. *Maybe he was another one of your tricks.*

You seem to know a lot of them, Carnelian remarked suspiciously.

Carnelian was getting heavy. How could she do that?

Maybe this is another trick, Carnelian went on. *Maybe your way* out *is just another way* down.

You can't lose us. This is our home. We will find a way back to your precious mountain and blow it all to pieces! Flare fought me even harder.

I loosened my human shape. I lengthened my legs and wrapped one around him, one around Carnelian, then clung to them with the strength of diamonds. For Meryem and Nory and Jayat and Spark, I told myself. I tightened my grip on their bodies and their ears.

They had to learn to fear my voice, not Luvo's! *You can't scare me, you two. I was beaten by imperial soldiers. I lived for weeks without undressing because it was so cold. I was sold for a slave and lived on my own for years on garbage. You call that temporary? Fine. But I'm going to be temporary for a while longer,* without *you destroying everything around me. Without you destroying* me. *And if you want to die so bad, then I'll help you do it! But you aren't going to defy me ANYMORE!*

We were nearly five miles out. I poured more magic into my grip. I let the diamonds' power fill the tentacles that I had wrapped around Flare and Carnelian. They squealed, feeling their own heat reflected back upon them.

It's not death, you stupid creature! Inside her skin, parts of Carnelian were moving. They raced through her, around and around. She was turning herself into the quartz trap, spinning her power. As it whirled inside her, it built. She got stronger as she fought. *It's not death at all. If you weren't so* temporary, *you would know. We go to the next place, the next part of ourselves. Who wants to swim around through all of time! We want to grow up.*

Getting out means we are worthy *to move on. We become part of the great world, not cooped up inside it.* Now Flare did the same thing as Carnelian, spinning inside his skin.

They got hotter, burning me. I moved faster, dragging them for all I was worth. The fault was turning deeper under the ocean floor. The canyon that was my goal was another two or three miles away, perhaps. We weren't near enough. Worse, at the edge of my senses, I felt my stone alphabet. The *ships* were sailing right overhead. There were breaks in the ceiling of the fault here. If Flare and Carnelian got free now, they might come up right under the escaping fleet.

Let us GO! roared Flare, slamming me into the wall of the fault.

We don't believe you anymore! Carnelian dragged me in one direction, Flare in the other. They were ripping me apart, blazing as their insides spun. The volcano spirits saw them fighting with me and screamed. They swamped us. Every inch of the open fault around me was filled with magma. They copied Flare and Carnelian, whirling in circles. Heat built up everywhere, blinding hot.

Then everyone squeezed in, crushing me. My diamond faces strained, trembled, then splintered. The volcano creatures stuck threads of magma into the cracks. They oozed into me, trying to swamp Evvy until all that was left was liquid stone magic.

I fought. I wasn't liquid stone! What of my body? I tried to feel the hands and feet that had done so much. I wanted to sense the mouth and belly that loved good food. I remembered the tooth that was starting to ache.

Deep inside I promised myself that I'd tell Rosethorn, so we could get the tooth looked after. The promise felt like a quartz shard, cracking in the heat.

I tried to rebuild myself. I needed Luvo's smooth and polished skin. I imagined him shedding water as I wanted to shed these fierce, hot creatures.

While I fought to be whole again, they spun faster.

Up, Carnelian whispered fiercely. *We're going up here and now, Evvy. You're going, too. You'll find out what it's like. And we'll shake the world when we go.*

Up, up, UP! Flare shouted. He and Carnelian darted to the top of the fault. They pulled me along.

I dragged on them, but my arms were noodles. My strength had melted. I was done.

Gods of all stone be praised, Luvo said. *We are not too late.*

We won't fall for this trick another time, Evvy. She said it, but Carnelian still halted.

Flare stopped too. *You don't fool us. We're going out right here.*

NO. I didn't know this great, female voice, but it was familiar. I knew the stones in it, from mica to obsidian to basalt. It sounded like . . . Starns. It sounded like the island.

NO. That male voice was strange, too, smaller, but solid and just as unmovable. I knew it was odd, but he sounded like the island I'd seen next to Starns.

NO, the two islands said together. Their mingled voices set the earth to trembling.

Power as great as the sea's wrapped me up. I felt Luvo in it, but there were at least five strangers there, too. They folded me around, shutting out the lava. I was enclosed in a globe of magic that was cool and solid. I would have cried if I'd had eyes.

Not here, fiery young ones, said Starns. *You will not destroy my waters.*

You will not shower death on our shores, said that second voice. *You must change. We know this.*

Once we too changed. Once we too broke free of the molten chambers under the earth. That was Luvo. *Each of us was born like you and leaped free, like you. But my friends here, the Battle Islands you would destroy in your new birth —*

We are not ready to change, Starns told them. *And now we have found that if we join together, we can stop you from your destruction. Change all you like.*

Someplace else, another island, a younger one, said. *We will not permit it here.*

You can't stop us! shouted Flare.

Actually, I think perhaps they can, Carnelian whispered.

Watch us, the islands said.

The entire earth around us *pushed,* away from the cluster of Battle Islands. The fault rippled, thrusting the volcano spirits onward. From inside the globe that the islands and Luvo had made around me, I shoved Flare,

Carnelian, and the volcano spirits down the fault. We couldn't go back: The islands wouldn't let us. We could all feel a solid, invisible wall at our backs. So I kept bumping them from behind in the safety of my globe. We headed toward the crack in the ocean floor, the one Luvo had shown me, what felt like ages ago. I was terrified the fault would shake loose, but the islands wouldn't let it. They held it in place and kept moving us away, their magic harder than stone.

At long last the ceiling of the fault opened up overhead. Far, far above I could hear the cold whisper of the sea in all her malice.

I retreated to the side of the fault. *Flare, Carnelian — this is it. If you go straight up through there, you can come out into the sea. You can form shapes, and make steam. . . . Well, you'll see how it works.*

Flare, Carnelian, and the spirits shot up into the crack.

We're free! Carnelian, let's go! Flare became a volcano spirit again in his shape. Only his hair remained of his old seeming.

Time to grow! Carnelian lost her human shape, until she looked like all the other volcano spirits. The only way I knew which one was her was from the blue, dresslike sheath that covered part of her.

They rammed themselves up into the huge crack that led to the ocean floor. The other volcano spirits followed.

298

They raced along in a river of fiery melted stone. I watched them flood the long crack that would carry them into the cold, cold sea. There they would go black on the outside, then billow along the ocean floor, still red-hot stone in their hearts. They would build on each other, climbing toward the surface. In advance, they would send out waves and steam to warn passing ships. Soon enough — there were so many of them — they would break the surface of the water, throwing up stones and ash. They would have all changed into something else. And sooner or later they would become an island with a volcano at its heart.

Did I know you could get these islands to help, Luvo? I asked.

We did not know we could command those terrors, replied Starns. *I thought my only choice was to wait for my own destruction, and hope the change would be good.*

But we like *being islands,* the male one said. *It's interesting. I wasn't bored yet.*

I did not know it would work, Luvo told me. *But I found I was not prepared to let you die, Evumeimei. I know it must happen. I learned that if I may put it off even for a drop of time, I will take that drop.*

You did not have to be so very rough with us, Great Luvo, the male island complained. *We were listening.*

You did not listen fast enough, Luvo told them.

22

Out of the Ashes

Luvo and the island spirits carried me back to Starns. I couldn't have reached it on my own. I had used up everything in that last fight with Carnelian and Flare. The islands even gave me some strength, after Luvo nudged them.

I will tell Rosethorn you are alive, Evumeimei. We will come for you as soon as we can find a ship to bring us, Luvo promised. *You know she will manage it.*

I *did* know that.

The strength the islands gave me was enough so I could crawl into a barn uphill from the place where I had left my body. I needed to be under cover. Ash still fell from the cracks that had opened on Mount Grace. I had no way to know if there would be any gadolgas from the volcano sprouting out to sea. I barely noticed the earthquake that shook the hill just as I began to climb it. My sense of everything was dull and distant. I wasn't too far from being a cinder.

*   *   *

As soon as I could do more than bleat like a sheep, I searched for food. Sooner or later I had to see if Meryem, Jayat, and Nory were alive. If I had only been unconscious for a day, they *might* be partway to Moharrin, if they lived. That day when I woke up in the barn, though, I could do little more than stagger. The bit of light that came through the clouds of ash was fading. In my present shape, I wouldn't make it as far as the river without food or a horse.

I had to find food before the light was gone. My feet — then my knees and my hands — crunched as I headed for a nearby farm.

In their rush to escape, the farmers had left plenty behind. I ate my food cold for two days. The house's fires were out. I couldn't bear so much as the heat from a candle flame, anyway. Even the touch of my own breath on my skin was too hot. I hoped that effect of being nearly scorched by volcano spirits would wear off soon. Normally I like fire.

That second day, the farm's goats came back. They were hungry. I fed them and milked a few. What milk I didn't drink I gave to the other animals that returned. I learned to walk like a sailor when little earthquakes shook us all. Those were more gifts from the Carnelian and Flare volcano, growing out to sea.

On the second day, I lurched around, sweeping ash off of grass, hay, troughs. I brought up water from the well until it was clean. I opened the doors of the house and brought the washtubs and barrels inside, to protect them from the worst of the ash. Then, slowly, I filled anything that would hold water for the animals, inside and out. I dumped grain out of sacks in the barns and sheds. Until rain came to rinse the ash away, they'd be able to survive. I hoped.

The ash stopped falling by the third day. From rumblings in the ground, I guessed a lot of volcano spirits had abandoned the chamber under Mount Grace entirely, going to try their luck under the sea. No one remained to try to escape the mountain. The skies were hazy, but it was clear, except in the southeast, where a black cloud hung. That would be the new volcano. Flare and Carnelian had led enough of their kind out that they had built a mountain on the ocean floor. They were coming into the open air.

I couldn't wait any longer. I needed to find my friends, if they were alive. They had to be alive. After everything — melting, the sea's meanness, fighting with young volcanoes . . . Meryem, Nory, and Jayat had to be here. They had to be breathing and walking around. I didn't know how I could bear it if, after everything, I found their bodies on the way to Moharrin.

I wasn't sure how easy it would be to reach them. The earthquakes would have knocked the road to pieces. Lucky for me, two of the animals who had come to the farm were mules. You can't beat mules for taking on bad terrain. I sweet-talked them into wearing saddles and packs I had stuffed with food and mule treats. I knew that nobody tells a mule to do anything. It's better to negotiate.

So what if I hobbled like an old woman? It was time to go. Otherwise, like the ferret in the old stories, curiosity would kill me. Or worry. Or fear.

Off we went, slowly. Each step sent up a puff of ash. Tree limbs sagged with more ash. It blanketed the grass and hid the stones. I had to wrap a scarf over my face to keep from breathing it. I even ripped up two shirts and gave the mules scarves for their noses. I envied them their long eyelashes. Every little breeze blew grit right into my face. My eyes watered all the time.

The mules warned me when a fresh shake was coming. That was good. My magic was still limp, so *I* didn't know. When the mules halted, their eyes rolling, I'd slide from the saddle. I'd talk soft to them until the ground settled again. I gave them apples and carrots and paid them compliments in every language I knew. They liked the compliments even more than the treats. Mules are pretty vain.

There's no good speaking of that journey. It lasted two and a half days. The road was just sad. In three places rockslides had wiped it away. Lucky for me that I had mules. Lucky, too, that the Makray River was changed, knocked into a new course by the bouncing earth. We picked our way along the old riverbed. The whole time I prayed to Kanzan the Merciful, to Heibei, and to the gods of the Living Circle. I wanted to see no tumbles of clothes, no bodies half buried by rock or ash. I wanted no sign that the people I searched for had died making this journey. Either the gods listened and they were safe, or they were under so much rock that I never saw them.

I wore out the three brooms I brought, sweeping ash from the mules' grazing and my campsite. I went through every spare bit of cloth. We couldn't drink the Makray's water. It was acid from the damage done by the volcano spirits. The mules grumbled as I measured out water from my canteens, but they could smell the river. They wouldn't touch that water. If I came back after death as anything, it would be as a mule.

It was like a journey through the hell of those who defy the Yanjing will of heaven. I thought I'd stopped believing in those hells, but they hadn't stopped believing in me. They had followed me all the way here. This one had, anyway.

Around noon that third day, we came down the crumbling road into Moharrin. I took one glance at the lake. That was enough. It was filled with dead fish. More acid from Mount Grace.

The village was a mess. The earthquakes had made a hash of it. Some wooden houses had collapsed. A lot of the rickety wooden barns and sheds were destroyed. Nothing moved anywhere. My heart dropped to my belly.

The ash was a lot worse up here, too. "It's like the *town* is a ghost," I told the mules. I'd been talking to them for a while. "Without people it's a ghost of itself, you know? No farmers, no kids. Everything's all gray. No smoke from the chimneys, no sounds. It's dead." My eyes were sulfur dry and bitter. It didn't matter. Nothing mattered in this world.

The mules just flipped their ears at me. They aren't good conversationalists.

I looked at the sun and choked. Smoke came from the inn's kitchen chimney.

Of course. The inn was stone. Its barns were mostly stone. People might come there for safety.

Quiet as a mouse, I dismounted. All this way I had named rocks and their shapes to myself so I would not think. I had plenty not to think about. I couldn't think that Meryem, Nory, and Jayat were dead. I couldn't think that rough types who had stayed behind might have gotten them. The problem was, rough types might be at the inn right now.

What to do? I didn't have any weapons. Talk about bleat-brained! I had always had my magic before. A little of it was coming back, but it wasn't enough to turn a crystal into a night lamp. As a weapon, my power was useless.

I took off my headscarf, though I kept the one over my nose and mouth. I didn't want to give myself away by sneezing. There were fist-sized rocks beside the road, smooth ones. A girl with a headscarf and stones always had the makings of a sling.

I tethered the mules in what was left of an orchard. With rocks in my pockets, I crept up on the inn. Instead of going through the main door, I went the long way around, to the kitchen garden.

Meryem sat on a clean bench in the swept-out kitchen yard. Chickens pecked all around her, looking for food. She'd been grinding chickpeas. The Dreadful Doll sat beside her for company. She was singing to it. She hadn't seen me.

I tried to breathe and blinked a lot, my eyes stinging fiercely. Only six years old, but like me, she had survived all the world threw at her. My foolish words hadn't gotten her killed. I had a second chance. I'd believed I would wear her death as a chain around my neck all my life.

I walked slowly to her, because I was afraid I would stumble. "I was wrong to say what I did." My voice was muffled by the scarf over my mouth. I pulled it down.

She dropped her chickpeas. "Evvy! You came! I thought you left!" She grabbed me and hugged me and started crying.

I hugged her back. So maybe I was crying, too.

306

"Wait. Stay there — don't run away!" Meryem ran inside the kitchen.

I heard barking. Dogs ran out, growling, their hackles up. They were a mixed crew of animals, but they all looked serious. I backed up, hands in the air to show I meant no harm. Behind them came Nory and Jayat. Nory was armed with a huge pot in one hand, a knife in the other. Jayat had an iron spit that he held like a staff. Both of them relaxed when they saw me. And I couldn't help it — I grinned. They looked good and alive.

Jayat gave a couple of tricky whistles. The dogs growled, circled around me, sniffing, then went back inside. I was glad to see them, not just because they were animals, but because they were protecting my friends. "Nice dogs," I said.

"They come from the farms around here. Nory collected them in case anyone nasty came along. She taught me the whistles. What happened to your volcano? We noticed when the mountain stopped smoking." Jayat pointed to Mount Grace. Clouds hid the peak. The outline I could see looked different, but I saw no plumes of ash and steam.

"It's poking up offshore," I told him. "You can see it if you go down to Sustree. Flare and Carnelian have all the glory they could want."

Nory is more practical, like me. "How bad is the road?"

"Impossible," I said. "I had mules and it took me two and a half days. We're stuck here for a while." As if the land itself agreed, it shuddered, making us stagger.

Nory looked at Jayat. "We keep foraging. Evvy can help. She owes us some hard work."

I glared at her, but she was right. It was my fault Meryem had left the group. "I brought two mules," I told them. "I'll bet there's plenty more livestock around if we can feed them. We'd better hurry, though. If they can't dig through the ash or find water, they'll start to starve."

Jayat leaned on his iron spit. "How will you get home? Is Rosethorn still in Sustree? Did you bring Luvo?"

I shook my head. "They sailed. But they'll return, eventually. Luvo will tell Rosethorn I'm alive — we're alive. As soon as she can bully someone into sailing here, she'll come. Once I get my magic back, I'll be able to tell Luvo you're alive, too. I'll bet you coppers to diamonds Oswin will come with her. He was half-crazy when he found out you weren't on the ship."

"You sound pretty sure of your Rosethorn." Nory's face was as sour as her voice.

I shrugged. I knew Rosethorn, and she didn't.

Nory shook her head. "Meryem! Where is that girl? Look at this!" Nory crouched and began to pick chick-peas out of the dirt. "It's not like we can afford to waste food!" She put them in the bowl that Meryem had dropped. "Evvy, make yourself useful here. Jayat, why don't you —"

"I'll go check the pot," Jayat said quickly. "All we need is for it to burn." He vanished inside the kitchen.

"Why are you so sharp with him?" I crouched beside Nory and started to gather peas. "He came to look after you two. He could have been safely away."

"I didn't ask him to come," Nory said, her voice clipped. "Now he's stuck. Maybe living with me for a few months will teach him that he doesn't want to marry me after all."

"You think the others will come home by then?"

"They always do," replied Nory. "Pirates, earthquakes, big storms . . . they always return once the people on the other islands start to get on their nerves. We're proud folk here on Starns. We prefer to do for ourselves. Keep gathering those." She got up and went into the house, her eyes sharp. Inside, I heard her scold Jayat. I did as I was told, thinking.

It was good to hear her, and good to hear Jayat as he argued with her about something. Staying here for a while wouldn't be so bad. Hard work would keep my mind off how little magic I had. I could be useful. Rounding up animals and getting them fed, collecting food . . . More people would come once they felt safer. They would need to eat. I could help with the cooking, too.

As my power came back, I could summon the big rocks from under the fields. They could turn the ground over so the ash would get mixed in with fresh dirt. And maybe I could clear the rockfalls on the road to the sea.

Sooner or later, though, Rosethorn and Luvo would come for me. We'd go home, to Winding Circle and a different life. I'd need a new direction then. It was as clear as the plink of the dried peas as they struck the bowl.

I'd lived two ways. I'd been one with Luvo, the islands, Flare, Carnelian, and the volcano spirits. All that fire and glory was splendid, but . . . It was nothing like the hot rush of feeling that swamped me when I saw that Meryem, Nory, and Jayat were alive. Being a creature of melting stone was powerful. It was as powerful as the earthquakes. Being with these meat creatures again was as warm and complete as my own blood.

I was a meat creature who had come close to being a monster. I had almost surrendered being human without knowing what I was giving up. Maybe only Rosethorn, Luvo, and Myrrhtide would know I had helped to save lives and this island. That made *me* feel good. Useful. As if I had earned my place among my fellow meat creatures.

I liked that feeling. I wanted to earn more of it. I could start here, with the fields, and the roads. In the end, though, I would have to take Rosethorn's path. Battling Carnelian and Flare had worked because I'd had Luvo, and because I'd been lucky. Left to myself, finding the way on my own, I might put my feet wrong, like I did with Meryem. Being useful doesn't come naturally to me. I'd have to study it, like Rosethorn did. Winding Circle could teach me to help on purpose. They could teach me to do it because I'd *planned* to do it all along.

So I'd go back. I'd tell them it was time for me to learn. I'd put on the white robe, and thank the gods of the Earth for letting me wake up in time.

"Here." Meryem poked me in the shoulder. "I came back so I could give you this." She handed me a chunk of amethyst the size of her fist. "To make up for the one me'n Treak broke."

"Nothing would make up for you dying. No stone is worth a person's life." Mostly I even believed that. I meant it about *her* life, anyway. Some people aren't worth a grain of sand on the beach.

I suppose Winding Circle will teach me not to think that way. *Maybe* it will be an improvement.

"Do you like it?" Meryem looked really worried.

"It's *beautiful*. I'm keeping it always. It'll make me think of you." I meant *that* completely. "Come on. You can help me bring in my mules. I have more dried chickpeas in my saddlebags."

Meryem ran across the yard and grabbed a cat. She carried her back to me. "This is Squeak. She had kittens in Azaze's room. Nory says I can have one. Do you want one?"

I swallowed a lump in my throat. Maybe it was time to have a cat, too. The temple's novices are allowed to have pets. Lark says it makes them more responsible. I think it makes them less annoying. "Maybe." I had to clear my throat and say it twice, because it came out a little funny the first time. "Maybe. Mules first. Kittens later."

Meryem ran ahead of me, skipping. Her feet kicked up puffs of ash and dust. At least this part of my being a better meat creature was off to a good start.